BY MEGAN CUMMINS

If the Body Allows It
Atomic Hearts

atomic hearts

atomic
hearts

A NOVEL

megan cummins

BALLANTINE BOOKS

NEW YORK

Ballantine Books
An imprint of Random House
A division of Penguin Random House LLC
1745 Broadway, New York, NY 10019
randomhousebooks.com
penguinrandomhouse.com

LIBRARY OF CONGRESS CATALOGING-IN-PUBLICATION DATA
Names: Cummins, Megan author
Title: Atomic hearts: a novel / Megan Cummins.
Description: First edition. | New York: Ballantine Books, 2025.
Identifiers: LCCN 2025014952 (print) | LCCN 2025014953 (ebook) |
ISBN 9780593875353 hardcover acid-free paper | ISBN 9780593875360 ebook
Subjects: LCGFT: Novels
Classification: LCC PS3603.U66333 A93 2025 (print) | LCC PS3603.U66333 (ebook) |
DDC 813/.6—dc23/eng/20250501
LC record available at https://lccn.loc.gov/2025014952
LC ebook record available at https://lccn.loc.gov/2025014953

Printed in the United States of America on acid-free paper

1st Printing

First Edition

BOOK TEAM: Production editor: Cara DuBois • Managing editor: Pam Alders •
Production manager: Sam Wetzler • Copy editor: Hasan Altaf •
Proofreaders: Barbara Jatkola, Vincent La Scala, Tricia Wygal

Book design by Debbie Glasserman

The authorized representative in the EU for product
safety and compliance is Penguin Random House Ireland,
Morrison Chambers, 32 Nassau Street, Dublin D02 YH68,
Ireland. https://eu-contact.penguin.ie

FOR MY MOTHER

This time I was beside you.
I waited, and I saved you.
I was there.

—Laura Kasischke, "For the Young Woman
I Saw Hit by a Car While Riding Her Bike"

part
one

December

THE PAST

I WAS SIXTEEN. I SAID I WOULD WALK. IF MY FINGERS FROZE OFF, MAYBE IT would be like I'd never touched him.

I slipped on a patch of ice when I was halfway home and landed on my wrist, breaking it in three places. Lying on the sidewalk with my head in the snow, looking up at the stars, I'd thought over and over: *You deserve this.*

A few weeks later, when we were all back at school, and Cindy and Gabe were back together, and I was wearing a sling and a splint, Gabe whispered to me, not kindly, "You should've let me drive you."

It had seemed so out of the question Gabe would like me back that I never told anyone—not even Cindy—about my desperate crush on him.

I'd been raised on secrets, I knew they weren't a good idea, but I was used to them and had found safety in them before. Everything was changing so fast. I didn't know what was real. My and Cindy's dads were using again, and I had to become a different, stronger person before I'd even figured out who I was in the first place.

When Cindy started dating Gabe, I didn't think about what could've happened if I'd just talked to him. He played drums and had swoopy black hair and bony hands that mesmerized and every girl, even the cool ones, had been in love with him for at least a minute. Gabe was messy, complicated. He thrived on making people feel uncomfortable, uncertain—he liked making people crave him, making people desperate to know when his attention would fall on them again. And once he was with Cindy his attention did fall on me—sometimes, anyway. "Gabe loves you," Cindy told me once. "He thinks you're weird."

She laughed like it was something hilarious, but she watched me, her expression sharp-edged. She needed me to know that she was aware that Gabe saw something in me, even fixated on me. That was her way—she needed control to feel safe.

"He does not love me," I said, making sure she couldn't see my face in case it showed the truth. For the first time in our two parallel lives, I wanted to keep her at a distance.

My shyness around Gabe might have, in some way, been self-protective. The small, private, painful longing was better as a secret. Better when it was held back by the elbow. I couldn't jump when I didn't know if the water was deep enough to catch me.

But then, the night of the party, I plunged, and I fell for a long time.

"We need to tell Cindy," I whispered to Gabe once the guilt had sunk in.

"Why hurt your best friend?" he asked. "It honestly meant so little. I barely remember it."

Despite his declaration, for some reason—cruelty, maybe—he kept talking to me, and texting sometimes. And I kept listening, because you always want the person who told you you're nothing to think you're something.

And when you start to keep a secret like that, a secret that big, it gets possessive of you—it won't let you go, even when you've realized it's long past time to tell the truth.

I'd decided to go to the party after chugging a cocktail of self-pity and a sad-girl playlist Cindy had made me.

"Go," Cindy told me on the phone.

She was away with her mom on a ski trip, their usual winter break vacation that Mrs. Fellows had insisted on even though their lives had turned upside down. My life, too. Her dad had left, she hadn't heard from him in weeks and didn't know where he was staying, and my dad was living in a motel with court-mandated rehab approaching after a second DUI.

"I'm not really in a partying mood," I said.

"You can't just be a sad girl the whole time I'm gone."

"Why did you make me a sad-girl playlist, then?" I asked.

"To remind you it could always be worse! You could have to be a sad girl for a *living*."

"That sounds awesome."

"*Go*," Cindy said again. "It will take your mind off things. I hate that I had to leave you for the holidays."

It would take a lot more than a keg of beer and a picked lock on a parent's liquor cabinet to forget our lives—but it was worth going to make Cindy happy.

For a while after that night, I found myself sinking into the seductive torture of wondering what could have been. All the other ways the night could've gone—they felt so possible, almost like I could make them real if I only believed they were. I started to understand the stories you hear about people becoming convinced of pasts that don't belong to them. If I'd listened to different songs that led to different feelings. If, when I took my headphones out, I hadn't searched the house to find it was empty. If Cindy hadn't been on vacation with her mom. In the end, though, I believe that life has a longer runway than that. Most of the things coming are a long time coming.

I'd stopped the playlist and put on red lipstick and a black dress and trudged through the cold night to the party. A girl from school was hosting: Alice, who lived in one of the sprawling developments of white brick McMansions on the edge of our small town near Ann Arbor.

Alice's trusting parents had gone out of town and left her alone. Cindy and I knew her from marching band; she was the cheerleader who played the trombone. During football games she marched in her cheer uniform, reveling in her contradictions. She was nice to everyone. She probably really meant it, but thinking about her cynically was more satisfying.

I stood outside when I arrived. Alice was laughing on the front porch, her parents' absence an opportunity to make the house her own. I was home alone a lot, too, but I drifted through the rooms, searching for nothing. Being alone looked good on Alice, like her parents were busy and cosmopolitan and she was independent, while I could tell that people—Cindy's mom, especially—thought of me as abandoned.

The uplighting on the trees in the yard made them look like ghosts, and the whole house was iced with sharp white Christmas lights—not like the chunky flashing ones we put on our bushes. So much light poured from the windows that even the front yard felt warm. I walked toward the door looking up at everything, and I ran right into Gabe. A winter hat covered his ears, but a loop of dark hair spilled out over his forehead. He puffed on a cigarette even though Cindy had made him quit.

I was dizzy from staring up at the lights. His image split into two and then floated back together.

He'd been with Cindy more than six months at that point, and for most of that time I'd been relieved that he was with someone so close to me that rules dictated he'd never be mine. He and I could never figure out a friendship after he started dating Cindy. But that had never mattered. We all hung out sometimes, it wasn't like Gabe and I hated each other, and it wasn't like she and Gabe were going to get married. We all seemed to understand that. Cindy and I were forever. Cindy and Gabe were for now.

"Cindy and I broke up," Gabe said, flicking ash. "But you probably already knew that."

Cindy had told me the news triumphantly before leaving, though I knew the crash would come soon—she'd get pulled down by his hold on her like she always did.

My attempt at a sympathetic smile twisted into a grimace. "She told me. I'm sorry."

I started walking around to the back of the house, hoping Gabe wouldn't follow, but he did. There was a fire going in a firepit. I brushed snow off the steps of the deck, and he did, too, and we sat on the frozen wood.

"She only broke up with me because her dad went off the rails. It's such bullshit. I wanted to be there for her, I *was* there for her, but she didn't give me a chance."

I hesitated. I could see what he meant, but when it came to her dad, Cindy had me.

"It's not always easy to talk about," I said, "with other people."

"She talks about it with you," Gabe spat.

"Well, you know why," I said. "She and I are the same."

"My parents have problems, too. They barely talk, and when they do it's just to bicker about stupid stuff. I wish one of them would do something insane. At least it would bring them out of their fucking comas."

I looked away. Heat from the fire barely reached us, only the suggestion of warmth.

"I wish my parents only fought about stupid stuff."

I felt his hand on my shoulder.

"I'm sorry," he said. "I shouldn't have said that. I shouldn't make what Cindy's going through about me."

"Well, she did dump you," I said, "so it is kind of about you."

Gabe laughed, and I did, too. The world got a little warmer. His fingers slid down my arm and landed on the deck.

"I've been worried about Cindy, too," I said. "I'm more used to this stuff with my dad. But it's been a long time since hers relapsed. And I know Cindy's mom blames my family for it. Maybe things would be better for Cindy if she didn't know us."

"Cindy's a good judge of character," Gabe said. "Without you she'd be really lost."

"Same," I said. "Me without her."

My eyes broke from the fire. I looked at Gabe and his face was close to mine, so close our breath touched, and then we both pulled away. I wiped my running nose on my jacket sleeve and said I wanted a drink, so we left the yard and went inside, where the warm air rushed through our bodies like fire up a chimney. Our cups stayed full, one of us or the other refilling for both, and Gabe was sarcastic as usual but warmer. He didn't take his hat off, and melted snow curled the ends of his hair. We were in a corner of the kitchen where no one else was, a knot of garlic bulbs hung above our heads, and when he laughed, he threw his head back over the sink and I felt embarrassed that I could make someone laugh with their whole body.

Is a mistake made out of loneliness, or sadness, as bad as one made out of desire or envy?

The kitchen got crowded, and loud. "It's kind of hot in here," he said. I followed him up the stairs, not thinking further than one step ahead, and he opened the door to a bedroom and beckoned for me with a jerk of his head. When I didn't follow, he took my hand. I hesitated, then let him pull me inside.

He backed me against the door slowly until my body closed it. A soft click and we were alone. He put his hand in my hair. He kissed me.

That house, Alice's house, it was so perfect. Nothing felt real about it; it was a stage for lives that would evaporate the next day.

There was the ice and snow outside, obscuring everything, and I wanted to know I still existed. That there was life outside the storm. Excuses, I know, but it's what I was thinking as we kept taking things one step further. There was a condom in his wallet, and we used it even though I knew it was probably meant for Cindy.

In the shuffle of clothing my dress bunched up beneath me, and I stained it with blood. I should've found a towel but part of me had frozen, thinking Gabe would be the one to know what to do.

After, when we were lying in the bed, the sheets rustling softly around us, he took out his phone and took a picture of me. I was laughing at something he said, and as soon as I heard the sound of the camera, I grabbed for his phone, but he dropped it on the floor and put his hands in my hair again and told me he would delete it later. I didn't ask for proof.

He kissed my neck, but the photo had sobered me. I pushed him away and sat up quickly.

"I have to go," I said, throwing off the blankets, and as I did, I hooked myself up to an IV of guilt that wouldn't stop dripping for a long time.

"Hey," he said, looking startled. "I'll drive you."

"I think I'd rather walk."

"Come on, Gertie. It's like twenty degrees."

"Please, Gabe, leave me alone."

After I picked myself up off the ice, I walked the rest of the way home cradling my broken wrist and the feeling that I'd never made a bigger mistake in my life.

The garage door was open when I got back to my house, and the bare bulb in the rafters glowed above the empty milk jug that my mom had hung from the ceiling so she'd know how far to pull in without hitting the lawnmower. Her car was gone, but my dad was just outside the door in the white plastic chair he sat in when he smoked, the one next to it—mine—empty. It was our spot, where we sat together and looked at stars and where, sometimes, my dad would bring out his guitar, and he'd sing softly, a cigarette embering in the ashtray next to him. The music accompanying the sky.

His wrist hung over his knee, and there was a cigarette between his fingers. The frigid air, the adrenaline from my fall, and now his smoke, too, cleared my head of everything and all I could feel was gravity pulling down on the broken bits of my bone. I sat down next to him.

He picked up a thermos of coffee from near his feet and handed it to me.

"Hi, hon," he said. "You look like you need this."

His eyes were bright, he might've been sober, and I took a sip.

"I'm not that drunk," I said, shy, though, at having been caught. "Or, I wasn't, anyway. I wish I'd been, though."

He laughed, then his laugh turned into a cough.

"You look a little feverish." He switched his cigarette between hands and placed his palm on my forehead. "Why is your hair wet?"

I winced as I held up my wrist. "I fell. I might need to go to the hospital."

"Oh, boy," he said, stubbing out the cigarette.

"In a minute," I said. "I need a little more coffee."

He leaned back in his chair. "Only a minute," he said.

Our garage faced a patch of woods. The trees were too serious and lifeless in the dark and cold and their branches had been iced into syringes. Now and then a clump of snow fell from a branch, thudding onto the forest floor. I couldn't feel my fingers. I looked down at them; in a flash before my eyes, Gabe's hand was there, leading me up the stairs of the festive house decorated with twinkle lights, two Christmas trees, a wreath on the door. I touched my cheek; his breath had been there.

"Did I tell you about the time I got drunk and jumped into the Charles River? I was living in New York, working my first advertising job, and I'd gone up to Boston to see Michael."

My stomach twisted at the name, Michael, Cindy's dad, who was also my dad's best friend since childhood.

"Mom would be mad if you told me."

"Well, it seems like it might make you feel better about yourself," my dad said. "If you want to hear it."

His eyes wrinkled with a smile behind his smudged glasses, his eyelashes so long they touched the lenses. One of his teeth was brown from nicotine. Somehow, he almost always looked serene no matter how bad things were.

"Sure," I said, hearing the splash of him hitting the water.

"I jumped in and cut myself—I don't know on what, something lodged in the river. I was bleeding, but I was so drunk I refused to go to the hospital. My brother—your uncle Ansel, you know, who died of AIDS before you were born—was there, too."

My dad hardly ever talked about his brother without bringing up that detail, that he'd died of AIDS, as though he still couldn't believe it.

"Ansel and I had come up from New York together," my dad went on. "I woke up the next morning and the sheets were covered in blood. I couldn't remember anything. I told the nurse who gave me the tetanus shot that I just woke up like that."

He laughed at the memory, and I laughed, too, but it didn't make me feel any better about myself.

"Before you met Mom," I said.

"Oh, yeah. She wouldn't have let any of that happen."

"Well, I just slipped on ice. It would've happened if I'd been sober. It would've happened if Mom had been there."

"Don't be so sure," he said. "She has a sixth sense for imminent disaster."

"Where is she?"

He shrugged. "Out somewhere. I told her I was coming over to get some things, so I think she wanted to make herself scarce."

"That's bullshit," I said. "She's avoiding the inconvenience of having a family."

"Hey," he said, "that's not fair. Get up. Time to face the music."

My dad moved his chair into the garage, reached up for the pull string to turn off the light, and drew his keys out of his jacket pocket. A taupe spring jacket with ribbed sweater cuffs he wore no matter how cold or warm it was.

His car, packed full of his things, was parked on the street. He opened the passenger door and took a box out and put it in the ditch.

"I thought you were just going to rehab," I said. "Mom said that you would come back when you got out."

"She said we could talk when I got out."

"I just don't see why you have to take all this stuff with you."

"I like my things."

"Dad . . ."

"Shh. Just get in. We gotta go."

The engine brightened the night. The headlights lit up the quiet. I held my hand to the vents even though the heat was still cold.

"I can't believe you have to go to Minnesota for two months. It's even colder than here."

"Well, I've tried all the rehabs in Michigan. Your mom thinks they didn't work."

"Isn't there one in, like, California or something?"

"It's only two months, Gertie."

All of this, a long time coming, but it still felt like being in a car that had flipped, waiting on the freeway for the jaws of life to come get me. The jaws of life—such an ominous name, like survival could kill you.

My dad was sober on and off over the years. Cindy's dad, on the other hand, had been sober since her birth—until the car accident last year. My dad, who'd been driving, was the one to get the DUI, but Cindy's dad got hurt—not badly, but there was back pain, and then prescriptions. For Cindy's mom, Annemarie, blame had been brewing even before the accident, like she'd known one day my dad would be the reason Michael started using again. She began acting strangely around me, distant. I tried to get Cindy to talk about it, but all she said was: "She thinks our dads are bad for each other."

Cindy didn't blame me, or my family, and her love kept me sane. We stayed close, which irked Cindy's mom, and it irked my mom that Annemarie wasn't nice to us anymore, and so she made a point of hugging Cindy tightly every time she came over, Cindy and I looking at each other wide-eyed over my mom's shoulder.

"One of these days she's going to squeeze you till your eyes pop out," I told Cindy, but, honestly, I would've preferred that her mom treat me that way, too. Instead of a tight hug, I got a tight-lipped smile, more grimace than greeting.

Cindy and I needed each other, so there was no splitting us up. No one else would ever understand what we were going through. Other people's parents were getting divorced, too, sure, but for me and Cindy, we were losing everyone, all at once.

That night I broke my wrist, my mom met us at the ER and told my dad to leave. Two months gone turned to three, the talk between my parents didn't happen, and then my dad met a guy who knew a guy who worked in advertising in Sioux Falls, South Dakota.

That's where he went next.

June

THE PAST

IT WAS EARLY JUNE, THE YEAR AFTER THE PARTY, AND I WAS IN THE YARD.
Cindy was inside making drinks. I put a match to a tuft of dryer lint
nestled between the logs I'd pulled from the woods. The lint succumbed to the flame almost instantly, curling up like a dying spider.
The twigs caught. Everything was bright and orange and contained
in the circle of cinder blocks I'd dragged from the neighbor's yard,
where a pile of construction garbage sat from their stalled addition.
Money problems, I guessed. We had them, too.

Cindy opened the screen door with her foot and appeared beneath the porch light. She rushed toward me with two cups that were
full to the brims. The drinks looked like the inside of a blood orange:
ruby and radiant, sloshing over the lip when I took a sip, burned
candy. I wouldn't normally drink at home, but my mom had gone to
Florida for a week with her new boyfriend, Vaughn, and my dad—
well, my dad didn't live with us anymore.

"Get it, Girl Scout!" Cindy crouched over the fire and held her palms over it. She loved to make fun of how I'd been a Girl Scout when I was younger.

"Whatever," I said. "I've got a better chance of surviving End Times than you."

"Gross," Cindy said. "Who would *want* to live through End Times?"

She had a point. We settled in, mesmerized by the flames, until Cindy's phone absorbed her. Her smile looked like a secret.

My mom and Vaughn were sailing on the boat he kept docked in Florida. They'd started in Miami and were winding all the way around the Keys and then up the Gulf Coast to Sarasota. I Google Earthed the route, zoomed in so I could see the sand beneath the blue glass of the shallow water. It looked pretty. It wasn't something we would've ever done together before, when we were a family, because my dad would've gotten seasick. When I told my mom I'd rather die than go on a trip with Vaughn, we got into a big fight. Plus, I told her, I had school. It was time for final exams. I couldn't just *go*. She did that thing where she pushed her fingers into her temples to let me know I was giving her a headache. Her thin lips trembled, and I wondered what she *really* wanted to say to me.

Finally, she relented, and let me stay home.

"Have you heard from your dad since the last time?" I asked Cindy. "Is he okay?"

She shrugged. "Aside from the fact he doesn't live at home? And that my mom won't even tell me where he is and won't let him call me? Fine, I guess. Has your dad talked to him?"

"They're not supposed to talk, remember? My dad led your dad down the path to drugs."

"You know I don't like it when you joke about that."

"I know," I said.

"God, I've told my mom a million times not to blame other people for our problems."

"I'm really sorry, Cindy. I shouldn't have brought it up."

Cindy sighed. "It's okay." She fished a few ice cubes from her drink and pelted me with them.

I shrieked. "Not fair, you said you forgave me!"

"I'm having fun here with you and all," Cindy said, "but I can't believe you passed up the chance to take a week off school."

"I told you," I said. "Vaughn would have pushed me overboard."

"Okay, sure, drama queen. So, have you talked to her? How is Carla McMahon enjoying life at sea?"

"I don't know," I said. "I think she's having fun, and in theory Vaughn knows how to sail, since he fixes boats for a living."

Vaughn was outdoorsy, a water person who grew up in Maine. Ever since he was eighteen, he'd worked for Boston Whaler as a traveling repairman, and we'd had the bad luck of them sending him here.

"Well, at least he won't sink the ship," Cindy said. "I'm glad Annemarie's not dating yet."

Cindy nudged my foot with hers. I grabbed her toes and squeezed them.

"You don't think your mom will let your dad move back?" I asked.

Cindy might not have known where her dad was staying, but at least she was pretty sure he was still in Michigan. When I tried to imagine Sioux Falls, I saw a grassy, gray-skied place, blank and peopleless.

"No," Cindy said quietly. "I saw her take the divorce papers to the post office."

"Oh, Cindy. I'm sorry."

Silence fell along with Cindy's face. Somehow everyone at school had found out that Cindy and I were the girls with drug addict dads. Somehow meant someone meant *Gabe,* who had parlayed our problems into social status—for him, anyway, since he was close to the drama but not in the eye of it, while Cindy and I lost whatever mild popularity we'd had and walked through school pitied or mocked. If not for Cindy, I'd almost be glad my mom wanted to sell the house.

We were just finishing sophomore year, and the thought of spending two more years in that school clouded the coming summer with dread. We'd be free for a few months, but fall would come soon enough.

There was also the secret.

If a new school year started and I still hadn't told Cindy what happened with Gabe at the party in December, I didn't know if I would ever be able to tell the truth. The idea that a lie—my lie—could last that long made my hollow mistake feel full of bad personality. I might have been able to defend myself against a moment of weakness—but six months of lies?

I twirled a blade of grass between my fingers, tossed it into the fire. I'd planned to spend tonight alone, but Cindy called to say Gabe had ditched her. I heard the sadness in her voice, though she tried to hide it with a laugh, so I told her to come over, that I was building a bonfire.

I'd been thinking about a novel I wanted to write. I was tired of my own life, wanted to throw myself into making up a new one—and in the book, the heroine will probably need to build a fire, so I needed to remind myself what it felt like. Smelled like. Smoky, damp, the burn of baking dirt. She's going to fall into a pond, and her foot is going to get caught on the root of a water lily. Just as she's about to pass out, the light above her will change and the sky will spin and the weed will disappear, and she'll be able to kick her way to the surface because she won't be in her world anymore. She'll be somewhere else, somewhere unknown.

So the fire was research. And everything was more fun with Cindy, so while I hadn't told her about my plans to write a book—I was new to writing then and afraid she'd laugh at the idea—I was happy she was there staring into the flames with me.

"Isn't it so crazy how our parents didn't figure their shit out before they had kids?" Cindy asked for the hundredth time.

"I guess it's worth it to be here. To know you."

"Aw," Cindy said. "That's the greatest compliment I've ever gotten. I'd rather know you than never have been born."

We giggled into our drinks. The flames we coaxed into existence hugged one another in the firepit. My thoughts wandered again to my novel, and names for my character. Jamie. Matilda. Elsbeth. And names for the brooding but beautiful guy she meets, the archer in the rebel army. Parker or Harrison. Or maybe Hayden.

Imagine how strange the world will feel when Jamie emerges from the pond, the sky above her not the blue she's used to, but violet, with gray clouds. The trees will bend to a thicker wind than her wind, a wind that feels like feathers brushing her skin, and the birds will be singing in different tones. She'll be confused, at first, and she'll want to find her way home because that's how it always is in books—though if I'm ever transported in space and time I'll think, *Yes, finally*.

But then, gradually, she'll realize the change has enhanced her life. She's trading in the boring details for the wild ones. She has a purpose, suddenly; she's emerged from the pond baptized, the old pains and boredom cleansed from her body. Emerging as someone new, but also realizing she was that new person all along. Love, war, valor—in fantasy books, they're all a disguise for the simple feeling of wanting to be someone a little bit special. A little bit worth remembering. Her fears vaporize as her clothes dry beneath some bright faraway sun that looks bigger than the only sun she knows. All her raw courage is re-forged into a sword.

My idea was good. I just had to get the words on paper.

The approaching night tricked my eyes into thinking the fire had gotten brighter. Cindy and I were alone, everything quiet and trees all around us—a good selling point, according to the realtor who'd stuck a big sign with her face on it in our front yard. And she'd hung a little box on our doorknob with a combination lock, and nestled inside was a key so she could get in anytime. It was like the house already wasn't ours.

Overhead, a hawk swooped gracefully into its nest. Cindy gasped and pointed. She loved birds. The stars popped out one at a time. I liked wondering what it would be like to live in a different part of the universe. What would be the same, what wouldn't be.

If I stared long enough without blinking, the stars began to vibrate. It was so peaceful in our yard, even if so much had gone wrong there. I'd asked my mom where we were going to go from here, but she was evasive. Somewhere cheaper, she said. Or to Vero Beach with Vaughn, where he lived when he wasn't traveling.

Cindy'd seen the For Sale sign. She knew what might come, but we didn't talk about it. Her mom was a lawyer, her dad had grown up wealthy: Money wasn't one of their problems. My dad hadn't worked in months, and my mom's antiques shop had gone out of business years ago. The sign made Cindy nervous. It made me nervous, too. But there was something else on her mind that night. I could tell. She kept taking a deep breath and then biting her lip.

"Cindy, spit it out!" I said finally.

Cindy's dark curly hair fell in her face as she looked down at the fire. Her brown eyes reflected the flames, and her lips moved almost imperceptibly with the words she couldn't say aloud.

Finally, she said, "This is super awkward and of course I know you would *never*—but, Gabe hasn't ever tried anything with you, has he?"

My heart went cold and dropped low in my chest. His name was a finger that jabbed me between my ribs. When I spoke, I had a hard time keeping my voice even.

"What do you mean? What did he say?"

"I don't know, just this thing," Cindy said. "The other night I didn't want to, you know, and he said, 'There are other girls who make it easier on me.' I was like, 'What other girls?' And he said, 'I've heard Gertie's pretty easy.' Which, oh my God, I'm so sorry to even tell you this, I know it's a shitty thing to say and not true, you've never even had sex! And even if it was true, it's none of his business."

Shame possessed me like a spirit. I could barely breathe, and I felt tears in my eyes, and maybe if I started crying she'd figure out the secret on her own and I'd finally be free.

How had I succumbed to someone so cruel? I looked at Cindy, who raised her eyes to look back at me, but then the wind changed and smoke forced my face over my shoulder.

"That's crazy," I said after a shaky breath. "What's really awful is that he was pressuring you."

My own voice strangled me. I hadn't answered her question. I couldn't even speak to her long enough to lie. I tried to tell if Cindy had noticed my omission, but she had started crying, tears that made it hard to see her face.

"It's been an awful week. My mom said this terrible thing, too. She said I should try to meet new people this summer."

"She wants you to break up with Gabe?" I asked.

Cindy shrugged. "I mean, always. But that's not really it. She's . . . started on this crazy idea that you're a bad influence."

Crushing, to hear someone say the worst you've thought about yourself.

"She's projecting because she's mad at my dad. And your dad. And she hates Gabe. I told her I couldn't abandon you—and she was like, 'That's sad, but we have our own problems.' She is being *so* cold. I keep telling her you're the only person I can trust—but she keeps saying if that's true, then there's a problem."

"Cindy," I said. "I have to tell you something."

I felt the pain piercing my thigh before I heard the pop of exploding metal and a loud hiss. I didn't scream, but all the air rushed out of me. I could almost see it, the way you could see air get sucked from astronauts' mouths in movies when they go out into space without their suits. A rusty aerosol can tucked into one of the cinder blocks. I hadn't noticed it before, but the heat from the fire had made it explode. I froze as I looked down at my thigh, at the shard of metal as wide as my big toe embedded two inches deep beneath my skin. I didn't breathe, not until I couldn't stand it any longer.

What I'd been about to confess popped apart over the fire. Cindy's hand covered her mouth; her drink was overturned next to her, juice and vodka crawling across the grass.

I stared at the shard of metal for a second, completely bewildered, and I reached for it, but my hand hesitated and all my strength disappeared.

"Cindy." Panic rose in my chest. "Pull it out. Please, get it out!"

Cindy grabbed the shrapnel and yanked it out quickly with the sickening sound of metal tearing through flesh. Everything was still; even the flames froze, and then the blood flowed out, and I rushed at the wound with everything I could find: my math homework from my back pocket, leaves from the ground, my T-shirt pulled down over my shorts.

"It's okay." Cindy grasped my shoulders, but her voice didn't sound convinced. "It's okay, you're okay."

Wasn't there an important vein in your thigh? I'd never seen so much blood in real life. It seeped through my fingers and ran down my wrists. I pushed myself up to my feet and almost fell into the fire. Droplets of blood went flying and were devoured with a sizzle.

"I need to go inside," I said weakly.

We left a trail of blood that dotted the grass like dewdrops. The fan sputtered on in the bathroom, one of the lightbulbs flickered, and I propped my leg on the counter. My knee knocked the clamshell soap dish to the floor, where it broke, and I lifted my hand and math homework and looked at the cut. It was a gouge, really, my skin completely open in a bloody trench. I pressed the flesh back together, but the pain hit me hard, and I leaned over and threw up on the floor next to Cindy's feet.

"Jesus," she said. "Okay, I'm calling my mom."

I could see it: Annemarie pulling up and surveying the bathroom, the vomit, spilled vodka in the kitchen and a cutting board scattered with lime wedges. Seeing our bloody house with the For Sale sign in the front yard because my mom didn't have a job, because her business hadn't survived, and she'd never landed anywhere else. Annemarie horrified—not out of concern for me, but out of concern that her daughter was with me. One more strike against me in a tally I'd always had a feeling she'd been keeping.

"Wait." I pressed my hand to Cindy's arm to stop her from making the call. She lowered her phone. I left a scarlet streak on her clean white sweater. In my memory she looks like the actress in a horror film that isn't very feminist.

"It's not that bad. Just give me a minute."

I tore through the cabinets, leaving bloody handprints on everything, and I found small Band-Aids and hydrogen peroxide. I couldn't wedge my thigh under the faucet, so I told Cindy to wait while I rinsed off upstairs. Each step turned our realtor-ready house into a crime scene.

I stood under the cold water without even taking off my clothes. I was flushed and feverish before the shower, and then I was shaking with cold after. Hydrogen peroxide dribbled over my cut, and I watched it fizz. I bit my lip against the stinging. The blood slowed a little but still flowed freely, a small rivulet draining from the wound. I folded a few paper towels and wrapped my leg with a long tear of duct tape I found in my mom's desk. I needed stitches. I needed wound evaluation. Maybe Cindy should call her mom.

But aside from the fact that Annemarie thought I was a screwup, our insurance had been my dad's insurance, and we'd lost it when he'd gotten fired from his job last summer. An ER bill would cost at least a thousand dollars. I didn't know how much my mom had in the bank. I had five hundred dollars saved from birthdays and babysitting gigs. More than anything, I didn't want to have to ask Vaughn to pay. He would demand a repayment plan. He'd take credit for saving my life. I'd have to work off my debt, emptying rattraps on his boat and scrubbing barnacles off the hull.

Downstairs, Cindy was sitting on the couch with her phone pressed to her ear.

"Okay," she said. "Bye."

As soon as she hung up, she said, "My mom called me. I didn't tell her anything. But she wants me to come home now."

She paused.

"Are you *sure* you don't want me to take you to the hospital?"

"I'm fine," I said. "I'm so totally fine. It's not even bleeding any-more. It, like, wasn't as deep as it seemed at first."

The morning, I thought. I would see how it was in the morning. I felt very tired, and very woozy, and so after Cindy left, I limped to my bedroom and wrapped myself up into a burrito with my blankets to hide from the pain. My brain kept latching on to what Gabe had said about me. *I've heard Gertie's pretty easy.* I tried to take myself far away.

Two questions I had about the fantasy novel: Why does the character get transported from her home in the first place, and does she ever come back? These questions were more important than whether or not she falls in love with the brooding archer boy. Also, let's face it, she definitely falls in love with the brooding archer boy. Who could resist?

There could be a section where the girl gets wounded, because she'll take naturally to a bow and arrow and join the army against the evil lord, or dictator, or whoever it is they're trying to defeat. She might get separated from her company, stumble into a forest, deliri-ous, with beasts roaming among the trees and their yellow eyes gleam-ing hungrily. But she'll mix a salve. She'll use her wits, because girls in fantasy novels always have hidden talents. They're always able to fend for themselves from the start. They make the right choices quickly, and they do it all themselves.

June

THE PAST

I WOKE UP LATE THE NEXT MORNING. THE SAME OLD SUN BLAZED ABOVE the house, except that there were spots in my vision that made the sunlight look moldy. I rolled over, and my skin tore away from the sheet. A new oozing of blood welled up, as sticky as glue.

In the bathroom, I repeated the procedure: hydrogen peroxide, new paper towels. The cut seeped but didn't gush. Maybe it would scab today. I just had to keep it clean. Everything would be fine.

The house, though. The house was a wreck. The blood would be easy enough to clean off the hardwood floors and the tile in the bathroom, but there were drops of it on my mom's rugs in the living room. And drying vomit on the bathroom floor. Blood on the doorframes where I'd touched them to steady myself.

I started cleaning. The thing with real life was that you had to do something to make yourself less miserable. You couldn't just fall into ponds and emerge a warrior. There was no lantern of fate like the one leading Hayden to Jamie as she splashes onto the banks of this new world through a corridor burrowed underneath her own. An Underworld.

The next day was Monday, and there was school. I packed the hydrogen peroxide and extra paper towels for the midday wound cleansing. As I drove my mom's car to first period I thought about what might happen to the girl if she slipped back into her old life. Maybe she gets struck by an arrow, and dying in her new world means returning to her old one. Would she go back to school? Would she try to get back to Hayden, or whatever his name is, to continue fighting for the cause? And why does she feel so attached to a cause she just found out about when she never really did anything to make her old world a better place? Maybe it's because suddenly everything that makes her comfortable is gone, her whole system of social support gone, with no one around who remembers it. That sort of thing would rattle a person, would maybe make her see things she ignored before.

I parked the car and limped into geometry late because I couldn't race the bell. A few people looked at me as I ducked into my desk, but no one said anything, and Mr. Simon was as oblivious as always. All day I dragged behind, walking slowly so it wouldn't look like I was in pain. At lunch I sat in the cafeteria, blinking at the long tables of mostly white kids, me and Cindy included, a fact everyone pretended was fine, and I started sweating. "Is it hot in here?" I asked Cindy, shading my eyes from the watery sun streaming through the block-glass windows. She shook her head. She looked at me with concern.

"I think it's kind of cold, actually. Are you sure you're okay?"

"What's wrong with McMahon?" Gabe said as he slid into the seat next to Cindy's.

"Nothing," I said quickly. "I'm good."

Gabe put his arm around Cindy. She smiled into her half-peeled clementine. She was a sweet beauty, a Jane Austen heroine, short and pale with full raven curls and a small nose between two blushed cheeks. Whereas I was long-limbed and sharp-featured and had a resting bitch face framed by short blond hair that Cindy had cut into an angled bob. She and I joked about it, that I could be having the best day of my life and still look like I wanted to kill someone. I liked the way we complemented each other, the sweet and the sour. Cindy was bubbly, I was gloomy, together we were happy.

As Gabe rubbed her back, his ice-blue eyes roved my face, intense enough to give me chills. The secret gave him power over me. Half leftover wanting, half shame. And now sharp anger—not just because what he'd said about me was mean, but because he'd come so close to telling Cindy, when all those months ago he'd forbidden me from coming clean, and I'd been dumb enough to agree.

Cindy melted into his affection, resting her head on his shoulder. I pulled bits of brown lettuce from the edges of my sandwich and flicked them into my lunch bag. Cindy and Gabe must've made up sometime yesterday. I smiled at them to hide my grimace. It was always tumult with Gabe, always some reason to be upset. He was like the angel of destruction, but instead of locusts, he brought forth an army of sulking hipsters. Beautiful and shadowy and sent from hell.

After lunch, I snuck into the girls' bathroom and propped my foot on the toilet seat, gagging as I peeled away the paper towel. The congealed blood had the consistency of molasses. A smell like rusty metal mixed with something putrid. My pulse beat inside the cut. More hydrogen peroxide, more paper towels. On my way home, I decided, I would get proper bandages.

By the end of fourth period, I felt dizzy, and by fifth period, fever smoked like kindling in my head. I thought I might pass out if I tried to play my flute in band, plus Gabe would be in the back of the room in the percussion section, smirking at me. When the bell was about to ring, I stopped by the main entrance. I could see my mom's car parked in the lot.

But there was no one to call me out of class. My mom had listed only herself on the form the school sent home. How to explain to the front office that I ran my own life, anyway? I opened the doors, peered outside. The parking lot attendant was nowhere to be seen.

The engine of my mom's car whined when I turned it on. I didn't look in the rearview mirror as I drove away. I had to squint to see the road. The light came from the sun, but it was also coming from inside of me, like white linens waving on a line in the periphery of my vision, fuzzing everything out.

At a red light I covered my eyes with my hands and tried to rub them clear. Maybe Jamie, after being sent home, will try to return to the other world to finish the fight and be with her love—only to find she can't return because she's already dead there. Her home is the only world her body can live in, and the only option is to find a way to get Hayden there.

A honk from the car behind me woke me up and sent me the rest of the way home. The day had lasted a hundred years. I wasn't hungry, but I made a plate of pickles rolled up in deli turkey with a side of Miracle Whip just because I hadn't eaten much over the past few days. I got cold again and wrapped myself in a throw blanket and shivered through episodes of *Gilmore Girls*. My homework surrounded me, spread out on the couch—biology and an essay on *Hamlet* I hadn't started—but none of it made sense. How did Hamlet recognize Yorick by his skull? I touched my own head with both hands, then closed the big tome of Shakespeare's collected works. I leaned back into the cushions, and the television washed over me. I'd seen all the episodes before, but the show was comforting. The world so impossibly small.

My mom called a little while later. I tried to be polite. I told her everything was fine at home, and she said she was having the time of her life. She'd held a hose over the dock at the marina that morning so she could give fresh water to the manatees that had swum up out of curiosity.

"They're very social creatures," she said. "It was Vaughn's idea to give them water."

She sounded happier than she'd been in weeks, and I thought it was probably because she was away from me.

"You know, it's illegal to interact with manatees," I said. "You're not supposed to give them water. You're just supposed to watch them."

My mother sighed.

"I'm just saying, if Vaughn claims to be so knowledgeable about sailing, he should know."

"Gertie, please."

"Tell him to stop messing with the manatees, or I'll report him!"

My mom's voice got really low, like her throat was full of gravel. "If you ruin this for me," she said, "I'll never forgive you."

There was silence. It beat in my ears like it had wings. *Never*—such a big, lasting word, a word that keeps expanding and never stops, never gives up. It's its own universe, that word. She'd already decided he was more important than I was. And maybe I shouldn't have been so defensive about the manatees—I mean, what was really so bad about giving them fresh water? It wasn't like Vaughn was shoving potato chips down their throats—but my gut reaction was to find something wrong with whatever Vaughn did because he was wrong for us, and mean, and it wasn't fair, and my mom was going to uproot us and make me move like it was no big deal.

Both divorced, both getting older, she and Vaughn were rushing to start something. And there's nothing scarier than adults who feel like they've wasted time, with the ends of their lives burning their heels like hot coals, like death is something that starts happening the minute you reach a certain age. And as far as Vaughn was concerned, I was in the way of the rest of his life.

I wasn't sure which of us hung up first. We'd already left the call, was the thing.

I fell asleep early and woke up sweating. I kicked off the blanket, rolled off the couch, and limped to the freezer. I pressed an ice pack to my forehead. The cut was sticky and inflamed; the veins surrounding it were a map of blue lines creeping farther up and down my leg. I thought of Jamie shaking with fever in the woods and waking up having made it through. She wouldn't need help. I popped a Tylenol and went back to the couch.

The hours crossed the border of night slowly, on foot, and I moved in and out of sleep like my brain was a pendulum—one side sleep, one side restlessness. When I woke up, it was maybe to raccoons knocking over trash cans outside or night-bruised headlights slicing through the windows. Time felt loopy. The clock on the wall ticked but didn't tock. Water didn't help my dry mouth. What if I was getting really sick? I wondered if there were any leftover antibiotics in the medicine cabinet, but I couldn't muster the energy to get up and look.

If Jamie were back in her home world, back in school, would she be distracted and uncertain? Would she think her time in the other world had all been a dream, or that she'd gone briefly crazy? She couldn't tell any grown-ups; they'd make her go to therapy, or worse. She'd stay quiet, burdened with a secret and heartbroken and not equipped to deal with any of it, but she'd get through it. At night, she'd go to the pond where she fell in and breathe in the muddy smell. She'd write messages on rocks and throw them into the water, but they'd go unanswered. *Fall in,* her messages would say. Or *I'm waiting.* Or maybe she'd realize that even though she can't go back to the other world as a human, she can go back as a ghost. And she'd fall in and emerge shimmering, floating, a specter gliding across the blood-soaked fields of war. She'll find Hayden in a field tent, injured and dying, and she'll cloak him in her invisibility and guide him back to the pond where for the last time they'll look upon his world and understand that they'll never be able to return because she's dead and *he's* dying and the war is almost lost. So they'll sink into the pool together, the water a silk cloth around them, the other world breaking into smaller and smaller pieces until it disappears. They'll emerge gasping for air on the banks of the pond near Jamie's house. Hayden will be fading, like a filament in a lightbulb starting to pop, and in Jamie's world she'll give him antibiotics and vitamins and clean water. And he'll recover.

I woke up hours later. My phone had been sounding its alarm for a long time. School had already started, first period was almost over, in fact. The landline rang, and I let the answering machine get it. It was the attendance office, inquiring about my whereabouts since no one had called to excuse me.

Yellow pus oozed from my cut. I tried to stand, but the ceiling spun, and I collapsed back onto the couch and put my head between my knees. I couldn't seem to breathe very deeply. I dug my phone out from between the couch cushions and dialed my dad's number. It rang and rang, and then a robot announced his voicemail. All the anger I'd been wrestling just felt like sadness now, and it went limp. My mom just wanted love, and for some reason we couldn't figure out how she could have it without tearing everything apart.

If you ruin this for me, I'll never forgive you.

I wondered if Jamie would begin to feel like she made the wrong choice after bringing Hayden back with her. They might have fun at first—they'll go boating on a lake, and he'll never have experienced speed so fast, and it will take his breath away, and he'll associate all those good highs with Jamie. He'll eat pizza for the first time and feel the tickling cool of air-conditioning. Everything will be fascinating for him, like it was for Jamie when she first went to his world. But then depression will sink in because his friends and family back home have been destroyed, and he wasn't able to save them, and he won't feel like he belongs in this new place (even though somehow everyone speaks English in the book). He'll be homeless, because there's no way Jamie's parents will let a boy move into her room with her. He won't be vaccinated against the diseases of this world. He won't understand the politics (though, honestly, who does?). He'll have no past he can talk about because his past doesn't exist in this place. They'll look at each other and think what a bad idea their being together had been.

"Oh my God."

I opened my eyes. Our realtor was standing across the room. I hadn't heard her open the door. The little box with the key—I'd forgotten about it. Usually she called before she brought people over, but maybe she had and I was sleeping, or maybe she'd called my mom's cell.

Behind the realtor stood a man and a woman. Their hands covered their mouths as they looked at me and at the blood on the floor and the handprints on the frame of the back door. The tangle of blankets and the serum that leaked from my wound onto the couch. They were horrified.

"Are you okay?" the woman asked.

Nausea swelled inside of me and I got up and tried to limp to the kitchen sink, but I sank to my knees and dry-heaved over the living room floor instead.

"Oh, honey," the realtor said. She dropped the folder she was carrying onto the coffee table and knelt beside me.

Without saying anything, I rolled up my shorts and showed her the cut. A horrified look darkened her face.

"Where's your mom?"

"I thought it would get better." I watched her dig her phone out of her purse. "Wait—don't call my mom!"

She wasn't. She was calling an ambulance.

I prodded the cut. It did look a lot worse today.

This—this was what my mom would never forgive me for.

Antibiotics dripped from an IV bag and ran through a catheter into a vein in my forearm. They were keeping me overnight, and a psych evaluation was in the works, though I insisted I hadn't done any of this on purpose. The hospital had called my mom, who was scrambling to find a flight out of Florida. She and Vaughn had been docked somewhere remote, they didn't have a car, but she told the nurse to tell me she was coming.

Why did you wait to come in? they asked at the hospital. I tried to think of an excuse. How must it make doctors feel, that people always want to lie to them?

I closed my eyes. I felt stuck in the bed, stuck in my book. Maybe Jamie and Hayden would run away and try to start a new life. Maybe they'd go back to the other world and live as ghosts, floating around for eternity as eerie balls of incandescence. It sounded good, but probably wouldn't be that much fun after a few days. All the things they loved had to do with being alive.

I didn't know how to make the story something that wasn't depressing. I didn't know how to end it. It all seemed so small and senseless, all my ideas, my book, my quest to get my mom to realize Vaughn was a jerk. Maybe one day I would be able to think bigger.

June

THE PAST

AFTER A LONG TIME SPENT ALONE IN MY HOSPITAL BED, I TEXTED CINDY TO tell her where I was. The ellipsis of her pending reply scrolled across the screen for a long time. Then a single word appeared: *What?*

I know. The cut got infected.

I'm coming to see you. Hold on.

Your mom will let you??

My phone didn't buzz. It took me a long time to stop bringing its screen to life, checking for messages but finding none.

My nurse's name was Cassandra. She had a short blond ponytail and small thin lips. She'd smiled at me once like she felt sorry for me, and told me to call her Cassie, but ever since, she'd been all business.

"Did you hear from my mom?" I asked.

Her expressionless face sank into a frown.

"She's on her way, but I don't know when she'll get here."

Cassie hung my IV bags from a new pole and wrapped a cuff around my arm. I didn't want her to judge my mom for not being there. It wasn't her fault I was alone. I'd wanted to be—it was a decision I'd made.

Outside the window of my room, the sun broke into orange and pink strips. The lights in the hallway dimmed but didn't go out. They left milky puddles of light on the floor. Through my open door I could see only one of these puddles, but I knew they repeated themselves all the way down the hall, past the nurses' station, to the elevators, smelling of antiseptic. I guessed that I was supposed to go to sleep now—no one had really told me what to do—but the quieter it got in my room, the louder the rest of the hospital seemed. I swear it was like I could hear the drip of medicine from every IV bag, and the rattle of pills, and the buzzing of surgical saws, sharp and spinning, somewhere in an operating room deep in the belly of the hospital.

My mom was probably stranded at the airport, stuck on an uncomfortable bench waiting for the planes to start taking off again in the morning. I called her, but her phone went to voicemail.

I tried my dad again, remembering the robot that had answered when I'd called him from home that morning. But this time, he picked up.

"Hi, Gertie," he said. "It's been a minute since you've called."

"Yeah," I said. "I'm sorry."

"Are you okay?"

I hated that—that a call from me made him wonder if I was okay.

"I'm at the hospital, actually. I . . . well, I'm *in* the hospital. This aerosol can exploded, and I got cut."

"Excuse me?" he said. "You're in the hospital again?"

I could hear an exhale of smoke.

"Yeah. It was stupid. I was, well, alone, and I thought it would get better on its own."

"Your mom wasn't there?"

"She's, um, well, she's in Florida. But she's on her way home."

"She went to Florida?"

"She's been seeing this guy. I wasn't sure if you knew."

"No," he said. "We haven't been talking."

He was quiet for a moment. Then he inhaled sharply and said, "Are you okay?"

"I'm fine. On the mend."

"Do you want me to come there? I can't believe you're all alone."

"You don't have to come," I said. "Mom's on her way. I just wanted someone to talk to. Are you at home? Tell me about it."

"I'm on the balcony of the apartment I rent in Sioux Falls. It was hot here today. I don't know if that's normal for June or not."

"Tell me more—what is Sioux Falls like?"

My dad talked, and I settled back onto my pillows. In rehab he wasn't supposed to talk to us, and I hadn't called him much since my mom had started seeing Vaughn. Everything had happened so suddenly.

At first she called his trips to rehab "business trips," but I remembered when she told me he was an addict. I was seven, and she asked if I wanted to take a walk with her. When we got home, I looked at my dad and mused that he didn't look any different than he always had. For a long time after that I thought what he was doing must not be that bad. It went against everything I'd learned at home and in school, but I wondered if there was a way he could just keep doing what he was doing, but not get worse.

Even when I'd seen him for the last time that night in December, at this same hospital, he'd looked as he always had. But a few weeks before that, he'd rolled through a red light, high on oxy, getting his second DUI in as many years. What if he'd hit someone? And I understood what my mom said to me when she told me she was going to divorce him: that every day with him felt like it could end in disaster, and she didn't want to live that way anymore.

"It's South Dakota's biggest city, but it feels like a small town," my dad said.

"Hm," I replied. I hadn't been listening. A hand wrapped around the doorframe of my room and fished for the light switch, plunging the room into darkness. And then I was alone.

"I know, it's riveting stuff, my new life in Sioux Falls," he said.

"I'm sorry. I'm sleepy from the stuff they gave me." I paused. "You would like it."

I'd meant it as a joke, but my dad didn't laugh.

"Well, I'll let you go," he said. "Get some rest."

He hung up and I lay there in the dark with my phone resting on my stomach. The voice on the other end didn't sound like it belonged to my dad. I wondered what I'd missed, every step of growing up, what I hadn't seen or what had been kept from me. Another past behind a hidden door.

My phone was facedown on my hospital gown, and suddenly light seeped from its edges.

You need to be more careful, McMahon.

I let the phone fall to my side. I turned my head away. There was a bed next to mine, but it was empty. I wondered what my parents' rooms were like when they were in rehab, when they'd first met and had their whole lives ahead of them—lives they were about to begin again. Hundreds of nights that could've been different. They branched off into futures that were boxed away with other dusty possibilities of time.

But if my parents' lives had gone differently—gone better—I probably wouldn't be here in the hospital. A lot of the stupid things I did in the past year I'd done because their lives were crumbling, and I thought mine might as well, too. Was there any way they could still be in love? Right up until the end there were good things between them, good things that survived a lot of misery. My dad brushing my mom's hair at night, my mom singing the songs he liked. My mom probably remembered more, or differently, but that's what I saw.

Would any good things last between Jamie and Hayden? I know I said it could never work out between them, but I mean, what if? The thought was as calming as a drug. Not every love had to have a half-life.

June

THE PAST

I OPENED MY EYES TO SEE A PAIR OF SNEAKERS RESTING ON THE FOOT OF my bed. Converse, with stars and hearts drawn in ballpoint pen on the soles. I followed the legs and there was Cindy in a chair, her fingers gliding over her phone.

She looked up and smiled. "I just posted a photo of you on Instagram with all your IVs. People are *flipping out*."

She turned her phone toward me. My eyes were closed, my lips slightly parted, my hair greasy. It wasn't a good picture of me, but even worse was that the girl I saw looking back didn't really look like me.

"I wish you hadn't posted that."

"I couldn't not." Cindy swung her feet to the floor and propped her elbows up on the bed. She spun one of her tight dark ringlets around her fingers, trying to get it to frame her face the way she liked. She wore a brown T-shirt that said *hello* in ten different languages. The clock on the wall read eight-thirty.

"How'd you get here?"

"I took an Uber."

"What about finals?"

Cindy shrugged. "I turned in my paper for English, asked to go to the bathroom, and walked straight out the front doors. Didn't look back. I told the nurse I'm your sister. She gave me a weird look, like, 'Oh God, don't tell me there are two of you?'"

"We should be careful or they'll do a medical experiment on us to find out what went wrong with our DNA."

"But the procedure will go awry."

"And we'll wake up zombies."

"And eat everyone at school."

"Hey, wait," I said, catching sight of a breakfast tray on a table by the door. "Would you bring that over here?"

Cindy plopped the tray down on the rolling table by my bed and swung it over my waist. A pile of rubbery pancakes wobbled on the plate. I stabbed one with the fork and jiggled it in front of Cindy's face.

"Get that away from me!" she cried.

We passed the carton of orange juice back and forth. Cindy wrapped an IV tube around her finger. She leaned in close to me and took a selfie. On the screen I looked normal and happy except for the hospital gown. Cindy turned on music, and it bounced brightly off the clean white floors. "Cool you don't have a roommate," she said, looking at the empty bed next to me.

The loneliness last night, the sadness, all the mopey thoughts about love—all that disappeared, and I felt better even though my mom, and her anger, was streaming north in an airplane, ready to land in this room.

"I almost forgot." Cindy pulled a folded piece of paper from her back pocket. "I bought us a star."

"A star?"

She handed me a certificate with cursive script embossed with gold foil that said: "Gerndy. HD 510204. Declination 14°32'35.8"."

"It's kind of bullshit, actually," she said. "I bought this but the certificate they sent doesn't tell us anything about it—like if it's a red giant or yellow dwarf or whatever. But I thought, you know, even if it's not official, like it's not a regulated industry or whatever, here's a place. Our place."

I clutched the paper hard. Even though we would never get there and even if it wasn't really ours, it was a place that existed. Burning atoms far away, as real as this hospital room. It's still there, assuming it was real in the first place.

"Cindy," I said, "this is amazing."

"Oh my God, are you actually crying?"

"We're just officially the most adorable nerds ever. How much did this star set you back?"

"Like ten dollars."

"Cheapest real estate in the galaxy, everyone."

We laughed, but then Cassie came in and we stifled our giggles as she changed the bag of fluids dripping into one of my arms.

She looked from me to Cindy like she knew I didn't really have a sister.

"Your mom is here," she said. "She's talking to the social worker right now."

My heart lost its footing and slid down into my stomach. Fear and relief: They were an unstable floor beneath me.

"Does she look mad?" I asked.

"She's very worried," Cassie said. "The infection was serious."

"I think you're avoiding telling me that, yes, she looks really pissed."

Cindy snorted with laughter. Even Cassie's serious face slipped into a smile. Then the door to my room opened, and the first thing I saw was my mom's gray bag, fake leather, swung over her shoulder and bulging with whatever she threw in hastily on her way out of Florida. Her short strawberry hair was greasy from her night on the floor of the airport. Fingerprints smudged her glasses, cloudy over her gray eyes, perched on her narrow nose.

She looked at me, her eyes wet with tears, and she rushed to my bedside.

"Mom," I said. "I'm really sorry. I didn't mean to get hurt."

She squeezed my hand. She looked worried, and relieved, and happy to see me, but most of all there was kindness in her face.

Cassie gathered the garbage from her needles and bandages and slipped out.

"There's another chair, Mom," I said hoarsely. I gestured to the corner.

It was only then that my mom noticed Cindy. Surprise filled her face, then concern. Cindy smiled weakly.

"Hi, Mrs. McMahon." She waved a few fingers, keeping her hand close to her chest. "Did you have a good trip?"

My mom pulled the extra chair across the room, grimacing as she took in my IVs. She hated doctors, hated hospitals.

"Cindy, does your mom know you're here?"

"That would be a big fat *no*," Cindy said, shrugging.

My mom usually laughed at Cindy's antics, but not this time. She sighed and settled into the chair. She looked tan, and her hair was bleached copper by the sun. She was still wearing flip-flops over polished toes—her Florida uniform, she'd called those sandals and a T-shirt and shorts when she was packing. Her hand covered one of my IVs, and her thumb rubbed my skin absently. It hurt, the needle getting nudged back and forth, but I didn't want to tell her to stop.

But then I noticed it. The ring on her finger.

"Mom," I said, pointing.

Cindy's gaze followed.

"Holy shit," Cindy said.

The diamond was the size of a firefly. It caught the light and sent twists of sparkles over my woven cotton hospital blanket. My mom looked down at her own hand with surprise, as though she'd forgotten.

"Yes," she said quietly. "A little bit of good news."

She smiled, and her eyes searched my face. I could tell she was waiting for it—for me to say something she'd have to scold.

I could say *congratulations*.

I could say *wow*.

I could even just say *okay*.

But I thought about the past six months, and searched again for any words that might make my mom slow down. I said, not for the first time, "Mom, remember how your divorce lawyer advised you not even to *date* until six months after the divorce is finalized?"

My mom bowed her head. A heavy sigh escaped her.

"Gertrude, please. I'm not in the mood."

"I'm just saying."

My mom raised her palm. "You're always *just saying*. It's time you listened. I have a chance for happiness after twenty years of putting up with your father's bullshit, and I'm not going to give this up, okay?"

"You mean after twenty years of being supported by him? Of him buying us a house and cars and food and clothes and paying rent on the antique store?"

My mom shot up. Her body was a sharp line above me. Cindy reached out and grabbed my wrist, startled, and my mom softened a little bit. She didn't like witnesses to our fights. She didn't like the idea of Cindy hearing, of Cindy telling Annemarie about our bitter voices ricocheting off the cold hospital tiles.

"We're not having this conversation here, Gertie."

"Why not," I shot back. "You think the hospital staff doesn't already know we're fucked up? You think Cindy doesn't know? I came in here alone. The realtor called the ambulance. You're off . . . *wherever*."

"Quit it."

"Mom." Tears flooded my voice. "Why, though? Why *him*? It's all happening so fast."

My mom went to the window. She stepped into the sun's glare and was devoured by the light. Her hands framed her hips and she tilted her head back so that the sun found her neck.

Cindy leaned in close. For a second, I thought she was going to get up and leave. "Please don't go," I whispered.

"Never," she said.

Finally, my mom spoke: "I don't know what to say, baby. Except I think we need a little time."

Baby. I couldn't think of the last time she'd called me that.

"That's what I've been saying," I replied. "*Time* for us to adjust."

My mom came back to the bedside, shaking her head.

"No," she said. "I mean, we need a reset. This summer. Vaughn and I—we need time together to figure things out. To make sure it's right for both of us—and for you."

She looked down at her ring again, angled her finger so the stone glittered.

"We're going sailing in the Mediterranean."

My mouth fell open. Someone's shoes echoed hollowly in the hallway. The sound stopped right outside my door, and all three of us—me, my mom, Cindy—looked expectantly at it.

Annemarie appeared, peering into the room skeptically, as though she didn't think that she'd find anyone. She saw Cindy, and she exhaled.

"Cindy," she said, tapping her foot. "Come on. I'll take you back to school."

"Shit," Cindy said. "Did you see my Insta? Is that how you found out?"

Annemarie ignored Cindy. She smiled quickly at my mom, still with her hand on the door. Then she looked at Cindy, Cindy looked at me, I looked at my mom. I picked up the thread that was dropped when Annemarie opened the door.

"Where am I supposed to go?" I said. "I doubt the social worker you had to talk to would like it if they knew you were going to leave me alone all summer."

"All this," my mom said, waving her hand in a circle to indicate me, the hospital, the wound. "It's all part of the same problem. We just need time to get used to new ideas. And I think you've made it clear you'd be happier staying with Cindy this summer, rather than with me and Vaughn."

She looked at Cindy's mom.

"If it's okay, that is, Annemarie," she said quickly. "I would of course reimburse you for everything."

Cindy and I both stayed silent. Our eyes met. By asking the question, my mom let go of the rope holding the guillotine. It fell. The truth was coming out now.

Cindy's mom released the door handle, looking reluctant to give up her claim to the exit. She looked beautiful in her white blouse tucked into a black skirt, her heels clicking across the floor. Her approach was wordless, and my own mother inhaled sharply, as though she wished she could suck her words back in. But they were out in the world, heckling her like flies, and by not saying anything Annemarie said everything. I could've saved my mom the embarrassment if I'd had the chance to share what Cindy had told me by the fire.

Annemarie's eyes flickered toward me. "You know, Carla, I was actually thinking it would do Cindy good to spend some time with new people this summer. Just a refresh after everything that's happened. Maybe you could find a camp for Gertie?"

My mom looked as stunned as if someone had thrown a Bible at her. Her face twitched, and she swallowed hard, and I could tell she knew as well as I did what Annemarie meant: *Everything* meant *everyone* meant *me*.

The bad influence.

The degenerate friend.

"Mrs. Fellows," I said weakly, "Cindy didn't have anything to do with the aerosol can. I was alone when it happened. She'd already gone home. It was just me there . . ."

"It's okay, sweetie," Annemarie said, and that word—*sweetie*—stuck to me like gum. "Come on, Cindy." She put her hand on Cindy's arm.

"Mom, stop it!" Cindy jerked free. "Gertie needs me."

"*Cindy.*"

Cindy rose reluctantly. "Gertie, I'll call you later."

Annemarie sighed and followed her, leaving me and my mom alone.

My mom frowned. "We'll figure something out," she said. "You can always come with us on the trip. Wouldn't it be fun to go to Europe?"

I looked at my hands. My veins, bruised from IV needles, traveled the length of my body in blue lines, but my thoughts shot to South Dakota, to my father. And how sad he'd be to hear my mom was getting remarried only a couple months after they signed divorce papers. That some new guy was taking her to Europe, taking his daughter to Europe. The loneliness he must have been feeling—I felt it, too. That little bit of hope for the family, hope that everything could go back to the way it was before, was gone. He lived in Sioux Falls, and he wasn't coming back.

"I want to stay with Dad," I said quietly.

"Oh, honey," my mom said.

"He's clean now," I said sharply. "And you heard what Cindy's mom said—this place is toxic. We need time away, and you said yourself you need time alone with Vaughn, so what do you suggest I do? Get emancipated? I mean, if you really feel that's best, we can look into it."

"Jesus, Gertie." My mom's gaze fell coldly on me. But I could tell she still felt the sting of Annemarie's judgment. Maybe in some small way she liked the idea of sending me to my sober father when Annemarie's husband was still using.

"Fine," she said, raising her hands. "Call your dad. See what he says. Don't be surprised if he doesn't want you to stay there. He just got out of rehab, honey, and you know he was never a very involved father."

"Don't be surprised if someday Vaughn isn't interested in you anymore."

This shook up my mom's anger, and she was about to pour it out when Cassie returned with a bunch of forms for her to fill out.

"Good news," Cassie said. "You can go home today."

She pointed to different lines on different pages, and my mom clicked her pen and started to sign.

"Get those signatures now," I said to Cassie bitterly, "before she takes off again."

"Quit it," my mom said.

"You quit it!" I snapped.

Cassie hurried the forms into a pile and left.

June

THE PAST

DAYS HAD PASSED SINCE I ASKED MY DAD IF I COULD STAY WITH HIM. I could hear his voice in my head. The long pause, long enough for me to want to take back what I'd said. Followed by, "Sure, hon. You can stay here." Then he'd cleared his throat with three quick coughs, a sound I hadn't realized I'd missed.

Did he not want me either? I'd tried not to sound desperate, but he'd heard it—that I had nowhere else to go. Maybe in the end it didn't matter if he wanted me or not—I couldn't spend all summer at camp doing crafts like everything was okay.

Before we'd hung up, I said, "You would hate this guy, Dad. Vaughn. He's the worst."

My dad chuckled, but it was a sound coming from a body whose heart had stopped.

Meanwhile, my mom had taken an *it's your life* attitude about my going to South Dakota, and she threw herself into planning for her own summer. I started packing, too, totally baffled by the idea of being away from home for almost three months. I threw my flute in the suitcase, knowing I wouldn't practice. I thought of my dad in December, saying he liked his things and needed to take all of them with him. I looked at the stuff in my room and wondered what I would need.

Soon the one thing I had left to do was figure out how to tell Cindy. School had let out, and our moms were keeping us apart. I should've told her right away, but I kept erasing the texts in which I started to say it. I knew she missed her dad. I knew she'd be sad that I was seeing mine while she couldn't see hers.

I had finals to make up. I'd missed them while I was recovering, so I spent the first few sweaty days of summer vacation sitting in school taking the exams my classmates were done with. The air-conditioning in the building was off, and the classrooms only half lit. I kept getting stuck in some memory—my mom by my hospital bed, my dad on the phone, Vaughn eyeing me. Triangles morphed into squares during my geometry final. I yawned and finished the last proof. I left the test on Mr. Simon's desk—he'd wandered away earlier and never come back.

In the hallway, the lockers were all thrown open, forgotten contents revealed, and dazed by geometry I abandoned the halls and stepped outside to where my eyes battled the sun. I found Cindy and Gabe sitting on a bench near the doors.

"You're finished!" Cindy cried. "Let's celebrate."

"I was just about to bike over to your house," I said.

But Cindy didn't hear me. She pulled a flask from her bag and held it out to me triumphantly. Gabe was looking at me, but I kept my gaze sternly away from him. My bike was locked to the rack, a few scattered cars were spaced out in the parking lot, but otherwise the school grounds were empty, and we were alone.

I swallowed the vodka that was hot from riding out the day in her leather bag. Little fires danced in my throat. "Thank you," I said, coughing. "So, look—"

"My mom is finally loosening up," Cindy interrupted. "Letting me come here, for example. I think I might be able to talk her out of the Gertie interdiction. She didn't say no when I asked her again this morning—she just didn't say anything. Giant leap forward for Gertie-kind."

She screwed the top back on her flask. "How much time do we have? Your mom didn't book a camp for you yet, did she?"

She looked at me hopefully.

"I have to tell you something."

This made Gabe look up at me.

"I have to stay with my dad for the summer."

Cindy's head jerked back in surprise. "What, in Sioux Falls?"

I nodded. Gabe tilted his head and looked at me as though he wanted to say something Cindy couldn't hear, but I fixed my eyes firmly on Cindy and nodded.

"What the hell? When did your mom decide this?"

"It sort of came together last minute. We didn't really know what else to do with me. I'm so sorry, Cindy."

"Is your dad clean?"

"I think so."

"Well, cancel!" Cindy gasped. "Call your mom, call him, call the newspaper. We can work this out."

"I don't know, Cindy . . ."

Could I back out, if Annemarie *would* let me stay? I'd have the whole summer to find the right time to tell Cindy the truth, and I could fix everything.

"I'm texting my mom," Cindy said, her eyes big and desperate.

Then I realized: I couldn't stay with Cindy until she knew about me and Gabe—in a moment when nothing felt certain, that was a beam from a lighthouse. I had two choices: go to Sioux Falls or tell Cindy the truth right there, outside the school, in front of Gabe.

"Cindy, it's okay," I said. "I think I have to go. My dad sounded happy, and I keep thinking of him alone in South Dakota. I miss him, and I want to be there for him to help him stay clean."

Cindy's face looked like it was searching for a way out of this.

"I'm sorry," I said again.

"When do you leave?" Cindy shoved the flask roughly into her bag.

I hesitated. "Day after tomorrow."

"Excuse me?" Cindy looked aghast. "When were you going to tell me?"

"I'm sorry, Cindy. It was last minute." I checked my phone. "I should go."

"Right, you have to pack."

"Cindy . . ."

"I guess I'll see you when you're back?"

"Yeah," I said, deflating. "See you."

She touched Gabe's elbow as she turned to let him know they were leaving.

"Later, McMahon." The way Gabe said my last name, it was like a punishment.

I lifted a hand, let it fall over. A gust of wind pelted my ankles with specks of dirt. Above, clouds freighted moisture across the sky. Cindy slid into her car, Gabe into the passenger seat, and they were gone.

June

MY MOM'S FLIGHT LEFT FROM A DIFFERENT GATE. EVERYTHING WAS planned with precision. She was going to meet Vaughn in Florida, and together they'd fly to Italy. She and I waited in the slouching security line, my mom periodically checking her watch and fixing the other passengers with a stern stare.

Hopping one-footed back into our shoes on the other side of the scanners, with my phone back in my hand, I saw a text had come through while my bags were rolling under the X-ray.

I have a stay of execution in the works over here. I'm really working my mom hard—she was so surprised you have to stay with your dad, she didn't mean for that to happen, she's worried he hasn't been clean long enough. She feels bad about what happened at the hospital. If she says yes will you stay? Have your mom call her? Please?

"If anything comes up, call me, okay?"

My mom was gathering all her things around her, but she stopped to look at me.

What could I do? Ask my mom to hold on, tell her I'd changed my mind, or just wait until we parted ways and sneak out of the airport?

"It's okay," I said. "I mean, everything will be okay. I'm sorry if I've made things difficult for you."

I moved my phone back into my bag. My mom put her hand on my shoulder.

"I know this has been a tough year, sweetie, but we'll get through it," she said. "Should we get a coffee together?"

"I think I'm just going to go to my gate."

"You sure? Do you need a snack or something?"

"Thanks, Mom. I'm okay."

She hugged me. Told me again to call her, to use the satellite phone if it was an emergency. If we both looked back at each other as we went in opposite directions down the crowded concourse, it wasn't at the same time.

Stepping onto the plane was like walking through ivy into another world. I folded myself into my seat and looked out the window. Planes glinted in the blue sky, coming and going. Clouds shaped and reshaped themselves then blew away in the wind. The airplane made its electronic whirring as the flaps went down. A hundred video screens lit up all at once and then went dark again, glitching out.

Just before I put my phone in airplane mode, a new text came in, not from Cindy, but from Gabe.

Hey, McMahon, what's going on? Text Cindy back. I'm worried about you. Why do you have to leave?

I inhaled sharply, and the woman in the seat next to me glanced up from her book. I wrote a text to Cindy and sent it right away so I didn't overthink it.

I'm sorry. I'm not allowed to stay. You're the best for trying. Don't forget about me. xoxo

I toggled the phone into airplane mode and closed my eyes. The plane backed away from the gate and the engines made their no-going-back noises. It was too late to change anything. My windpipe felt as thin as a gold chain.

The plane rounded a corner and came to a stop. All at once, the engines roared and we picked up speed and the nose tilted off the ground. There was a quick upward lift and we banked over Detroit, turning west. I pressed my fingertips to the window. The trees of the suburbs bunched together in large squares, cut up into grids by the streets. The lines of houses thinned, replaced by stamps of farmland.

At the other end of this plane ride waited my dad. I could see him standing outside the terminal holding a cigarette, gazing into the distance like he used to do from the garage.

What was I going to say when I saw him? It felt like ten years had passed in the last six months. Did he still watch the late shows, and did he still keep the Sunday paper in his car all week, reading it, I didn't even know when—glancing down at stoplights, resting a moment before getting out of the car when he went places? He used to move the loose sections off the passenger seat so I could sit down whenever we went somewhere together. Would he try to quit smoking for the hundredth time? Did he still talk to his sponsor from Michigan on Fridays? *Hey, Tim, it's going okay.* Did he have any ideas for what we'd do this summer? What we'd say? How we'd be?

I could have been with Cindy right now, sprawled on her floor with the television on and bowls of popcorn balanced on our stomachs. Her happy dog, Ralph, would be chasing her cat, Steve, who just wanted to yawn and sneeze and get high on catnip in peace. Cindy shooing them out of the way of the television screen. Between movies we'd hop on Cindy's laptop and look for apartments in New York, where we wanted to go to school in two years. We could never believe the prices, but we ignored that part for now, imagining we lived there and were making it work, absorbed by it and lost to it, meeting all the people we were destined to meet. All those plans with Cindy felt like they were already in the past. We'd lived some version of them, I guess, just in their imagining, and they felt as real as the lives of Jamie and Hayden did, everything so carefully crafted they took on a second skin of truth, hiding the fiction underneath. My book was turning into my lifeline—if Jamie and Hayden could survive, I had no excuse not to. If I could solve their problems, I could solve my own. So I gripped their arms and kept them close, hiding in their story and desperate to believe that if they could forgive each other for the things that were to come—unknown but sure to be terrible—then Cindy could forgive me for a brief moment in a bedroom that I'd entered who I was and come out who I wasn't.

part
two

December

THE FUTURE

AIRPORTS. AS IF THEY AREN'T BAD ENOUGH ALREADY, THEY ALSO REMIND me of that summer I got on a plane and didn't come back the same. Lately, in my mind, I've been back in Sioux Falls, turning over rocks, looking for a better story.

It's just after Christmas. A year is wrapping up. Fifteen years earlier, Mom and I had parted ways. I flew to Sioux Falls, and she flew here, to Florida.

Ciarán and I deplane in Orlando and walk straight to the rental car agency. One day was the minimum rental, though we'll be here only a few hours, the time it takes to pick up Mom from Vaughn's house—which until recently was her house, too, though she'd never been added to the deed. It's been months in the planning; we're here to take her home with us.

"Can we promise each other this is the last time we'll ever go to Florida?" I ask Ciarán. The engine starts quietly and our phones connect to the dashboard automatically, fighting over the Bluetooth.

Ciarán rubs his eyes, then looks at me with the skin of his face pulled down toward his chin.

"Don't do *The Scream* at me," I say.

He breaks open with a laugh. "You Americans can't resist Florida's swampy allure. I expect we'll be coming back one day."

"Don't underestimate me."

Ciarán slides onto the freeway and cuts a line through the middle of Florida; it's damp and hot and black-eyed Susans thrive in the full sun alongside the road. I never could've imagined, at sixteen, that Mom and Vaughn would stay together this long. More recently, I never could have imagined that they, having been together so long, would ever split up.

"I've been writing a new book," I say, after some silence.

Ciarán's eyes widen but he doesn't take them off the road. "You didn't tell me."

"I do it alone. On my lunch break. When I can't sleep."

"What are you writing about?"

"My parents. The summer I spent in Sioux Falls with Dad."

"Uh-oh," Ciarán says.

"I know. Mom won't be happy."

"It's been a long time, though, since all that. Maybe she won't mind anymore."

There's more I could say, but I don't. For all I've written about myself—twisted versions, anyway, shaped into fiction—I've never touched that summer. I couldn't write about it because I didn't feel ready to change anything that happened. Now I'm finally stretching the limits of my imagination as far as my heart in concert with my conscience will allow.

Does time make you safe? What about fifteen years' worth of it? People tend to choose: *I became who I am despite the past or because of it,* which aggravates me since it is so clearly both. Sometimes I think of the book I wrote at sixteen as an example: I learned how to write and how not to write from it. But more than anything I'm just fond of it, even more so lately as I think so much about that summer. Jamie and

Hayden's book leaned toward sadness—from the very beginning I put them in an impossible situation—but I admire the instinct I had then, to hunt for hope even where it seemed there was none. I haven't lost that.

After an hour in the car, Ciarán eases off the highway and the road gets narrower as the ocean gets closer. I catch glimpses of the blue through steely condo complexes on A1A, and then we turn off the beach and stop in front of Vaughn's sand-colored bungalow capped by a turquoise tile roof.

"If you'd flown into Melbourne, I would've come get you," Vaughn says through the half-open screen door. "And then I would've dropped all three of you back off."

Which airport we flew into was an argument Vaughn insisted upon every time we visited. He thought it was silly to pay for a rental. We didn't like connecting flights, an excuse we used to cover the truth: We wanted our own car, an escape hatch.

"Connecting flights are harder for Mom," I say, knowing he hasn't considered her.

Vaughn doesn't reply; he already seems impatient for us to leave. His face has sagged with age, and his hair would be white except he's gone bald. He's tall and has always slouched because of it, and now his stooped shoulders crouch even lower, and the same put-upon scowl covers his face. I did everything I could to get between him and Mom when I was a girl, and I can feel again the spittle that landed on my cheek the time he towered over me and said, bitterly, "When are you going to grow up and learn to respect people's privacy?"

He got what he wanted, in the end. I built a life away from Mom, away from him.

Mom comes to the door, perched on her scooter, waving as Vaughn pulls the portable ramp from the garage.

"Hold on," he snaps at her. "Back up."

My heart takes an angry leap toward him. Ciarán puts a hand on my elbow. "We're getting her out of here," he whispers.

Mom goes past Vaughn without a word—either they already said their goodbyes, or they aren't going to. "I'll get her bags, then," Ciarán says, ducking inside.

I help Mom into the car. "You're leaving your orchids?" I ask.

"They don't travel well."

"But Vaughn is going to kill them."

"Better them than me." Her sigh pulls her shoulders up into a shrug. Vaughn ambles over, looking about the world as though it's pleasanter now that Mom is on her way to being gone. He smiles detachedly and rests his elbow on the top of the car door.

"So, how's your writing?" he asks me.

To myself I say: *I hope you die soon.* To him I say: "Fine."

"Nice little first book you put out," he says. "I can't tell you how relieved I was when your mom told me you didn't quit your day job."

I turn to Mom and put a finger gun to my head and blow my brains out all over Vaughn.

He ignores me.

"You're doing the right thing," he says to Mom. "I'm getting too old to take care of you. You should be with family."

I thought he was my family. That's what Mom said on the phone when she and Vaughn decided not to live together anymore. He never married her. She never got on his insurance, which is why she couldn't treat her disease. That small glinting ring he'd given her sat on her finger for years before she finally took it off.

"Boy," Ciarán says when the car doors have shut. "He's a piece of work."

Mom, in her previous role as Vaughn's advocate on our rare visits, would've once bristled at a comment like this. Now we get a snort and a closed-mouth laugh.

"You ready to go home?" I ask.

Except we're not going home, not to New York, anyway, where Ciarán and I have lived for almost ten years. The city scares Mom, its infrastructure unsupportive of her condition, the crowds unkind to her scooter. When she first asked if we could all live together in

Michigan, I thought I could change her mind. I spent months looking for an accessible apartment in the five boroughs and found none
we could afford, none that would've offered me and Ciarán a sem-
blance of privacy.

We had jobs that could be done at home. Ciarán was the tech
editor for a magazine, I was an administrator for a parks conservancy.
We agreed we would ask our bosses about going remote.

"I am ready," Mom replies. "My story started there. Now it's going
to finish there."

I feel dizzy and upset in the back seat. Ciarán catches my eye in
the rearview. I exhale and say, calmly, "You know I get sad when you
talk like that."

"Why? I've had a good run. A few more years of B cells attacking
my myelin, a few more black holes on my MRIs, and I'll be ready to
check outta here."

"That's not the plan, Mom. We talked about this. You're going to
be with us a long while—"

"Let's settle for a little while," she says.

"Should Ciarán just crash the car now?" I butt my way into the
front of the car, an elbow on either seat. "Is that what you want?"

"All right, girls," Ciarán says.

She's joking, he's been insisting from the beginning. She's not
really going to kill herself. She looks out the window, smiling in-
wardly at a secret.

Still a Catholic boy at heart, Ciarán has been able to take her morbid outlook in stride. "You're telling me we could've just moved to
New Jersey?"

Righteous for someone who isn't a native New Yorker, I said, "If
we go eighteen miles we might as well go eight hundred."

The security line at MCO moves slowly, a late-December super-
hangover of Disney and Christmas. Mickey Mouse ears look aggressively similar to the horns of a satanic goat. I'm happy Mom is with
us, but the uncertainty about what comes next fosters a somberness
that overtakes all other feelings.

"There's part of me that wishes I could go and live with your father," Mom says. "He wouldn't give me a hard time."

"You really think that wouldn't have been a disaster?" I ask.

"Not after all this time. And then I wouldn't be a burden to you."

"You're not a burden, Mom."

Her scooter has been whisked away to the cargo hold, and she digs in her purse for a bill to tip the woman pushing her airport wheelchair.

"Don't fret about that, Carla," Ciarán says, pulling out his wallet.

"Thank you, Ciarán," she says.

She pulls out of the line near the scanners, ready to stand unsteadily, holding on to the metal detector for balance, and be patted down.

She thinks her life is over, that she has nothing left to give. She's been approaching her death like a joke. How could she not have anticipated how much this would hurt me? How devastated I would feel when she revealed, after the lease was signed and movers hired and goodbyes said, that she wanted to move back to Michigan because it had recently become a right-to-die state?

June

THE PAST

SIOUX FALLS. THROUGH THE WINDOW, GREEN-AND-GOLD PLAINS GES-
tured beyond what I could see, and the prairie rose up toward us with
great speed, and then we came even with it. The plane bounced a few
times before connecting solidly with the runway.

I waited to get off with everyone else, my notebook clutched in
my hand, and then we funneled out into the muted terminal. Everyone else from my flight streamed past me like they knew where they
were going. Baggage claim came into view and my eyes circled the
space in search of my dad, but he wasn't there. A second look proved
the first right.

I wandered outside, but he wasn't in one of the cars idling at the
curb. The bags from my flight made their slow rotation. My two
suitcases arrived side by side. I heaved off the first and chased after the
second. Then I checked my watch, checked my phone, went and
checked my face in the bathroom mirror.

I called his landline, and his cellphone, but both routed me to voicemail. I didn't leave a message because he must have been on his way to get me. I sat on a bench outside the terminal, compulsively checking my phone for a missed call, but the screensaver—me and Cindy at the beach, wearing big sunglasses—stared back at me. It was hot, hotter than I was expecting, and a dusty wind whipped through the pickup lane. One by one, the other people waiting for rides reunited with their friends or family. It came in bursts like this: A flight landed, the terminal spewed people out, then they dispersed into the rolling land that went on forever.

I called my dad again. Without admitting to myself he wasn't coming, I checked Google Maps for a bus route.

Did I give him the wrong time, the wrong day?

Did he forget?

Was I really there at all? Maybe I had died in the hospital, and my purgatory was to sit outside the Sioux Falls Regional Airport forever—which to be honest was a real bummer as far as purgatories went.

No one seemed to notice how long I'd been waiting. Behind the fortress of my bags, I brought my knees to my chest, lifted my feet off the sidewalk, and stared at coins of flattened gum.

There was a sign for a shuttle that stopped at a bus terminal downtown. I looked over my shoulder toward the pickup lane, but my dad wasn't there. I could always get out of the shuttle line if he pulled up. But he didn't, and eventually the bus picked me up and took me away.

At the downtown bus depot, I waited alone on a bench in the shade until another bus came that took me to the outskirts of the city. I got off where Google told me to, and there was still a long walk to go. Partway there the sidewalk ended and I pulled my suitcases over the grass. My dad lived in an apartment complex called Rolling Prairie, and finally I saw its green-and-white office and its clubhouse with a pavilion shading the entranceway. Rows of buildings multiplied beyond, all the same, their parking lots mostly full. It was evening now, getting toward dusk. Numbers printed on the sides of the buildings directed me toward my dad's, and I stood outside the entrance and took everything in. The rain gutter hanging down into a bush, a dented metal house of mailboxes outside the building.

The outer door was wedged open with a brick, and I shouldered my way in, heaved my things up the steps one at a time, sweating, and came to face my dad's door.

There was no answer when I knocked. I tried the handle and found it was unlocked. The door caught on a pair of shoes, and I gave it a shove to push them away. The first thing I smelled was smoke.

"Dad?" I called.

There was the sound of a fan spinning, but no answer.

A hallway with brown carpeting led to a single bedroom, where light came in through a rectangular window crosshatched with vertical blinds. There was a small, unclean bathroom. A kitchen to the right, with a metal sink full of dirty dishes and, for some reason, a toothbrush perched on the edge of the basin, and through the kitchen a table and an armchair. And a balcony, and there I saw my dad sitting in a white plastic chair just like the ones we had at home in the garage, smoke smudging the air around him.

"Dad," I said again. This time the sound caught his attention, and he looked over his shoulder, blinking like he couldn't quite place me.

"Oh my God," he said, his voice muffled by the closed door. "Hon, what are you doing here?"

I opened the sliding door and stuck one shoulder out, about to demand why he hadn't picked me up, why I'd had to walk two miles from the bus stop with my bags, but my falling heart crashed through all of these questions. As soon as I looked into his small, drooping eyes half shaded by their lids, I could tell he was high.

Even though I knew coming here was my only option, I'd had doubts about it, but I never thought he wouldn't be clean. He'd lost everything, at least I thought he'd lost a lot—how could he stand to lose more?

His voice when he spoke again was as slow as oil glugging out of a bottle. "What are you doing here?"

"What do you mean, what am I doing here?" My voice was tight and angry; I was trying so hard not to cry.

I held my elbows, worry replaced with bitterness at having been forgotten. I'd thrown his question back at him, but he was silent. We stared at each other; now we had to decide between the two of us who would say the next thing.

I caved. "Do you not remember that I'm staying here this summer?"

He sat up and shakily stubbed out his cigarette. His tired eyes looked more alive with a scowl in them. "Of course I remember, Gertie. You said you were getting in tomorrow."

"Today." I spread out my arms obnoxiously to indicate my presence. "Obviously."

He didn't say anything. I looked out over the balcony, trying to make sense of things. Below us was a pool with a small hot tub next to it. No one was lounging by it, but someone had left a towel draped over a pool chair that was missing some plastic belts. The fluorescent blue water shimmered. Beyond, past the rooftops of the buildings, golden prairie unspooled.

"So you forgot," I said finally, and flatly, trying to prompt him to say something. I met his eyes. He lit a new cigarette.

A sigh forced its way out of my closed throat. My dad laughed through his nose.

"I missed that sound," he said. "Frustration mixed with disgust. Look, I thought it was tomorrow. I'm sorry."

I ran my hands through my hair. I was greasy and tired from the plane, and more than anything, more than being angry or annoyed or scared that he was using again, I wanted this to work. This *had* to work.

"I missed you, Dad."

He stood up and opened his arms, and I stepped into them, my ear against his chest. He held me close. His lungs crackled with smoke. Maybe I did say the wrong day on the phone. Maybe he was just really busy.

Even as I allowed for these possibilities, I knew they weren't real.

"Sorry, hon," he said, calling me that again. "My antidepressants make me a little tired."

"Are you taking lithium still?"

He laughed. "C'mon in."

He led me inside with the slow, plodding gait of someone sleeping on their feet. He stopped to grind his mostly unsmoked cigarette out in an ashtray on a small table next to a recliner, the only chair in the living room, which faced a television set up on the floor. Cords snaked to an outlet a few feet away, stuffed with plugs.

"Look, Gertie," he said, "I'm not feeling so great. I think I'm going to get a little rest. And then we can have dinner, but help yourself to anything if you're hungry in the meantime."

He said this without looking at me, and then he disappeared into the bedroom.

The door clicked shut, and I was alone. The dirtiness of the apartment closed in. Everything was gritty and soaked in smoke, and beneath the scent of a million inhaled cigarettes was something stale and sour. Fruit left to rot in the sun.

The landline was cradled on the kitchen wall. Next to it was a desk with an old computer and a corkboard hanging above. Seeing the phone, I couldn't help but wonder what would happen if I called my mom and told her he was high, he hadn't met me at the airport, and I wasn't sure if this was going to work.

I would be asking her to get on a plane *again* to come and rescue me. But when she heard he might be using, would it matter? She would do it . . . right?

My hand touched the receiver with a flat palm. Then I saw a box tucked in the corner. It was a new air mattress, the receipt still stuck under the cardboard flap of the box. I looked at the date; my dad had bought it yesterday. There was a new pair of sheets propped against it—pink with white polka dots, still folded around cardboard.

For me.

I picked up the phone and sank to the floor. Flakes of ash from an overturned ashtray on the carpet stuck to my sweaty hands. I didn't know what I'd say, I just knew I'd told my mom I'd call her, and she was probably getting worried.

Her voice woke up the other end of the line. She asked how my flight was. I stared at the box, the sheets, the ash on the floor, the empty living room.

"It was good," I said. "I'm at Dad's place."

As soon as I said it, I knew I wasn't going to tell her the truth. She went into the details of her trip—she and Vaughn were leaving Florida for Europe tomorrow—and then she asked if she could talk to my dad.

I froze. It was only eight-thirty. She used to get suspicious when he went to bed early; she thought it meant he was hiding something.

"He went to pick up dinner," I said. "I'll have him call you tomorrow before your flight."

"A little late for dinner," my mom said. "Did he not ask if you were hungry when he picked you up?"

"No, he did," I lied. "I just wasn't hungry yet. And we're an hour behind you, remember."

"Okay. Make sure he doesn't just let you eat crap all summer," she said. "Have him call me tomorrow, yeah? Early, if possible. We have our flight to catch."

She sounded relieved she didn't have to talk to him. We hung up, and in fact I was really hungry. When I opened the fridge my eyes fell on a few bottles of beer. I was sad to see them, but also relieved, because I grabbed one and cracked it open and took a few heavy sips. I rested the cold bottle on my forehead, then took it back out onto the balcony and sat down in my dad's chair.

He'd left his soft pack of Marlboro Reds on a low glass table, along with his lighter, and I flicked the spark wheel and watched the tiny flame burn out and reappear. I used to shred his cigarettes when I was little before I grew to like the smell of secondhand smoke. He would get so angry; he told me I was wasting money because he was just going to buy more. Now I'd rather he smoked all he wanted and give up the other stuff.

I finished the beer, and then another. Thick patches of stars emerged. The Milky Way seeped through the darkness like a stain. My dad didn't wake up like he'd said he would. I could hear his snores through the wall.

I slapped a mosquito away from the wound on my thigh. The doctor had told me I needed to find somewhere in Sioux Falls to have the stitches taken out. I was supposed to do that tomorrow, or the day after. I couldn't remember.

The lights beneath the pool's surface made the water glow green. There was a text from Cindy I hadn't replied to yet. The secret was turning me into a terrible friend.

The last time I saw my dad, I'd almost told him what I'd done with Gabe—it had been that night in December when he took me to the hospital. My blood was on me, staining the dress, and though it was hardly visible against the black fabric, I burned with shame when the nurse made me take off my heavy coat, certain everyone could see it, smell it, know what I'd done. The story threatened my lips, a desperate urge to come clean, to come unstained. But we'd never talked about things like that before, and in the end I told him nothing.

My beer was empty, I was feeling a little drunk, and my stomach growled. The memory of that December night and the IV of guilt still in my arm made me think that if my dad didn't deserve forgiveness, then I didn't either.

After a long time outside, I went in and inflated the air mattress, not worrying about the noise because my dad's sleep would be deep for a long time. With the sheets on and a blanket shaken over the top, it looked inviting. It looked like a little place for me there. I climbed onto it without eating anything from the fridge; all the food was unhealthy and I could see my mom wrinkling her nose, angry at me for eating junk and mad at my dad for buying it.

I would have to get used to it being just the two of us. Who else was going to be there for him, if not me?

June

THE PAST

"LOOK, HON, I'M SORRY ABOUT YESTERDAY," MY DAD SAID THE NEXT MORN-
ing, yawning as he filled the coffee maker.

He wore a loose, stained T-shirt, with the logo of his old ad agency
on it, tucked into gray sweatpants.

I opened a box of Cheerios and peered inside.

"Don't sweat it," I said.

"You know you can always come here, though. You're always
welcome."

"Thanks, Dad. I appreciate it. Mom didn't think . . ." But I didn't
finish what I was going to say. It didn't seem fair right now, first thing
in the morning. "I mean, will you call Mom? She wanted to talk to
you."

"I called your mom this morning and left a message."

"Oh."

We shook cereal into bowls and waited, bleary-eyed, for the coffee to brew.

"So, look," he said. "I've got something to do today. But maybe you saw the pool outside. There are towels. It looks like a nice day."

"What do you have to do?"

"Just errands."

"Whatever happened to that advertising agency, the one your friend knew about?"

"No dice there."

"Have you had any interviews?" I asked.

"You always did ask so many questions."

He cleared his bowl and went sighing into his bedroom, and there was the sound of drawers opening. He said goodbye on his way out, and I looked around, in full daylight, at the messy apartment. I was faced with my first day in Sioux Falls.

I called Cindy and waited through four rings for her to answer. I imagined her in Michigan, looking at her phone and wondering to herself if she wanted to talk to me.

"Hi." Her voice was flat.

"Hi. How are you?"

She didn't answer. She sounded mad, and my whole body stiffened as though her anger were a freezing agent.

"I'm sorry," I said. "Really sorry. I know this is really hard. I wish I had a choice."

"You didn't call yesterday like you said you would."

"I'm sorry, it was crazy, my dad *forgot* me at the airport—"

Cindy cut me off. "This isn't *only* about you, Gertie. Now I'm all alone here this summer. My mom was going to let you stay here, with me, because you needed us. Your mom would've let you. It was her idea in the first place, remember? You could've changed your plans. But you didn't think about me."

I fell silent. She was right. I'd only thought about getting away.

"I'm sorry," I said again. "About everything. It all happened so fast."

"I'll forgive you, I guess, if you promise to call and text me a lot."

"All the time," I said quickly. "If things get really bad with your mom, will you tell me?"

"Yeah," she said. "What about you? If, like, something goes terribly wrong—what's our code word? How will one of us know if the other needs help?"

"Can I just tell you I need help?"

"C'mon, Gertie. Think about it. One word that will make me know you're not okay. *Really* not okay."

"Well . . ."

"You claim to want to be a writer, and you can't think of a word?"

"How about . . . *aerosol*. But I promise I'll only use it if it's a serious emergency."

"I guess that's fitting," she said. "Last time you crossed paths with one of those bad boys you almost lost a leg."

"So, we have our word," I said. "Sioux Falls isn't exactly a tourist destination, so I wouldn't drag you here for nothing. I'll only use it if I have no other choice."

"If all other lights have gone out."

"If I really, really need you," I said.

There was a voice in the background, Annemarie calling Cindy from below.

"Ugh," she said. "I have to go."

"I miss you so much."

"Me, too," she said. "I mean it—I want actual phone calls, like we're boomers or some shit."

"I will."

And then she was gone, and the apartment was quiet. I went to the bathroom and read labels in the medicine cabinet, but I stopped when I saw the names I was hoping wouldn't be there, all prescribed by different doctors. The most recent had been filled just a few days ago. I wasn't that surprised to see them—that might have been the worst part—but I did wonder how much longer until this round of MDs cut him off and he'd have to go looking elsewhere.

He was always so good at convincing doctors that he hurt. The fake injuries, broken toes, the chronic shoulder pain. And maybe he was in pain, somewhere. I thought back to the way my leg had ached in the days after the aerosol can exploded, thought back to the power of pain.

I let the mirrored door of the cabinet fall shut.

I rubbed my eyes hard, and then I searched the bathroom cabinets and found gloves and a sponge. I put Spotify on my dad's computer and played Taylor Swift on full volume. There was an open bottle of bleach underneath the kitchen sink that might have been left by the last tenant, and I scrubbed the toilet and counters and table. I wiped the ash off my dad's nightstand and plucked cellophane pull tabs from his cigarettes out of the carpet where they'd been dropped. I knocked on a neighboring door, and a skeptical-looking old lady with gray hair paused at first when I asked to borrow her vacuum, but she nodded when she peered over my shoulder into my dad's apartment and saw the bucket and bags of garbage tied up. I filled the vacuum's canister. I stood in the middle of the living room and looked around. There was still a black smoke stain on the ceiling above my dad's armchair, and the fridge was sticky with spills, but the apartment suffocated me a little less.

I wrung the sponge out into the bucket, and a little bleach splashed onto my thigh, and the skin around my stitches stung.

"Shit." I'd forgotten to ask my dad about taking me to a doctor. Then again, did I really need a doctor? The stitches were loose, pushed up by my healed skin. The cost without insurance, and the hassle of it, when all I needed was a pair of scissors, made me wonder if I couldn't just do it myself.

The internet told me there was a grocery store called Hy-Vee down the road. I'd never heard of that chain, but I took the key my dad had given me, and just as I was pulling on a sweatshirt my phone chimed with a text.

From Gabe.

Hey.

My brain was numb from bleach fumes.

You didn't reply to my text from yesterday. Are you ok?

I could block his number. I could do it right then. Only a few days ago I'd told him he was awful, exactly the type of attention he craved, so he could build you back up before tearing you down again.

Maybe, a little, I craved it, too. It was a distraction, the velvety feeling of regret.

Hi. I'm okay.

June

I SET OUT FOR THE GROCERY STORE ON FOOT, BUT I COULD FEEL GABE'S text sucking me back to Michigan as though through a pneumatic tube.

It was hard not to think about him when Hayden looked a little like Gabe, and no matter how hard I tried Hayden refused to go to the plastic surgeon for a new face.

Whatever. If anyone ever read the book, they'd imagine Hayden for themselves, so there was that to take solace in. I wouldn't be passing Gabe on to their imaginations. He'd just be living in mine, where Hayden finds poor, bewildered Jamie in the Underworld and has to figure out what to do with her. *I* had to figure out what to do with her. Taking this next step in the novel felt like having a body to get rid of.

Maybe she's emerged onto a battlefield, and there are bodies twisting and burning, blood soaking the grass. He takes her to the rebel safe house—a simple, inconspicuous farmhouse preparing itself for dusk. A lantern flickers on a table within and candles shine in the windows. A bevy of chickens poking around in the dirt are inspired to run by some invisible force. Beyond the house, there's a field thick with grapevines clinging to wooden trellises. From the barn comes screaming, and toward the sound rushes a woman with a bowl of steaming water, an armful of clean rags.

I had to keep remembering that Jamie was still a stranger to Hayden, that he didn't trust her yet, so next, I guessed, he'd have to take her inside and lock her in a closet while he talked to the others and figured out what to do with this strange person, wearing strange clothes, who claimed to know nothing about the war they were fighting.

While Jamie was in the closet with her growing problems, I was in Sioux Falls and had to deal with my own. Hy-Vee devoured me into its fluorescents. I looked for hydrogen peroxide and bandages from the pharmacy, tweezers from beauty, and kitchen shears from home goods.

Before my dad lost his job, I had my own credit card for emergencies; now I had twenty dollars my mom had given me as we parted ways at security. I used almost all of it, the cashier tipping change into my palm after she bagged my purchases.

On my way out I paused at a Now Hiring sign pinned above an application kiosk, but I looked down at the scissors and peroxide and decided I'd have to think about that later. There was a pavilion with picnic tables lining the building, and I went to the farthest one and ensconced my foot on the bench. The spidery black stitches lived in raised skin, and flecks of crusted pus clung to the threads. I brushed them away, grimacing. I poured a little antiseptic over the wound and remembered being in the girls' bathroom back in Michigan, doing the same thing.

I tore the zip tie holding the scissors to their cardboard backing with my teeth, poured disinfectant on their blades, and opened and closed them a few times. I took a deep breath and gently lifted a stitch with the pair of tweezers and brought the scissors close to it, preparing to make the cut.

"What are you doing?"

My breath fell into a sinkhole. I dropped the scissors and they fell on the ground. "Fuck," I said, diving to retrieve them.

Collected behind me was a group of Hy-Vee employees wearing their checkered button-downs pinned with name tags, holding cans of soda and salads from the prepared-food section. One of them tore a bag of Skittles open as he raised his eyebrows. Next to him, a boy with curly red hair and a long face looked at me like he was trying to place me in his memory. Two girls exchanged glances that suggested they'd be having a conversation later about this. And behind them, the only one not in a Hy-Vee uniform, was a boy with glasses and soft brown hair with a deep side part. A twin, I realized, of the boy with the Skittles, but they'd done everything possible to look different. They were all young, my age about, and all white except for one of the girls, who was Black with warm brown eyes and straightened hair that shone in the sun.

I looked down at the scissors.

"Oh, is this your table? Sorry, I can move."

"Whoa," the boy with the Skittles said. "Are you taking out your own stitches? Is that what you're doing right now?"

The group closed around me, each of them peering at my leg.

"Why don't you go to a doctor?" the white girl asked. She had a honey-colored mess of curls piled on her head, and as she talked, she pulled on a gold chain around her neck that held a chunk of tangerine quartz the size of a thumb. Acne dotting her cheeks somehow looked as lovely as freckles.

"Why pay the co-pay, I guess?" I said, and without moving to another table I poured more peroxide on the scissors and shook excess drops from the blades. I was getting close to losing my nerve.

"Are we really going to stay for this?" the Black girl asked.

"Hey!" the red-haired boy interjected. "I think I saw you outside yesterday. Do you live at Rolling Prairie?"

My eyes widened. "I just moved in yesterday. Well, not really moved in. I'm staying with my dad for the summer."

"We're neighbors," he said, smiling, ignoring the fact that every-one was looking at me and the scissors and my puffy stitches.

"So, are we doing this?" Skittle-boy said, rounding the picnic table and leaning closer to my leg.

"Yeah, I'll watch this," said quartz-girl.

She sat down next to me. Her necklace swung like a pendulum.

"Go ahead," she said.

"Jill, don't encourage her," her beautiful friend cut in.

"No, this is good practice." She looked up at me. "I want to be a nurse one day."

"Well, nurse," I said, extending the hydrogen peroxide toward her. "Hold this."

I lifted a stitch with the tweezers.

"I'm Gertie, by the way," I said.

The group returned a chorus of heys. Skittle-boy was named Aus-tin, and his brother was Adam. My new neighbor, Lucas, sat down next to me at the picnic table. Willa stood next to Jill, looking at me like it wasn't the first time she'd thought white people were crazy.

"Aren't you not supposed to perform surgery on yourself?" Adam asked. "Like, isn't that against the Hippocratic oath?"

"I'm not a real doctor," I said, "and this isn't real surgery."

Adam bit his lip as though he wanted to say something more, and I met his eyes, but he rocked backward and looked at the ground.

"Okay," I said. "Deep breath."

I slowly snipped the first loop, trembling, but the second one was easier. "This is gross," Willa muttered. The thread crawled under-neath my skin as I pulled it out, wormlike, and I grimaced and gagged a little and then the stitches pulled free from my skin.

Lucas and his friends stared at me. Then Jill said, "That was kind of badass." She said it plainly as she stood up, like it was just a fact.

"What would you have done in my situation?" I asked.

"I would've gone to a doctor," Adam said.

Everyone ignored him.

A gust of wind swirled through the pavilion, drying the sweat that had sprouted on my skin. I was left in that silent moment following a performance, and I soon realized I had to be the one to do the next thing, so I gathered up my materials. "I guess the show is over," I said, and was about to turn away when Lucas told me to wait.

"Hang out a little," he said.

They asked me where I was from, and how long I'd be there, and then they started talking about people I didn't know and I clutched the scissors and the peroxide and nodded along to stories whose context was foreign to me. And just when their lunch break was over, I remembered the Now Hiring sign.

"Are you guys really hiring?" I asked.

"We're always hiring," Willa said, in a way that told me how she felt about her job.

"I was thinking I might apply."

"Truly rad," Lucas said. "Do it. We need more friends to make work bearable. The more of us here, the better the chance you'll get scheduled with at least one cool person."

"You're awfully quick to call me cool. You don't know me."

They were standing up, collecting their garbage, and when I realized Adam wasn't coming with them, I waved to him and followed everyone else inside. They disappeared back into their shifts, and I filled out an application at the kiosk, listing Cindy as a character reference as well as the woman whose toddler I used to babysit.

When I went back outside, Adam was still sitting on a picnic bench, but he'd moved to one closer to the entrance.

"Hey," I said. "So, you don't work here like the rest of them?"

"Oh, no. My brother and I would kill each other. I'm working for the school district this summer, installing new computers. I just came to get the car keys from Austin."

"I was going to say that would be a lot of time together. But I'm an only child, so I wouldn't know."

"Does that mean nonstop attention from your parents? I'd *almost* rather see too much of my brother."

"Not really. A lot of time alone. I don't mind it, though."

I looked down at my leg, at the shiny pink skin that seeped a little bit where the stitches had been. I fitted a bandage over it.

"Well, I guess I'll go," I said. "I hope the bandage doesn't come off on the walk. If you see a trail of blood, don't worry, it's just me."

Adam put his hands in his pockets and twisted at his waist, looking out at the road. "You're walking? How far?"

"Not that far."

"I'll drive you. If Austin ever comes back out with the keys." He peered beyond me, into the store.

"It's not far."

"I'm literally not taking no for an answer," he said.

"Fine. I *choose* to accept your not taking no for an answer. Last time I refused a ride I broke my wrist and had to have surgery."

"Seriously? You need to be more careful."

Gabe had texted me the same thing in the hospital. Gabe and now Adam. Maybe they'd meant it out of concern, but when they said it, it felt like they'd chiseled away a little piece of my body and kept it for themselves.

"Finally," Adam said when Austin appeared in the path of the automatic door, whistled to get our attention, and tossed his brother the keys.

I followed Adam to a green Jeep parked in the lot. He was oblivious to the way his words had brought up a past and feelings he'd played no part in but that, for me, were never far from the surface. He opened my door, and, chided, I almost didn't get in, just squinted at him, annoyed. He was tall, and I had to look up to meet his eyes. But then I thought about how easy this had been, meeting these people, and I folded myself into the seat. Maybe we'd be friends. Maybe we were already.

Adam started the engine, looking down at my leg as he did.

"Are you sure you shouldn't go to a doctor?"

"I'm fine," I said, a little tersely. "Don't ask again."

"Just, you know, don't get sepsis."

"Very funny."

"I'm not joking," he said, but his voice broke with laughter.

"I'll keep an eye on it," I said. "I didn't think anyone would see me do it. I didn't mean for it to be a big deal."

"It probably made Austin's day," Adam said. "Everything's a joke to him."

"Oh, yeah? What about Lucas?"

"What do you mean, what about Lucas?" Adam glanced at me sideways.

"Just like, what's his deal? I guess he's my neighbor now."

Adam shrugged. "We're not that close. You're just here for the summer?"

"I think so."

"You don't know?"

"There are a lot of unknowns, Adam."

He laughed again. "You know, I'm meeting some friends at Falls Park. Do you want to come? The people at Hy-Vee are okay, but it might not hurt to meet other people."

"What does that mean?"

"They're just a clique. Like, they're cool, but Jill gets to decide who's in and who's out."

"And you're out?"

"I'm halfway in, but just because of Austin, and also by choice."

"All right, then," I said. "Let's go to this park you speak of."

"Really?"

I shrugged. "Why not?"

He'd been heading toward Rolling Prairie, but he pulled off onto the shoulder, looked around, and spun a U-turn.

"I get to text my dad and say I'm hanging out with a friend."

"Have you never had a friend before? That's so sad for you."

"Shut up," I said. "I have friends in Michigan. Like, two of them."

I opened my text thread with Cindy. *I'm in a car with a boy who is taking me to a park.*

You're not serious!

I looked out Adam's window at the new streets rolling by. It was the first summer of my life that I wouldn't see Cindy, wouldn't see home. I knew I wasn't the only person in the world facing something new, but I still felt alone.

December

THE FUTURE

CIARÁN AND I RENTED A TWO-BEDROOM CRAFTSMAN ON THE OLD WEST Side of Ann Arbor. A walkway cuts through a small lawn, but it's still more green than we're used to, coming from New York. There's a narrow driveway, with dead tufts of plants in its cracks. Ciarán turns in to it.

"Give me a second," he says, pulling bags from the trunk of the new-to-us car we'd bought. He doesn't close the hatchback, where Mom's scooter still sits, folded up. "I'll be back."

We're already on bad footing with the landlord, who we made install grab bars in one of the bathrooms before we moved in. We pointed out the city law that said he had to pay for the renovations to fortify the wall. "It's an old house," he grumbled, as though its ableism should be legacied in.

Mom pushes her door open and takes her right leg, the one that can no longer move or feel anything, and lifts it out of the footwell. Her scooter weighs fifty pounds and I haven't been to the gym in a year, but I struggle it out of the back and heft it over to her. She grabs the roof of the car and pulls herself up to an unsteady stand.

Ciarán, who's set the bags on the porch, hurries back over. "So impatient, you two." He takes some of the weight of the scooter as I set it down.

A few front steps are taken care of by a ramp. Mom wheels into the house, her exploration tentative at first, as though she isn't sure someone else doesn't already live here.

Ciarán and I moved all our things from Brooklyn a few weeks ago. In Mom's room, we set up a new bed and dresser. We framed a Maud Lewis print for the wall. Ciarán swings her suitcases onto her bed; they contain only her clothes and shoes and toiletries, some jewelry and files and a few old Christmas ornaments of paper-thin glass wrapped in newspaper. Everything else was Vaughn's.

"There's an orchid in the kitchen," I say. "We got it at Home Depot."

She goes into the open kitchen, an island separating it from the living room. "It looks happy." She digs her fingers into the pot to check if the bark is damp. I stand apart from her, watching.

Ciarán joins me. "The stork didn't bring us a baby," he whispers, "but it's brought us a baby boomer."

Laughter overwhelms me, and I wonder why I can't stop. I've been so worried—worried she would hate it here, worried we would hate it here, worried Ciarán would change his mind about me, about all of it, and go back to New York alone.

"What's funny?" Mom asks.

December was damp, mild, with leftovers of green. Winter hits hard and quickly as soon as January arrives. We go online shopping; winter clothes for Mom arrive in boxes, sit in snowdrifts on our porch. It's a polar vortex year, freezing here because it's too warm in the Arctic, a contradiction I find beautiful on the weather map, the thick white freeze curling down from the north and settling over the Midwest. It's a small comfort, romanticizing our doom.

"This type of weather reminds me why I always wanted to throw myself out the window every winter," Mom says. She sits on the couch, looks despairingly at the patterns of ice that crawl up the windows, at the thermometer tucked between the screen and the glass that reads fifteen degrees.

"This house is only one story, so I doubt it'll do much," Ciarán says.

"At the right angle, maybe," she muses.

"Stop it, both of you," I scold.

Mom laughs from the couch. She moves to get up, lifting her legs and placing them in front of her scooter. "Untwist, you dumb legs," she says, slapping her numb right calf that, in response, stays completely still.

"Don't do that!" I rush over, grab her elbow as she hoists herself up onto the scooter.

"She doesn't like it when I slap myself around," Mom says to Ciarán. "I don't need help," she adds, brushing me away.

"She doesn't want you to hurt yourself," he replies diplomatically.

Frustrated, in need of a break, I go into our bedroom, mine and Ciarán's, the small one without a bathroom attached because Mom needs the walk-in shower. I open the curtains wide to watch the snow. The city is different from when I lived here with Adam during college. Downtown, the small restaurants have gone away, high-rises have gone up, and while campus is in many ways the same, school spirit is a poor fit on me, so I don't see myself walking through the Diag brimming with nostalgia.

There are still as many trees, though, big old-growth oaks claiming seniority over the neighborhoods. Whenever things were messy with Adam I took long walks from campus to this part of town, probably even past this very house, carrying a notebook and writing down any thought that came to mind, looking back later for a gem in the rubble. Everything was abstract; the stories I wrote for class tried lines on for size. Until recently, I've been taking a long break from writing, something my absolutist, *tie me to the chair* writer friends can't believe.

The answer I give them, that artists need rest, doesn't suit them. The answer I want to give them, that often it's better not to write, would only make them think me unserious.

It might be hard to write about Mom now that she's here, sharing my space. For a long time, I thought my annual visit to Vero Beach to see her and Vaughn was going to be it, forever. Ciarán knew better.

"Someday soon we're going to need to figure out what to do about your mom," he said not long after we got married.

At that point, I'd only known about her disease for a few years. Diagnosed with multiple sclerosis when I was a child, she revealed the truth only when her long remission ended, when the illness became progressive and her mobility deteriorated. Dad knew, too, I found out, but neither of them had told me, another secret for the ledger. Even Vaughn knew before me, and Ciarán, who'd come from a long line of men who'd left, had spotted Vaughn's decision well before Vaughn let us know it.

Ciarán slips inside the bedroom not long after, joins me on the bed in the cold light.

"I'm wasting my writing day," I say. "Sundays are writing days."

The hours are ticking away.

"It's okay to take a break." Ciarán pulls a throw blanket from the foot of the bed and wraps it around me.

"No! Now I'm going to fall asleep."

To be alone, Ciarán and I close the door to our room. Teenagers again, when your bedroom is your whole world. I'm sinking back in time, becoming younger. At the same time, the mirror shows someone older. Cindy gets Botox, which I might try if I could afford it.

"I didn't realize the cold would make Mom want to kill herself faster," I say.

"She's only joking."

"You don't know how stubborn she is."

"I know how stubborn you are."

I turn on my side and throw a leg over his middle. "I'm not. Do you see how she wears hats and gloves inside? And the heat is boiling and costing us a fortune."

"The poor dear!" Ciarán puts his arm around me and shakes me lightly. His in-between accent gets more Irish when he makes fun of me. He grew up with his mother in Dublin, spending summers with his father in Boston—that is, until his dad's second family got too big, nudging him out. I laugh, too.

"I'm sorry," I say. "We have to promise to talk about things other than her."

"Don't worry, Gertie, we're not going to change."

The sky turns dark blue as we lie together. Soon I'll go back out, where I'll find Mom sitting in the dark. She hates artificial light but will allow me to brighten the kitchen to cook dinner. The stork didn't bring us a baby. Ciarán had always wanted one. He'd be such a good dad, everyone said.

June

THE PAST

I GOT HOME LATE THAT NIGHT, AND MY DAD WAS ALREADY SLEEPING. THE smell of smoke was fresh, dirty, and invigorating all at once. Maybe he was avoiding me. So much had changed since we'd lived together. It was hard for me to know how to be around him. *Who* to be around him. A daughter, or a roommate? A protector, or a friend?

I lay in the dark on my air mattress. I'd ended up catching the bus home when Adam and his friends left the park at ten P.M. They were on their way to get food and see a midnight show. Adam looked disappointed, offered to drive, but I waved him off. I'd been sad thinking about Cindy, and my dad, and I was aloof and distracted and I didn't pay attention to any of Adam's friends. They were rising seniors and had been friends forever, and it wasn't hard to tell they didn't really like my being there and were wondering why Adam had brought me.

"I'm sure I'll see you around," I'd said to Adam.

My phone rang. It was Gabe. The question of whether or not to pick up was as obvious as a single-solution equation, but I answered anyway. There was so much debris in my math with him.

"Why are you calling?" I asked. "Is Cindy okay?"

Gabe sighed. The air mattress squeaked as I stood up, and I went out onto the balcony.

"What do you want?" I asked. "Whatever mean thing you're going to say, just say it."

"If you'd given me the choice, I wouldn't have gotten back together with her. And who knows where we'd all be right now."

"Why would you call and tell me that? Why would you bring that up?"

"I just want you to know. You shut me out, but maybe it didn't have to be that way."

"Gabe," I said, "you told me I meant *nothing*. If you didn't want to be with Cindy, you shouldn't have gotten back together with her."

"It was stupid of me to say you meant nothing."

"You're torturing me on purpose." My hands were shaking so hard I thought I might drop my phone into the grass below. "I can't do this right now. In fact, I can't do this, ever. We're only talking to each other because it's late and we have no one else to talk to."

"You keep writing me off, like I'm incapable of any real feeling, but I *liked* you, Gertie."

My sinuses seized up and a tear fell down my cheek because I'd liked him, too, but I wasn't going to admit it to him, not now or ever, because what I felt didn't matter. Only Cindy mattered.

"I have to go. Maybe don't call again."

I hung up, feeling like a coward. *Maybe* don't call again. I'd cauterized my feelings for him again and again but they kept on bleeding.

I sat in my dad's chair. Gabe wasn't the first time I hadn't been able to resist doing something to nudge a feeling I'd had forward. There was a night at the end of freshman year when things between my parents were changing from sometimes bad to always bad. My dad left for a two-night business trip, but when my mom called the hotel in Toronto where he always stayed, the concierge—who knew her by then, my dad traveled there so often—said in a hushed voice that he hadn't seen Mark in a month or so.

When my dad got home from wherever he'd been, I listened to their fighting from my chair in the fume-filled garage. The yelling stopped, and my mom appeared with her purse and car keys. She told me she was going to stay with a friend, and she didn't look back as she got in her car and spun out of the driveway. Then my dad came outside, and I thought he was going to sit with me—but he just left, too.

The quiet pooled at my feet and grew deeper until it held all of me.

I watched the sun sink into the tree line, stabbed by branches. We lived right at the edge of the suburbs and the country, and even though a half mile down the road brought you to a main artery, with sidewalks and strip malls, looking around you might think there was nothing for miles except for our next-door neighbors, their lights winking through the trees. Maybe I should've been embarrassed by my parents' yelling, but instead it made me sad that no one had heard it except me.

I remembered something I'd discovered not long before that. A bottle of painkillers in my closet, hidden in a dusty black garment bag holding only one other thing: the black dress I would wear to the party with Gabe later that year.

Those small pills seemed just as weightless as the fabrics that hung in my closet. I started to wonder if they were still there, or if my dad had found another hiding spot for them. Wondered so strongly that I left the garage and went up to my room. I shuffled through hangers until the garment bag appeared. I fished its bottom until my fingers met smooth plastic and I pulled out a little orange canister, glowing nuclear at its core.

The curiosity grew. Why did my dad sacrifice so much for these? I'd read about it, heard about it in school, always feeling ashamed during DARE lectures because for almost everyone else in the room it was hypothetical but for me it was real. But even though it was real for me, I didn't know what the pills *felt* like.

I opened the bottle and shook two into my palm. Looked at them. And then I put them in my mouth.

As soon as I swallowed them, a fluttery feeling of vindication flew through me. I was a part of this now, even if my parents didn't think I was. Almost immediately I felt buoyant, not because the pills had started working, but because the pills were so metaphorically powerful—they ruined lives, they changed the course of history, and now they were a part of me, too. I couldn't wait to tell my parents, to make them feel bad for causing so much trouble. I was sure my act would make my mom feel admonished for her tough love; I was sure it would slap my dad awake, make him realize that even though this wasn't his fault, he needed to try harder.

But the giddiness faded, and the pills did nothing but make me drowsy, and my parents didn't come home. I crawled into my bed and fell into a sleep so deep that when I awoke it was like I'd been cut away from an iron anchor holding me to the ocean floor.

I thought about how different I'd felt finding the pills in my closet then—betrayed, used, lost—compared to finding them in his medicine cabinet here. I was resigned, accepting, if anything inconvenienced— couldn't he have waited a little while to relapse? I'd just arrived. Was the thought of a summer with me really that unbearable? Why did this have to happen *now*?

I was sure Jamie was probably feeling that same feeling but times one thousand.

By now her parents, who have been wondering when to worry, have started worrying. She doesn't know what will happen to her— her fate is in the hands of these strangers.

Someone guards the door to the closet where she was taken. Now that I was inside the house, I imagined things differently. There were Edison bulbs, and wallpaper, even though I said before that Hayden was medieval, with a bow and arrow. I could change it to a gun. I could do whatever I wanted.

Maybe Jamie gets the chance to flee. Maybe Hayden unlocks the door to her closet because he doesn't sense she's there to hurt anyone.

After all this time fighting, he's learned how to tell. But when Jamie reaches the door at the end of the hall, and opens it, she realizes she has nowhere to go. Her freedom, shot in the leg. Her heart, a statue pulled down by ropes.

She asks to stay. She asks to help them. When asked where she comes from, she says only that she got lost somehow, that there are things about her past she doesn't remember.

January

THE FUTURE

"HOW DO THESE LOOK?" I ASK CIARÁN, SHOWING HIM THE CUTTING BOARD, where there's a pile of chopped carrots for soup.

"Grand, sure," he says, not lifting his eyes from the bouillon cubes he's unwrapping.

"I know so little about you," Mom says. She's in the living room, watching us.

Ciarán and I, standing on opposite ends of the kitchen island, look over at her.

"Me, Carla?" Ciarán asks.

Mom is silent for a moment. "Yes. Gertie brought you to visit so rarely. I didn't meet your mother until the wedding."

"Well, Ma doesn't get over here much," Ciarán says.

"What are you talking about?" I cut in. "You know Ciarán. I told you about him right after we met, when we hadn't even started dating."

"Don't remind me," Mom says. "That trip to Europe you didn't tell me you were going on. I was so worried about why you weren't answering your phone. I finally called Cindy, who informed me my nineteen-year-old daughter had gone to Spain alone on some sort of medieval pilgrimage."

She's repeated this indignity often enough over the years that I no longer feel the sting of an attack. There might even be something close to pride in her voice.

"Cindy won't let me forget that either. She says hi to both of you, by the way."

College had put more distance between me and Mom than ever. She was starting her life with Vaughn; I was starting mine, whatever that meant. Once Ciarán and I were together, I kept him away from Vaughn, as I had Adam. The distance was calculated. Vaughn had always found me rotten. Would it change what Ciarán thought of me, to see someone hate me so much?

I'd gone abroad after my freshman year to hike part of the Camino de Santiago, a pilgrimage through Spain to the shrine of James the Apostle, and though I went for reasons more personal than spiritual, I admitted that all the walking made it easy to believe in something bigger than myself. I took the Camino Francés from Sarria to Santiago de Compostela, traveling seventy miles over five days. Yellow scallop shells—the symbol of the Camino—guided me through green Galician countryside and medieval villages, a dedicated-enough trek for me to take my Pilgrim Passport to the Pilgrim's Office in Santiago for my Compostela certificate. I went to the cathedral and looked dutifully through the bars of a closed gate at Saint James's reliquary. From there I went on to Finisterre, another four days of walking. There was blood in my brain and blisters on my feet and all I cared about was taking the next step. When I reached Cape Finisterre my head cleared for the first time in what felt like years, and the immensity of the Atlantic was a wind that went roughly through me.

I'd done the pilgrimage for the walking, and the time to think. Ciarán had come for more complicated reasons having to do with faith, and if he still had it. I must have passed him as I rounded the lighthouse—he told me later he'd been there an hour already when I arrived—and sometimes in my mind's eye I remember seeing him among the other pilgrims taking photos of themselves at the end of the earth. Other times it seems like I was completely alone as I stepped off the concrete path to the rocks beyond, as near to the edge of the promontory as I dared, and looked out at the incredible expanse of water. Alone until I heard Ciarán's voice, barely cutting through the wind, when he tried to pass around me.

"Sorry to bother, but I didn't want to startle you." He gave me a wide berth, his head ducking into his shoulders as though to apologize for his presence.

"You're fine," I said.

We didn't say anything else to each other. He looked at me like I was someone who would stay a stranger, but one he might remember. I'd felt the same. I lingered at Cape Finisterre long after he moved on, and we wouldn't have ever seen each other again except we found ourselves staying at the same hostel that night. He was sitting outside with a book when I arrived, and this time it was me who waved shyly, unsure if he'd prefer that I ignore him.

"It's the girl from the end of the world," he said.

We shared protein bars and beers and talked until everyone else at the hostel drifted to bed and our voices became bothersome. I noticed more about him: We were the same height, almost exactly; his coarse hair fell somewhere in a Venn diagram of red, blond, and brown; his green eyes with starbursts of amber near the pupils. We'd been assigned beds in the same room and we each stood outside the bathroom as the other changed. I fell asleep quickly, as I had every night on the Camino, and when I woke up Ciarán had already packed his backpack.

"She wakes," he said.

I hadn't seen him before because he'd taken the northern route, but we both had bus tickets back to Santiago, and plane tickets to Madrid, and from there he'd go home to Dublin, where he studied computer science and journalism, and I would go back to the States, where I took writing classes. We sat next to each other on the four-hour bus ride, trading Instagrams and phone numbers at the end, and still I thought I'd never see him again, which is probably why it felt safe to call Cindy from Madrid and tell her about the boy I'd met.

"How could you not tell me you and Adam broke up?" she asked.

"We haven't."

"Does this Irish boy know that?"

He didn't; in fact he didn't know anything about Adam at all. I'd hardly talked to anyone for two weeks, and Adam didn't come first to my imagination when a stranger asked for the story of my life. I didn't want to talk about home at all; leaving it behind for a while had been the whole point, so I could see who I was on my own after years of not knowing.

"I made a new friend, Cindy, that's all."

Cindy was projecting because she'd never liked Adam—at least, that's what I told myself as my flight was called, and I hoisted my backpack over my shoulder, and listened to Cindy's voice in my ear as I ducked into the plane.

But I could use Cindy's dislike of Adam as proof I wasn't falling out of love with him only for so long. Ciarán called a few months later from back in Dublin. I could hear he was a little drunk, there was the noise of passersby, he might've been standing outside a pub, his friends inside.

"I was telling someone about the Camino and I thought of you," he said. "How's things?"

I was stricken on the other end of the line: For years I'd more or less just let things happen to me. To leave Adam, I'd long felt, would be less like a choice and more like being orphaned. But then Dublin seeped into my ear. *Here's a choice,* Ciarán seemed to say.

June

THE PAST

"JESUS, GERTIE, WHAT KIND OF QUESTION IS THAT?"

It's what my dad said to me when I asked him at breakfast if he would ever consider trying methadone, something I'd read about online.

"Would you, though?"

He scowled and shook a section loose from the paper he was reading. *The New York Times,* just like at home, except there wasn't local distribution and the paper was two days old by the time it arrived in Sioux Falls.

"I don't need it, Gertie. Lighten up, okay?"

"I'm as light as they come. Fucking hydrogen over here."

My dad couldn't resist a laugh, a sound that reminded me of a creaking wheel. "As flammable, too."

"You know what happens next, though, don't you? I mean, we all do."

Dust trembled in the sunlight that cut through the room. A moment passed before my dad smiled and sighed, but he didn't answer me, just took his coffee and the paper out onto the balcony. I put my head in my hands. I was tired. I'd gone to Willa's last night after Lucas knocked on my door and asked if I wanted to hang out. I'd almost said no, but I needed to keep the promise I'd made to myself. If I was going to *really* be there and not think about Gabe, whose memory was a tribunal I kept getting dragged in front of, I had no reason not to accept.

Even though I was tired, I lugged a kitchen chair outside and sat next to my dad. We both looked like we'd already spent a whole day in the sun, though we were only watching morning from the balcony.

"Did I ever tell you about the first song you heard when you were born, in the hospital room?" my dad asked. "It was 'Did She Mention My Name' by Gordon Lightfoot. I don't know why your mom let me play it. She was probably in too much pain to care."

"You never told me that."

I looked up from my coffee into the sun until I was forced to blink. The sky was such a snarky blue, so bitter and bright, like it thought it knew everything. And in my mind the fuse blew on the hope for my parents, those two people who'd once been young, because I arrived and became the reason they were miserable. My dad sang a few lines from the song, breaking my anguish into pieces. His fingers twitched almost imperceptibly against the guitar that wasn't there.

"Why that song?" I asked.

"I was feeling melancholy. About the idea that people leave and stop talking to each other."

"That's depressing. Also, you left first."

Luckily, he laughed.

"I played it for you when you wouldn't sleep. You never slept. You were a baby tyrant, you know."

"Me and every other baby that's ever lived. I can't have been that bad."

"Don't gaslight me," he said. "I was the one who had to be at work at eight A.M. And your mom was drinking then."

A wave of silence rolled over us.

He lit a new cigarette off his old one. He had never smelled like anything but smoke; all his clothes were steeped in it, reminding me of our home and of my face pressed to his jacket when he hugged me goodbye in the garage on my way to school all those mornings. But today the smell planted a headache between my eyes.

"You and Mom never really had the same taste in music, did you?"

"No. One of our many differences."

"I don't think she has much in common with Vaughn either. Except AA, where they met. I don't know where he came from. He just appeared one day. You wouldn't have seen him while you were there."

"Your mom has always had a thing for strays."

"Yeah. And then taking them back to the pound."

A deep laugh erupted from my dad, so loud it made me jump. It was a rare sound flown straight out of the past.

"So this is the pound?" He gestured inside.

"I mean, sort of. Mom basically put us both up for adoption."

"Thanks. I needed to laugh today."

"Why, what happened?" I asked.

"Oh, it's just another day in the middle of nowhere."

June

THE PAST

I GOT A CALL FROM HY-VEE; THEY WANTED ME TO START WORK ON THE Fourth of July. "It's fitting," I told my dad after dinner when we were sitting on the balcony. "To celebrate the birth of our nation I will take my place as a cog in the capitalist system that's killing us all."

My dad snorted. "Easy there, Karl Marx. It's a summer job."

"A summer job," I repeated, looking down at my notebook. I flipped through the pages. A job would mean less time to write, but I was tired of being broke. And maybe it was a good thing, writing less, thinking more. I had no idea what to do with Jamie next.

"What are you writing?" my dad asked.

"It's just this thing I'm working on."

"The sooner you learn to talk about your writing, the better."

All my life, I'd seen my dad's commercials on TV—even after he'd lost his job, they still played, a mocking reminder of better days. He could tell a good story in thirty seconds. About anything, too. Cars, fast food, Dramamine.

"You work in short-form," I said. "I'm working on a novel. It's harder to explain."

"There's a healthy ego. What's it about?"

"A girl who gets transported to another world and joins a war against an oppressive regime."

He laughed, draping his cigarette hand lazily over his knee.

"I know you're laughing at me, but it's not just a fantasy book. It's a book about how fantasy makes us feel."

"I'm not laughing at you," he said. "I was just wondering what Ansel would think about another writer in the family, and a sci-fi one at that. His work was painfully literal."

"Maybe he had enough outrageousness in his life, dealing with you and Mike Fellows."

I couldn't help but feel judged by him, Ansel-the-serious-writer. What would he think of my book?

The rebels will realize pretty quickly that Jamie is totally useless; they'll have to start from scratch with training her.

"None of us could at first," Hayden says when Jamie confesses that even as she trains for war she can't imagine killing someone.

They puzzle each other. The details of their worlds don't align. A massive public school for Jamie, tutors and apprenticeships for Hayden. He was to have gone into medicine, but the war started and he escaped the capital, smuggled out in a truckload of munitions, each bullet destined for someone's heart.

Still, even with the great divide between them, they talk about their lives. It's how they start to matter to each other. It's how they'll eventually fall in love.

And then a morning dawns warm and damp and a spy crosses the threshold of the safe house and in moments has a knife to Hayden's throat. The man is down so quickly Jamie doesn't see him fall. She only sees the smoke tremble from her raised gun.

She must love Hayden to have killed that man. And the love hits her so hard it feels like a crisis.

This part of the book is supposed to be a turning point. A realization that she is committed, that she will do whatever is needed to protect Hayden and the rebels. I wondered if it was stupid. She kills a man without asking a single question. She doesn't know anyone in this world other than these so-called rebels—they're her friends, or else her captors, and now she's Patty Hearst in the bank with a gun. Will she ever worry about her soul? Her weakness? Her war crimes?

My dad had been staring at a page in his book for a long time without turning it. My ideas for my book felt frail, like they might not make it through the winter.

"You start your new job Monday?" he said. "How many days a week?"

"Five."

"And you're really allowed to work that many hours as a minor?"

"According to the guy, yeah."

"Just a tip: You probably shouldn't call your manager 'the guy,'" he said.

I rolled my eyes.

My dad closed his book. "Well, then we should go to Mount Rushmore this weekend."

"Really?"

"Yeah. If it's your only chance before you have to work all summer. I haven't been yet."

"Okay. Let's go."

"That was all I ever wished for when you were born," my dad said. "That if my child didn't share my interest in history, she'd at least tolerate visits to national monuments."

Fort Sumter in South Carolina, the Shipwreck Museum in northern Michigan, the Vietnam Veterans Memorial. All our trips growing up had been about history—but years had gone by since we'd gone anywhere, visited anything. At the mention of Mount Rushmore, I could see his spirit stand up and start walking again.

There was hope for both of us.

July

THE PAST

"IT'S NOT AS BIG AS I THOUGHT IT WOULD BE."

My dad and I were looking up at Mount Rushmore from above the park's amphitheater.

"What are you talking about?" he said. "It's massive. They blasted a mountain apart with dynamite to make this."

To me, though, it was dwarfed by the mountain it had been carved out of, dark and gray and studded with green pines.

My dad and I followed the trails, mobbed by holiday crowds, and wound up the hill and closer to the presidential faces. I'd never noticed that Washington's lapels were partly carved, and in the museum I'd read that the original plan had been to have whole torsos for all the presidents, but the sculptor, Gutzon Borglum, had died before the monument was finished.

"Listen," my dad said, squinting up at the stony faces. "Make sure you don't let this Hy-Vee job get in the way of having experiences this summer. Best advice I can give."

"I'm trying to save for college."

"Your uncle Ansel was sixteen in 1969, when I was nine. He was bagging groceries that summer, and his friend Franklin invited him to Woodstock. He didn't go. He knew it would mean a ten-hour car ride in his friend's beat-up Ford Falcon. It had holes in the floor and a carburetor that caught fire all the time, and when it did you had to pull over and beat the flames with a roll of paper towels that Franklin kept in the car for that purpose. Ansel always regretted not going, though."

"He didn't know Woodstock was going to be *Woodstock*."

"I'm just saying, take the more adventurous route whenever you can."

I felt a little annoyed—I was the one trying to work, I was in Sioux Falls so he wouldn't be lonely. "I'm here, aren't I? At the friggin' national monument."

"You cannot compare Woodstock to Mount Rushmore. We're at a shrine to the white patriarchy that includes two slaveholders. And Gutzon Borglum was in the Klan."

"What? I didn't know that last part. Why are we here?"

My dad shrugged. "History."

"They should really get rid of this." I lowered my voice to a whisper. "Should we blow it up?"

"Shh," my dad said, patting the air with his hand as though to tamp down my words. "Keep your voice down if you're going to plan a terrorist attack, won't you?"

"When it's closed, I meant, obviously," I said. "So no people die."

"Well, I think you have your What I Did Over the Summer essay."

I took a selfie before we left and posted it on Instagram. A comment from Cindy appeared almost immediately: *South Dakota kidnapped this girl and they must be stopped.*

My dad had booked a motel down the highway, and the sun was setting when we arrived. He looked tired as he pulled his shoes off and leaned back in his bed. I turned the TV on so no one would have to talk if they didn't want to. The room had two beds spread with dark green quilts, the old TV the size of a Smart car, a mini fridge that, when opened, revealed a half-empty bottle of a local wine made from berries. The more adventurous path had led here.

"Do you like it here? South Dakota, I mean."

My dad's eyes were closed.

"I can hear your grandma," he said. "She would say, 'Goddamn it, Mark.'"

"What for?" I asked.

"Everything. She didn't mince words when I messed up. I preferred that to your grandpa, though. With his plans and outlines, trying to quietly control everything."

"I never told you this, but he was my least favorite grandparent."

My dad laughed. "Ah, well, may he rest in peace, and your grandma, too. I should tell you, when I die, I want to be cremated. Just in case it crosses anyone's mind to bury me next to my father, which strikes me as a difficult way to spend eternity."

"Don't be morbid. But, duly noted."

My dad drifted off, and I kept the TV on, but I couldn't pay attention. With everyone, I felt like I was living a double life. Whenever I talked to anyone, I disappeared into wanting to please them, no matter what I'd promised someone else.

I connected to the Wi-Fi and notifications rolled in on my phone, including a text from Gabe—*Can we talk tonight?*—and a few Sioux Falls numbers I didn't recognize.

Willa's tonight. You coming? This is Jill by the way.

This is Willa. Confirming you're invited, you should come.

I'm leaving Rolling Prairie now—you home? I can drive.

Hey, Gertie. It's Adam. You going to Willa's?

I felt the warm glow of their interest in me—won so quickly, and yet they knew so little about me. For now, at least, I was whoever they wanted me to be. I sent a group text telling them I was at Mount Rushmore with my dad. *Touring yr great state.*

I turned the lights off and took the berry wine from the fridge. Outside, leaning over the railing of the exterior hallway, I drank straight from the bottle until I felt the first rush in my head. Gabe texted again: *Please?*

"Is everything okay?" I asked when he answered.

"Yeah," Gabe said. "I just wanted to hear your voice."

For a long time I believed the worst thing I'd done, I'd done the night of Alice's party. But this. This was what Cindy would never forgive me for.

July

THE PAST

ON MY FIRST DAY AT HY-VEE, I SAT OPPOSITE MY MANAGER IN HIS OFFICE, A small and dark room at the end of a bright, messy hallway, a secret lair in the store just off the produce department. His name was Anthony and he had small shoulders and big hips and a surprised look on his pinkish-red face that never seemed to fade, and I found myself staring at him as he thumbed through stacks of plastic-wrapped button-downs, looking for a size small.

Once he'd found it, I went to meet Lucas at checkout to train on the register.

"Just can't stay away from me, can you?" he said.

His grin snapped a rubber band against my wrist. Beneath the tingle I felt at his flirtation was a film of revulsion, but a blush rose against my will.

"You wish," I said. I was doing what I did so well, turning into a mirror that reflected Lucas's feelings back to him. I ran my hands over the register. "Let's look under the hood of this beaut. How does it work?"

"Okay, first lesson," he said, "is not to steal the money."

"Hold on, I better write that down."

"That's basically it," Lucas said. "Let's take lunch."

"No way," I said. "Show me how to weigh produce. And where's the binder with photos of fruit in case I don't recognize something exotic?"

Lucas laughed and reached over my shoulder for a beat-up binder filled with laminated pages.

"The fruit bible," he said.

"A sacred text."

We flipped through the binder, pointing out star fruit and kumquats until Lucas was called away to a cleanup. I spent the rest of the day at a desk in the break room watching videos about customer service. It was comforting to absorb these solvable problems. Unhappy customers who wanted to return something without a receipt. Rainchecks for sold-out sale items. I hugged my knees and looked at my phone because the videos were mostly common sense. Jill was texting me after-work plans for a driving tour of Sioux Falls, though as far as I could tell from the week I'd been there, the city was a collection of wide, empty roads and low strip malls with a squat, glimmering downtown.

I got Adam to agree to drive us, so we can imbibe. I've always found Sioux Falls more fun after a shot of tequila.

Lol ok. Just watching videos back here, let me know when you're off.

Beneath all the motions of the day—working, texting, flirting— I floated in the aftermath of the sharp ping I'd heard that morning from my dad's cellphone, left unattended on the balcony, me next to it with my coffee in both hands. I looked down; the text hadn't yet faded from the lock screen. Whichever doctor he'd found must've been a writer, taking money for prescriptions.

Your prescription beginning with OX is ready for pickup.

. . .

When I got home that night, tipsy from Jill's tequila, my dad was watching television, awake but peacefully entranced. He acknowledged me with a small wave.

"Hi, Dad," I said. If he noticed I was drunk, he didn't care.

January

THE FUTURE

DESPITE MOM'S CLAIMS THAT SHE ISN'T LEAVING THE HOUSE UNTIL SPRING, on dry days I can usually convince her to go for a walk with me on my lunch break. We take up the whole sidewalk; oncoming pedestrians make her anxious as her scooter inches over the invisible halfway mark. Sometimes, students lost in conversation don't move over, and I stare them down. I feel my protectiveness of her growing, because the world isn't making room for her, and she's starting to disappear.

We usually end up at a coffee shop near downtown, where we stop for something warm.

January's almost over; acceptance of the cold has settled in. Mom's fingers don't seem able to negotiate the sugar packet. "It's getting on in the afternoon," she says, meaning she's no longer at her best.

"Do you want me to get that?"

She shakes her head, nods toward my glass. "I don't see how you drink iced coffee in the winter."

"I worship it," I say.

"I'd be praying to God I don't freeze to death," Mom says.

The coffee shop has an almond croissant we like. It sits whole on a plate between us. Conversation with Mom is difficult sometimes. It's a struggle to break the surface, and we're afraid the past will give us the bends. We have a different view of what was and a different plan for what will be. From my perspective, she hasn't gotten a fair shake in life, but she's uncomplaining, even serene, about everything that brought us here. And as for the future, she doesn't plan on being here much longer, which makes everything medical a struggle: The flu shot she refuses to get. The appointment with the neurologist at U of M she keeps canceling. The Medicaid spenddown, which she won't consider. A home aide, an idea she won't entertain.

"When I get to the point of needing an aide, it's time to go," she told me when I suggested it.

You already need an aide, I wanted to say. *We're your aides.*

Humans can adapt to almost anything. Before she knows it she'll be the person she swore she wouldn't live to become. And she won't be prepared for it. Then I remember I've never been able to force her to do anything.

"You're lost in thought," she says.

"Aren't I always?" I tear the croissant in half. "Ciarán calls it my thousand-yard stare."

"Are you writing another book?" she asks. "Is that what you're thinking about?"

"Sort of," I say. "I've been thinking about an idea."

I've never been a bolder writer than I was at sixteen, but fifteen more years have gone by, and, as I think about how to tell the story of that summer, the urge to grow something wild and brambly on the page has returned.

"I loved your first book."

"You did?" We'd never talked about it, my precious, quiet book of stories that grazed the bottom of one or two longlists.

"You know I love short stories."

"I didn't know you loved *my* short stories."

"They were beautiful," she says. "Although you were too hard on me and too easy on your dad."

Our table is pushed against a window. On the other side of the glass, a thickly matted spiderweb fills one corner, abandoned in the cold except for a yellowjacket curled around itself. It's so surprisingly brightly colored that at first I think it's alive, escaped from summer, struggling against the web. But it's long dead, a corpse shaking in the wind.

"You're probably right," I say, not wanting to do the work of explaining that I didn't write about real people, not really. I took their shadows and turned them into someone else—which is what makes people angry. Not that they were written about, but that they weren't.

"You and your dad were so close when you were young," Mom says. "Sometimes I felt like a stranger."

She's right. When I was young, it had always been easier to talk to him than it had been to talk to her, but I don't know if I can call it closeness. He was always hiding parts of himself from me back then. Even so, love passed easily between us. I have just as much love for my mother—I know that, I feel it—but it's a tincture locked away in a cabinet, dispensed in droplets. I don't know why, when I know it's plentiful. I suspect there's some rot of misogyny holding me back.

"You were the glue in the cracks," I finally say to my mother. This seems to please her.

July

THE PAST

"MY MOM'S TAKING ME UP NORTH FOR THE WEEKEND," CINDY SAID OVER the phone.

"Where?" I asked. "Why?"

"I don't know, bonding? We're going to this place called Calumet in the Keweenaw Peninsula. She was born there."

"That sounds like the name of a town that would be the last place you were ever seen."

Cindy laughed. "I might not have great cell reception. But you'll be okay, right? Things are good with your dad?"

I still hadn't told Cindy that my dad was using again.

That I had spoken with, and texted with, Gabe—several times.

That I'd slept with him in December.

Instead I'd kept my stories superficial—the Mount Rushmore trip, details about the new people at work, whom I didn't call friends, not to her.

"Gertie? Things are okay, right?"

I hadn't intended to drop a pregnant pause in the middle of our conversation. But I couldn't take it back. It was a gap big enough for Cindy to pry open further.

"I think he's using again," I said.

"You think or you know?"

I knew.

"I just wonder about it," I said. "There are some signs. But he's also depressed. He acts a little stoned when he's depressed. You know, detached, aggravated, sleeping a lot."

"Have you told your mom?" Cindy asked.

"Who, Ms. Mediterranean with her very expensive satellite phone? No. I'm not sure what she'd do, but she'd be mad. Don't tell your mom, please? I'll let you know if it gets worse."

Cindy was quiet on the other end.

I changed the subject, spent the rest of the call telling Cindy about Hy-Vee and the people I'd met, except I tried not to make it sound like I'd been having too much fun. There was this girl named Willa, I said, and we went to her house after work because it was big and she had a pool and her parents worked a lot. And a guy named Lucas who lived in the same complex as my dad, so I could usually count on him for a ride, and he would sort of flirt with me, but he also flirted with everyone, girls and boys. It was just who he was, gregarious.

"You and I used to drink, Cindy, but man, these kids can *drink*. I got drunker the other night than I had in probably six months, the night of—well, the night I broke my wrist."

"It seems like Adam likes you," Cindy said.

"Oh, you mean Lucas, my neighbor. He's the one I was saying flirts with everyone."

"*No*. I mean Adam, the dorky one."

The idea of Adam snaked through me, touched my spine in a way that made me recoil. It was a different response from the one I had to the thought of Lucas liking me. If Adam flirted, I had the sense he would mean it.

"I don't think so," I said to Cindy. "He has a friend named Regina who is in love with him. I told him, 'You realize she has a crush on you?' And he sort of mumbled that he didn't know."

"So, he basically had the same response you're giving me now? Gertie, you know it's normal for boys to like you, right? You're smart and pretty and kinda funny. You've never had a boyfriend because a guy could be holding a boom box beneath your window and you'd be like, 'Oh, it must be for the neighbor.'"

"I'm *kinda* funny? Ouch," I said, laughing even as guilt dripped faster, because as far as Cindy knew I was still a virgin. I tried not to think about it, tried to believe what Cindy said, that I could be with someone if I wanted. I knew she was right, theoretically, but I still didn't think it was *true,* even if I couldn't explain what the difference was.

"Fine," Cindy conceded. "You're *funny* funny."

"I've never had a boyfriend because I don't want one. They just take from you."

"You should write a romance novel," Cindy said.

"An austere story," I laughed, "full of hard-hearted people."

"And misery," she said.

"And no happy ending."

July

THE PAST

I NEEDED A PLACE TO SIT ON THE BALCONY. I'D BEEN USING A CHAIR FROM the kitchen and the other night the padded seat got soaked by rain. During my break, I bought a white plastic chair just like my dad's from Hy-Vee's garden department.

My dad was picking me up after work so we could go see an anniversary showing of *Jaws*. I left the chair by my locker and at the end of the day I brought it outside, waiting for him to come. Evening shoppers rotated in and out, the same types of cars replacing one another in the lot as the sky grew orange. I checked my phone; he was twenty minutes late.

A voice called my name, and I looked up in search of it.

It was Adam, waving.

"I'm glad I ran into you. How's it going?"

"Glad you ran into me?"

Adam ruffled his hair and looked intently at his feet, a look I recognized, as though he was hopeful the ground would swallow him up. I thought of what Cindy had said on the phone, and my stomach knotted. Butterflies felt the same to me as dread.

"I just mean it's good to see you again. God, everything is an interrogation with you."

"Sorry," I said. "It's good to see you, too. But I think Austin already left."

"I know," he said. "No one else works as many hours as you."

"You're not here for Austin?"

"No. What are you doing with that chair?"

"I'm going to take it home and sit in it."

"Fair enough," Adam said. "I was just trying to imagine the décor of your apartment based on that chair."

"It's for the balcony. And whatever, this chair could be in the Museum of Modern Art."

"Yeah, you're probably right." He looked over his shoulder, though we were alone. "I was actually here to see you."

He gestured to the bike rack.

"You want me to look at your bike?" I asked.

"Not my bike," he said, pointing to the one next to it, a red Schwinn with white tires. "*That* bike."

"What about it?"

He reached into his messenger bag and pulled out a new bike lock still trapped in plastic. He handed it to me.

"What is this?" Bewildered, I took the package and turned it over in my hands.

"You walk everywhere," he said. "This bike was abandoned at one of the schools I've been working at. They cut its lock today and were going to cart it off to the dump, so I asked if I could have it."

I touched the handlebars gently. It was a little scuffed, but perfect.

"I filled the tires," Adam said. "Enjoy life on wheels."

"No," I said, handing the lock back to him. "It's too much."

He put his hands in the air. "It was going to the scrapyard. You're just rescuing it from the trash compactor."

"Like in *The—*"

"*Brave Little Toaster?*" Adam interjected.

"God, that movie traumatized me." I bit my lip, looked at the bike. "Well, if you're sure there's no better home it could go to."

"It's yours." He sat down at the table opposite the bike rack, hands clasped between his knees. He looked up at me. "So, is it hard being away from, like, your mom and friends and stuff?"

"Yeah. I don't know, my mom and I needed a break. And I only have one really good friend."

"You must have more than one friend. It's only in the movies that people only have one friend."

"Okay, I guess I live in a movie then," I said, trying not to sound defensive.

Adam looked momentarily panicked, and then he deflected. "I think I get it. There aren't that many people we can feel really close to."

"You guys are kind of too nice, though. This bike, Willa letting me come over all the time. Suspiciously nice. I'm worried this is going to turn into a *Carrie* situation."

"In case you haven't noticed, there's not much to do here. Fresh blood is always welcome."

"You mean fresh pig's blood to douse me with?"

"You know what I mean." But Adam smiled.

My dad's car turned in to the lot. We were just in time to miss the previews. Talking to Adam, I'd forgotten to worry that my dad wouldn't come, and so in one big rush I felt the worry and the relief at the same time.

"That's my dad," I said, lifting the bike out of its spot in the bike rack. "I can't believe I have a bike."

"It should fit in the back." Adam was looking at my dad's Ford Escape. "I can put it in if you want. With your new chair."

My dad pulled up to the curb and rolled the front windows down. He surveyed the bike and the chair and Adam. "Are you bringing all this home? We live in a one bedroom, so there's no room for the boy."

"Dad," I grumbled. "It's just a chair and a bike. Adam gave it to me."

"Wow," my dad said, but in a dry way that meant he'd ask more questions later. "Nice to meet you, Adam. I'm glad you're not wearing a backward baseball cap."

"Why?" Adam said nervously.

"Never mind him," I said quickly. My cheeks burned. My dad had always said he would turn away any boy who came to the door for me if he was wearing a backward baseball cap. "We're going to miss the movie."

I opened the hatchback and Adam and I hoisted the bike in. My dad, to my horror, had gotten out and was standing by Adam as I struggled to wedge the chair in on top of the bike.

"She's a leftie, but she has terrible spatial awareness," my dad said to Adam. "I want a refund."

"Are you *done?*" I said to my dad.

"Okay." He winked at Adam.

Adam was smiling, but I could tell he was torn between amusement and confusion.

"Thank you so much for the bike, Adam. It's amazing."

"Like I said, you're rescuing it." He turned to my dad. "Nice to meet you, Mr. McMahon."

"Well, I'm sure I'll see you around." My dad climbed back into the car.

"Ignore him," I whispered. "Please."

Adam shrugged. "It's good to see where your weirdness comes from."

Gabe thinks you're weird, Cindy had said all those months ago. I must have seemed stricken because Adam looked at me oddly as I retreated, folding myself into the car. He backed away from the curb, his hand raised in a low wave.

"He's cute, if a little quiet," my dad said as we pulled away, "and he could've laughed more at my jokes."

"Do not start." I sighed. "I'm not getting involved with any corn-fed Great Plains boys this summer."

"Says the corn-fed Michigan girl."

. . .

We sat in the back of the theater. A giant bag of popcorn glistened in my lap, and my dad's Diet Coke sweat through its waxy cup. As the movie started and a pair of legs kicked innocently beneath the waves, my dad reached into his pocket and popped a few pills.

"He gave you a bike?" Cindy said.

"It was going to get thrown away."

"You won't get anywhere in life being self-effacing, Gert."

"Don't call me Gert," I say. "Gertie is already a nickname."

"I'm doing it because you're being annoying and I want to annoy you back."

"Don't make fun of me," I said. "My dad is like a zombie these days, and you're the only person I have to talk to."

Cindy cleared her throat. "Is he using? Tell me the truth."

"I think so," I said. It was as close to the surface of the hot truth as I could get without getting burned.

"If I tell my mom, she'll let you stay here, Gertie."

"I'm going to talk to him. Please don't tell your mom."

I took her silence as agreement.

"I won't tell, but I should," she said finally. After a pause she went on: "I was watching the news the other day, and did you hear about the drug the FDA approved? If someone overdoses, you give it to them and it, like, reverses it or something."

"Brings them back?"

"I guess so. My mom changed the channel—anything about drugs makes her mad. But I did hear you can get it at the pharmacy."

If Cindy hadn't watched the news that night, if she'd forgotten, if for whatever reason she'd chosen not to tell me—everything would be different.

February

THE FUTURE

ANN ARBOR IS SO DARK AT NIGHT, THE QUIET SO DENSE, AND THE EMPTI-
ness outside our house broken only occasionally by a slouched figure
walking home from campus. In the kitchen, I turn Mom's orchid
plant beneath a thin stream from the faucet. "Is this enough?" I whisper to Ciarán, tilting the pot to let the water drain through.

"You'd know better than I," he says.

The flowers give off a cold white glow, moths in moonlight. We're
being quiet, trying not to wake Mom, who went to bed in her room
off the kitchen. The orchid goes back to its spot on the table where
the best diffused light reaches it—"It wants sunlight through the forest canopy," Mom has told me—and I fill the humidifier that lives on
the floor beneath it. She tracks the orchid's progress closely, each day
pointing out new buds growing from the woody stems. Meanwhile,
I convinced her, once again, to put an appointment with the neurologist on the books. Nothing will make her better, but it's possible
something will keep her from getting worse.

Ciarán comes up behind me and rests his lips on my neck, wraps his arms around my waist. We stand close in the dark and his hand moves slowly down.

"C'mere," he says, pulling me into our room. He always kisses me before anything else. The warmth and safety turns into an ache of longing, and I open myself up to him and tell him to do what he wants to me. He takes both my wrists in one hand and pins them over my head, touches me with the other and tells me how wet I am. It's probably hormones, but lately when we have sex my eyes water until tears, unavoidable, run down my face.

"Is it crazy, Gertie, that I want to see you again one day?"

That's what he'd asked me the night he'd called from Dublin. That was the choice he presented.

I was in Adam's apartment when the phone rang. So much had happened between Adam and me, a whole archive of pain and long-ing that I'd been cataloging for years. My freshman year at Michigan, his sophomore, had brought us back together, then torn us apart. The pattern was always the same: We'd argue and then a burst of passion would reunite us; the DNA of all of it was jealousy on Adam's part, insecurity on mine. We spent most of second semester not speaking before renewing our relationship in the spring, right before I left for the Camino. Adam was it for me, I thought then, and so I always went back to him, unable to convince myself it wouldn't work just like it always hadn't.

I took Ciarán's call and went outside to the parking lot. A train track cut through a grassy gully between Adam's apartment and the road, used only in the middle of the night by a string of graffitied cargo cars that shook the bed and threw me awake while Adam slept. I sat on one of the low concrete barriers lined unevenly at the end of the lot, there to keep cars from getting too close to the tracks.

It was October, fall, and I wasn't dressed to be outside, frigid in a T-shirt and shorts, but the cold made Ciarán's voice seem clearer, louder, closer.

"Gertie, are you there?"

"Sorry," I said. "I'm here."

It was getting dark. Adam's bedroom window tossed light into the parking lot. He would ask me who had called when I got back inside. Up until Ciarán said those words—*I want to see you again*—I had believed it wouldn't matter how I responded to Adam because in my heart I wasn't lying. But Ciarán had made my composure brittle; he flicked it and it shattered. I wanted what I thought he might be offering, unknown as it was.

Adam moved within the frame of his window, flipping through a textbook cradled on his forearm. I could imagine the thick veins in his arms, all those times they held me going back so many years. As quickly as the feelings for Ciarán had advanced, fear overtook them; one by one the cities within me fell to it. He didn't want me; no one but Adam ever would. When you've been through so much with someone, your sorrow becomes part of your love, even if you try every day to banish it.

Adam, for his part, didn't want to talk about the past; Austin's drinking had gotten bad, we'd heard he was using, too, and anytime I brought up that summer Adam flinched, as though in it he saw the moment his family had been touched by poison. He was ashamed of it, ashamed of me, maybe.

I told Ciarán I'd love to see him again. If he came to the States, I said, he could meet my boyfriend, Adam.

Ciarán went quiet; later he told me he'd stood there on the street outside the pub in a crowd of drunk people, so embarrassed it was physical, doubling over as if in pain and biting his knuckles to swallow what he'd said.

I called Cindy right after. She was in New York, often checking in to express her dismay at whatever was the latest state of my relationship with Adam. "I think you're making a mistake," she said that night.

"About what?" I asked.

"Everything!"

Sophomore year passed, and the next summer I moved with a few of my friends from the dorms into the apartment across the hall from Adam's. Foolish, but at least he and I hadn't signed a lease together. Everything was difficult and intense with him, love that had strayed far from home, the sex passionate and rough and without any laughter. I worked two jobs and took five classes and Adam consumed any time I had left. There were happy times, too, as there usually are. We'd always been good at digging through the mess and finding meaning. Late nights walking home from parties, touching the whole way, hands or arms wrapped around each other. Reading with my head rested on his chest the times we lay on blankets in the warm fall glow of Alex Dow Field, where there was a remnant prairie that made us think of Sioux Falls. Humid summer days when everyone had left town but we stayed, and in that desertion the feeling of finding our place as adults in the world. And during all of those years it was true that I loved him.

For a year after Ciarán's call, I was a silent onlooker to his Instagram, my mood lifting anytime I saw his face. From where I gritted my teeth through life in Michigan, his seemed so comfortably European, cheerful even beneath Dublin's changeable skies. I paused one day at a selfie he'd posted, with friends on some cliff near the ocean, and his hair was flattened by the wind and his smile full of laughter.

Looking good old friend, I commented.

There you are, Gertie McMahon, he replied, almost instantly.

Here I am.

The flirtation was blatant and public, there for anyone to see. Most important, maybe, it was there for *me* to see, something beyond what I had, a sign of life, in its own small way like a water sample sent back from Mars. Meaningless unless I decided I wanted to go there. I did want to go there. With Ciarán, even though I hardly knew him, *old friend* felt true.

Given the distance, given our youth, I might have let Ciarán slide past me if not for the fact that it was wrong to want him. With Ciarán there was cause and effect, a story, it wasn't just Ciarán I wanted, but

Adam I didn't. At times in my life, I've tried to work out the meaning of this—that I'm not sure I'd be with Ciarán if I hadn't had to leave Adam for him—and the closest I can come to an answer is that the pain from that summer in Sioux Falls was indestructible. To leave it behind, I had to leave it with Adam.

July

THE PAST

MY DAD WAS USING. I WASN'T HELPING HIM; HE WAS AS LONELY AS BEFORE, or maybe lonelier. Deep into summer, July was slipping into a long fever dream, and I was going to wake up this in-between person who'd soon go back to Michigan and start a new school year still not having changed or made a difference, not having told Cindy the truth about anything.

On a whim I dyed the ends of my hair pink in the employee bathroom at work just so I could send a photo to Cindy. The dye would probably fade before the end of summer, so she would never even see it in person.

My dad noticed my pink hair outside somewhere in the middle of his long chain of morning cigarettes.

"Why did you do that?" he asked.

"I thought it would be fun." I touched my hair.

"As far as rebellion goes, I guess your mom and I can be thankful this is all you can muster."

Your mom and I. It had been such a long time since I'd heard either of them talk that way, like they were still together. Their marriage already seemed like a cobweb, as abandoned as the ashes in my dad's ashtray. A pile of cigarette butts lived there—exoskeletal, unalive, while the lit one between his fingers looked so much a part of him that it could have been made of his cells.

I swung my feet up on the railing so my toes blocked the sun from my eyes. My dad's voice was already a little wretched from the day's smoking. It was early still; he was probably only a few pills in, his eyelids not yet fluttering closed mid-conversation.

"Dad," I asked, "have you found a good AA or NA meeting in Sioux Falls?"

He flicked ash absently. "I don't do NA. The AA meetings I've been to have all been depressing."

"Depressing how?"

"I'll give you an example. One of the first meetings I went to, there was a guy who told a story about his Antabuse. Do you know what Antabuse is?"

I shook my head.

"It's a drug that reacts with alcohol, to help you quit. If you drink while you're on it, you get violently ill. He was taking Antabuse, and one day he got a vanilla milkshake. The alcohol in the vanilla extract reacted, and he projectile-vomited all over the McDonald's counter. It happens that fast." My dad snapped his fingers. "He told this story, and I just thought, 'That is fucking grim.'"

I chewed on my lip. Maybe he thought he wasn't as bad as the man throwing up at the McDonald's, but at least that guy was doing something to stop drinking. My dad thought his mistakes didn't count in the same way. But look at how they'd counted.

"I mean, sure, that's grim, but isn't everyone's story? In one way or another."

He didn't reply.

"Can you find another meeting? Somewhere else?"

"No," he said. "I'm used to Michigan meetings—that's what they call the style of meeting where you have small tables, breakout groups. Here it's just one big room like you see on TV. That doesn't really 'vibe with me,' as you kids say."

He stubbed out his cigarette and said he had an errand to run. I checked my phone miserably. I didn't want to know where he was going. His restlessness seeped through the wall as he moved about inside. A minute later I saw his car pull around the building and toward the main road. The past few days, it was like I was a piece of furniture he kept bumping into. His sad, thoughtful eyes hadn't looked anywhere but inward as he sat stiff as a statue on the balcony, one ankle rested on the other knee, a baseball cap shadowing his forehead. Depression that led to more pills that led to more depression. That was the way it worked with him. A vicious cycle.

Methadone, meetings: Everything I'd suggested, he'd waved away. Reluctantly, I heard my mom's voice in my head: *You can't help someone who won't help himself.*

What if I could, though? What if there came a day when I *had* to?

And then, as if he knew I was feeling alone, my phone lit up with a text.

Cindy showed me a photo of your hair. Didn't know you had it in you.

And maybe it was because I was feeling miserable, maybe it was because my dad was losing hope, and I couldn't do anything but watch, but I wrote back.

Are you with Cindy?

She just left. U look great.

I wanted my life to be like it was before, when I felt in control of what happened to me. When Michigan summer afternoons took all day, and all we had to do was show up and savor each one.

I went to the pharmacy the next day, slipping away as my friends took their lunches outside.

Jenny, the pharmacist, held up her hand when I approached the counter, and I waited for her to finish shuffling pills around in her counting tray. She looked up. "Picking up?"

"No." I scooted closer to the counter so I could lower my voice. A man with a baby strapped to his chest was browsing allergy pills nearby. "No. I'm wondering . . . do you have that drug here, um, the one that can reverse an overdose?"

I looked at my palm, where I'd written down the name.

"Nalox . . . something?"

"Narcan?" Jenny said.

"Is it expensive?" I asked.

"Insurance might cover it."

"Without insurance?"

Jenny tapped her fingers on the counter. "The nasal spray is about two-fifty or three hundred dollars per package for two doses."

"Do I need— I mean, would you need a prescription?" I asked.

"It's not over-the-counter yet, but a healthcare provider can offer it." She paused, looking at me. "A pharmacist counts."

That morning I'd emptied my bank account of all I'd made so far at Hy-Vee. Sabrina, the woman who managed my dad's apartment complex, had stopped me as I sorted through our mail at the pavilion of metal boxes outside our building. She saw I was opening the box with my dad's name on it. July's rent was overdue, she said.

"What do you mean?"

"I mean you haven't paid rent." Sabrina looked at me like I was stupid. She was a platinum blonde and she wore dark rectangular glasses and black heels and a black wrap dress, stalking the apartment buildings like a vampire doing its monthly administrative work.

"Can I buy the nasal spray now?" I asked Jenny. At the look on her face, I hurried to add, "My dad just had surgery. I read that even short-term opioid use can be dangerous."

I told myself it was only a precaution, that I probably wouldn't need it, but I still felt ashamed. Seeing the way Sabrina looked at me that morning, and then the way Jenny looked at me in the pharmacy, sent a wave of resigned understanding through me: They believed they knew everything about me.

Sabrina would have to wait until I got my next paycheck. I handed Jenny two hundred and fifty dollars in cash.

February

THE FUTURE

MOM HASN'T ASKED AGAIN ABOUT MY WRITING. IN FACT, WHEN WE TALK I steamroller her with questions about her health as though I can badger her into getting better. The neurologist's office calls; there's been a cancellation and the doctor can see her sooner. I take the phone from her—"Gertie!" she scolds—before she can decline. "Yes," I say. "We'll be there."

"You're acting like it's Christmas," she mutters in the car.

"Getting you to go to the doctor is about as miraculous as the Word made flesh," I say.

"Doctors haven't done anything for me before." She's next to Ciarán in the front seat; he's forced to take the afternoon off work, too, because I let my license lapse in the city. "I don't see why this one would be any different."

When Mom is checked in, I point to three seats in the waiting area. "Are these okay?" I ask Ciarán, who shrugs. Mom struggles off her scooter, and as soon as she's seated, a nurse calls her back. I follow her so I can intervene in case she tries to refuse any treatment options.

"Just in case you need any help, Mom."

"I'm fine," she says, batting me away with her hand, but she doesn't stop me from following.

Her doctor is young, dark-haired, with very pale white skin. He's probably my age but looks even younger, a baby in a grown man's body. He wears a bow tie and nice shoes, maybe to look older, and when I'm done judging his appearance I come to appreciate that he talks to Mom, not to me, and he doesn't assume the scooter belongs to her—instead he asks.

"If this is worth a dollar," he says, stroking one side of her face, "how much is this worth?" He strokes the other.

"Fifty cents."

"Sometimes she has a little trouble getting words out," I say, desperate to tell him the things she won't say herself.

"No, I don't," Mom says.

The doctor looks at me, then at her. He types into the computer. "You've never tried any treatment before?" he asks, ignoring us both.

"There wasn't much by way of treatment when I was first diagnosed."

"And since?"

"I didn't want to kill white blood cells. And for the amount those drugs cost, I could've taken pool boys to Tahiti!"

"Mom." I'm mortified.

"She's allowed," Dr. Berglund says.

I fall quiet, chastised. She didn't take any drugs because she couldn't afford them, couldn't even see a doctor until she turned sixty-five last year. Vaughn wouldn't pay for anything; she wouldn't appeal her disability denial. Now she and Dr. Berglund discuss what treatment at this late stage might look like.

"We might be able to keep you from getting worse," he says.

"See?" I say. "Mom, we can stop you from getting worse."

"I don't know," she says. "It's an injection? I don't like needles."

"An auto-injector," I correct.

"I suggest you think about it," the doctor says. "It could make the future easier."

"I have a plan for the future." She gives me a sly look. I return a fierce one. "They'll put you on a psychiatric hold," I warned her before coming, "if you bring up your plan."

Dr. Berglund doesn't notice. "You can't get pregnant on these drugs either," he says, smiling, "no matter how cute the pool boy is."

July

THE PAST

"LUCAS KISSED ME IN HIS CAR LAST NIGHT," I SAID TO CINDY.

"What? You told me you weren't into him."

"I thought about stopping it, but I just feel really tired, Cindy. And, I don't know, why not? It's a distraction."

"I guess you can be commended for coming out of your shell. Oh my God, is this going to be your first boyfriend?" From her voice I could tell she was teasing me.

"Don't infantilize me. He's definitely not my boyfriend. I say here under oath that I do not want a Sioux Falls boyfriend."

"I bet Adam's jealous," Cindy said.

"Probably not. I'm just new, you know? It's the only thing about me that's ever mattered to anyone."

"That's so sad, Gertie."

. . .

Postcards arrived all at once from cities with names that rang with luxury. Paris, Cannes, Nice, Milan, towns that looked like you might find a sundial there and actually use it to tell the time. My mom's notes were short, her handwriting large: *Hello from the sea. Hello from an inland jaunt. Tomorrow we go to Naples. Greetings from Corse. Love, Mom.* I knew she didn't have a lot of time to write, but all I'd learned about the places she'd been was from the short descriptions in tiny print on the postcards. Still, though, I liked them, and I pinned each of them to my dad's bulletin board.

When I wasn't working, I practically lived at Willa's, along with everyone else, in her big house on the outskirts of town. Adam joined sometimes, but he told me he could handle only so much of his brother and Lucas. He *did* seem to like me, though, and we'd become friends. A few times he and I had explored the bike trails, sometimes with his other friends and sometimes just the two of us. As I got to know the city, I was starting to get to know him, too. Most of the time, though, Regina was trying to stand close to him, and I could tell: She was in love. If things were different, Adam's affection for me would've already made me fall in love. But they weren't, so it hadn't. I didn't want to get in the way.

Lucas drove me home every night after Willa's. He'd kissed me as I was reaching for the door handle. The only thing I could think while his lips were all over mine was, *Well, we've found ourselves here, so I guess this makes sense.* We lived in the same complex, worked in the same grocery store, partied with the same people. That first time, I let it happen because it was easy. The next, because I'd gotten used to the idea I might want it eventually.

Lucas told everyone. Willa and Jill descended on me.

"Does Lucas know you hang out with Adam? That he gave you the bike?"

"I don't know. Why?"

"No reason," Jill said.

"There's a reason," Willa cut in. "Lucas gets jealous."

"But Lucas and I aren't *dating*. Just hanging out."

"That's Lucas." Jill looked sideways at Willa. "Wanting things both ways."

"Please," I said. "Drama is a self-fulfilling prophecy."

I didn't need any more priestesses in my life, unspooling yarn and deciding when things started and ended. My dad was giving me enough to worry about. Along with the pills, he'd started drinking again in earnest. Halved lemons shriveled on the counter in pools of gin, like dried-up sunlight. He thought he could choose pills or booze, but they always found their way back to each other, fated or something. Romeo and Juliet dead together in the crypt.

More often than not, though, he wasn't home, and when he was, there were times he seemed normal, and times I watched the fork miss his mouth when we ate the food I brought home after work. One night, I watched him pull into his parking spot as I was locking up my bike. I could tell he was drunk. When I'd gotten him to lie on his side in bed, I said, "You shouldn't drink with these," plucking a blister pack from his nightstand. If he heard, he ignored me.

Get through the summer. I felt myself slipping down a slide with those words written on it. Who knew what I'd do, what would happen, but I could keep my eyes closed. Good or bad, I felt myself letting go.

I would trade Willa's pool and the Sioux Falls bike trails and Lucas and everything else for like five minutes with you, I texted Cindy.

July

THE PAST

MORE AND MORE I LEFT MY NOTEBOOK AT HOME BECAUSE I DIDN'T WANT anyone to see me writing in it. I thought about Jamie and Hayden less and less, embarrassed by my own imagination.

I biked to Willa's, chasing the sky south into the prairie, new houses rising enormously around me. These houses, Willa's house, reminded me of Alice's, the party. Willa's was the only finished house among bare outlines of half-built homes in her cul-de-sac, which meant we could be loud. Bottles of liquor stood clear or amber on the patio table, Willa in the pool draped beautifully over a heart-shaped inner tube, yelling for Austin to bring her a drink. Jill complained of earaches from all the swimming. Willa swam over and tried to peer into her ear—"I wish I had an otoscope," she giggled tipsily—and I was laughing when my phone lit up with a call.

"Dad."

"Gertie," he said.

The shock of his voice sobered me. He never called, only texted.

"Are you okay?" I asked.

"I'm sorry, hon. I need you to come get me."

"Where are you?"

"I'm sorry," he said again, his voice getting farther away.

"Dad, tell me where you are."

"McNally's. Off Western Ave."

"I know where it is," I said. "Stay there. I'm coming."

I turned around and bumped into Adam.

"Everything okay?" he asked. The look on his face said he'd heard the phone call.

"Fine," I said.

"If something's wrong, you can tell me." He put his hand on my arm.

"Please don't," I said, brushing him away.

I found my dad passed out in his car in the parking lot of McNally's. I drove him home and stayed up the rest of the night worrying. I couldn't deny things were getting worse, but I hoped we'd reached the lowest point. And the low point didn't seem like the right time to leave—to call Cindy and fall on the sword in front of Annemarie. If I left, who would be there to take him to a meeting if he finally decided to go? And if this wasn't the low point—if there was lower still—who would be there to give him the Narcan?

I clocked in late the next morning, and Anthony, already in a bad mood, yelled at me.

"You're too new here to be pulling this crap."

"Sorry," I said, annoyed, and my tone made him roll his eyes.

My phone kept going off, igniting my nerves. Lucas had been texting me all day.

Did you leave with Adam last night?

?? no

I saw him touching you.

I left alone.

I looked and you both were gone. Where did you go?
It was a family thing. That's ALL.

"Hey! No phones on the floor." Anthony was standing near the Coinstar, his arms spread open in exasperation.

"Shit," I said.

"What did you say to me?" He took three quick steps toward me, and my heart clutched the bars of my rib cage. Vaughn had charged toward me once, just like that, the time he'd asked when I was going to learn to respect his and my mom's privacy.

"I'm sorry," I said to Anthony. "I didn't mean to."

"On your break, come to my office." He pointed one finger before he turned and stormed off.

A woman who had been veering her cart toward my lane stopped short, pivoted, embarrassed to have overheard.

"You've been a great addition to the staff so far," Anthony said later, after I'd clocked out for my break. "I don't want to see this type of behavior again."

"Yeah," I said, fidgeting. I pinched a bag of chips between my fingers. My lunch. I was the only one working today among my friends, and I was going to eat outside alone.

"Look, you're a good kid," he said. "But maybe you don't realize how important a first job is. You might need a reference from me one day."

His gaze was hot and awful. Not lustful or leering, really, but like he thought I was his to control.

"I don't get involved in drama except when it affects my house." He tapped his finger on his desk. "I can tell you need this job, not like the others, who just need something to do so their parents get off their case. Don't let them get in your way."

"Okay," I said.

His eyes lingered on me for a second longer, and then he peeled them off me. I slipped away before he could say anything else.

Outside, I opened the chips and ate them slowly, one by one. When a shadow fell over me, I looked up and saw Willa.

"Hey," I said. "I didn't think you were on today."

"I'm not." She sat down next to me. "I just forgot something in my locker."

I flipped the bag of chips in her direction, and she reached in for one.

"Is this all you're eating for lunch?"

"I've been, like, kinda too stressed to eat a lot lately," I said, which was true, but there also wasn't a lot of food in my dad's fridge. He lived on Cheerios and cigarettes.

"You left abruptly last night," Willa said. "Everything okay?"

"Yeah. Sorry. Did Lucas tell you I left with Adam?"

"He thinks so," she said. "But I know you didn't. I've been wanting to tell you—I know it can be hard sometimes, being somewhere else than where you're used to. I was new here in middle school. Not to mention one of the only Black kids in my class."

"Wow," I said, willing my voice not to sound anxious. "I didn't even think about that, how much harder that must've been for you than it is for me, moving here."

"Just let me relate to you, okay?" Willa said.

I blushed, embarrassed that she'd caught me in my hand-wringing. "Sorry. Where did you move from?"

"I was born in Georgia, but my parents were from Chicago. They moved to Atlanta for their medical residencies at Emory. So, like, I had Northern parents, but I was Southern, and then they got jobs at Sanford USD, which was recruiting talent, like, hardcore, so it was a hard offer for them to turn down. So now I live in the Great Fucking Plains."

"What about after high school?" I asked. "Do you want to go back to Georgia?"

"No. I want to go to New York. I think I'd like to be a doctor like my parents, but practice in a big city. I won't get poached by high salary and low cost of living."

"Me, too! The New York part, I mean. My friend Cindy and I, we have a New York dream. I want to be a writer."

As soon as I said it, I wished I hadn't. I hardly ever admitted that to anyone.

"That's really cool," Willa said. "Are your parents okay with it? Not exactly a slam-dunk career move."

"They've never really said anything about it," I admitted, which felt worse than saying they disapproved.

"Are you mad your mom ran off for the summer and made you move here? I would've complained to the president."

"It wasn't exactly like that," I mumbled, embarrassed. I was thinking of how to explain myself and my parents, why my mom needed to get away, but Willa stood up and checked her phone. "I should get going, I have to meet my mom. Glad to hear you're okay."

"Thanks," I said. "Hey, you're, like, the only one who has asked me any questions about myself. Except for Adam."

"That doesn't surprise me. They're not super curious people." Willa smiled at me. "They're our friends, though. We make do."

My dad was on the balcony when I got home, and I sat down next to him.

A few moments of silence passed. "I was so worried last night. All day I've just had this terrible feeling about how bad things are and how they're just going to get worse."

"It's all going to be okay." My dad closed his book.

"Dad," I said. "That can't happen again."

"Gertie," he said, slicing the air with his palm, "lighten up."

Tears sprouted in my eyes. "I'm not joking. You said you'd go to a meeting."

He didn't reply.

"Let's look one up right now."

"Gertie," he said again. "Why didn't you go to camp this summer if you needed something to do?"

"What do you mean?"

"Look, it's fine that you're here. But I don't need a nanny. I don't need anyone. Why do you think I still live alone in this godforsaken place?"

Whatever fight I had, that killed it.

"I'm sorry to intrude on your solitude," I said miserably.

My eyes were closed, fighting back tears. I felt his hand squeeze my shoulder, and his smile when I looked at him shot through me like sunlight through a rusted metal roof. His charm was his greatest weapon. It made us all love him so much.

"You're not intruding, Gertie," he said. "It's strange, what we're going through. It'll take some getting used to."

I tried to smile back. Right before me and somehow in secret, he'd built a stone wall around the part of me that could help him. I had to be content just being there with him, by his side, but in that closeness I felt distance grow.

A text from Willa summoned us to her house, and when I left the balcony I felt like I was leaving a sacred space. What hit me, the feeling, was the same one I'd had the first time I saw my dad's chair in the garage without him in it, after he'd moved out for good.

July

THE PAST

AFTER A FEW DAYS, LUCAS SEEMED TO FORGET HE WAS MAD AT ME ABOUT Adam, and we were back at Willa's together with his arm around me. When he drove me home, he pulled into his spot in front of his own building, not mine, and as he kissed me, he told me his mom and sister were gone for the night. "I have a headache," I said, slipping out of the car and trekking across the complex to my dad's. Inside, I sat on my air mattress and listened to the fan blowing in his room.

I couldn't sleep. I tried to write, to pick back up with Jamie where I'd left her, by the fire with Hayden, having just killed someone. I'd set up the people and the places and even the rickety start of a story, but what was I supposed to do next? Jamie couldn't just flirt with Hayden for the entire book.

What if Jamie tells the truth about who she is? Not to Hayden, but to the people in charge—two women, partners, named Dove and Briony. She has to tell someone, but she's afraid of admitting to Hayden that she lied to him. And Dove, who knows secrets Hayden doesn't, realizes immediately that progress has been made on a weapon that until now had only been a rumor: deportation corridors to other worlds. Jamie got there thanks to a weapon malfunction.

"You can't tell anyone," Dove tells Jamie. "Not even Hayden."

I looked back at my notebook and flipped through the pages I'd just written, and suddenly I felt hot with how bad I perceived the writing to be. I couldn't write a war. I couldn't write about different laws of physics. I couldn't write about portals to other worlds that a despotic government was using to deport dissidents. I didn't even understand my own life. I ran my finger over the words—*They've found the corridors, Jamie. They don't know how to control them, but you're a key. They'd do anything to find you if they could.*

Dove went on and on—*I* went on and on—explaining, explaining, explaining, but nothing made any more sense. Suddenly furious, because why would someone like Jamie matter at all, I tore out the pages and ripped them to pieces. The first and only time I'd ever ripped up my writing. It felt good.

March

THE FUTURE

THE SNOW MELTS IN ANN ARBOR; IT'S GRAY AND PEACEFUL AS THE STU-
dents leave for spring break. Melted ice rivers down gutters, and
Mom perks up.

"You survived the worst of winter," I say, and she replies, "Barely."

She allows her doctor to prescribe physical therapy. My license
renewed, I take her to her first appointment and follow her into the
big room of mats and machines, and after a few minutes of strained leg
lifts and stretches, Mom points to the set of rehab stairs in the corner.

"I want to try those," she says. "I want to get walking again."

"Mom," I say, but she's already climbing unsteadily onto her
scooter.

"Whoa," her therapist, a young woman named Marjorie, says.
"Wait for us."

"You can tell her no," I say to Marjorie, who comes up behind
Mom as she's reaching for the railings. She starts to wobble. I reach
for her shoulders, the therapist for her arms.

"Get off me!" Mom cries, throwing back an elbow that grazes, just barely, the tip of Marjorie's nose.

In one jerky, involuntary movement, I cover my eyes with my hands, hiding. From Mom. From Marjorie, who's cupping her nose. From the other therapists peering across the room at us.

"Do you realize," Marjorie says, "that your elbow made contact?"

"Why were you pulling me backward?"

"Mom." I lower my hands. "Please get down. You elbowed Marjorie in the face."

"I did not," Mom says, but she lets me take her arm and guide her back to her scooter.

We sit in the waiting room. After a few minutes of conference with Marjorie's boss, it's decided. No report needs to be filed. Marjorie would be happy to try again. "Maybe next week," she says.

"I'm never going back there," Mom says in the car. "If they won't let me try to walk, what's the point?"

I decide I'll have to write about that scene in the physical therapists' office one day, which is how I disassociate from the reality that Mom elbowed someone in the face today.

We drive through campus on the way home, and I'm hit by memories of college, and the writer I became during it. I abandoned my pursuit of fantasy, rebelling against it because I believed it hadn't helped anything. Any world I created would be worse than the one I was already in. I seemed able only to elevate misfortune, the characters wandering deeper into the maze of their own worst impulses.

I was devoted to realism and brought little imagination to it. I worked doggedly throughout those four years, mostly in secret. I wrote only the strictly possible, things that had happened to me, embryonic feeling steeled within indisputability. In writing classes, I was praised only for my sentences, but I never submitted my stories for campus prizes, and I never wrote in front of Adam, who knew I took those classes but didn't question where the stories I sent to his printer had come from or when I'd found time to write them.

I was as ashamed of writing as I was of sex. There was fault to find in me for both. My classmate lazily flinging my story across the table, having written on it, *I find it hard to care.* Adam stormy in bed next to me, asking why I hadn't said anything when I was dry and he'd entered me anyway.

Writing became miserable, each story a poll of others' interest in me. What had been real pleasure turned to struggle with Adam, vulnerability I masked with sounds and movements.

In the winter of my junior year, I fell ill with a sinus infection. For two weeks I struggled through work and class submerged in white noise, unable to hear or breathe, sleep distant. I went to a walk-in clinic, where they gave me a sample antibiotic, anthrax-grade, for free, which cured the infection but gave me thrush in my mouth. When I needed a private place on campus to dissolve the antifungal tablet under my tongue, Adam, who was so disgusted I realized the disgust must not be new, mentioned the fourth-floor cubbies in the graduate library. They were big enough only for a chair and a wooden slab of a desk, but each one had a large window overlooking the president's mansion.

I tucked myself into one of those cubbies every day to take my medicine, and when the treatment was done, I still found myself going to the grad library between work and class, as well as after, before going home. I wrote, and in that privacy, my work was anonymous—I could've been any student, working on anything. I felt a shred of the boldness I'd had at sixteen in Sioux Falls. Any real courage was far away still, just an inkling, a sense that I would one day be somewhere else, and someone else. My writing didn't become better, but it was important that I glimpsed that shimmer when I did, or else I would've quit.

I talked often with Ciarán in those winter months. I told him what I should've been telling Adam, everything about my days and all the rest, what I was working on and what I was reading, and by the time I got home each night I had nothing left to say—but Adam didn't notice anything had changed.

Ciarán was a secret, and he knew it. "I couldn't encourage you to be honest with your boyfriend right away," he told me later. "I had to make you fall in love with me first."

I would stay in the library until it was late, later in Ireland, in a space so small it could fit only me, with no chance of anyone entering and laying claim to me. Ciarán came off warmly even in his texts, but the dream was inevitably broken by a message from Adam asking when I was coming home. Though we didn't live together, we slept in his bed almost every night, performing something we'd never really arrive at. Some mornings I woke up almost unable to move, aware that if I got out of his bed I could choose not to come back. Our roommates thought we were the rare exception—real love at our age. And it was real, or had been, but it didn't feel like it belonged to me anymore.

One night, I left the library, but instead of going straight to Adam's as I usually did, I found myself in my own room, in my own bed, curled around myself and holding on to the knowledge that the next time I saw Adam would be the last as his girlfriend. It was a delicately formed thought. I could crush it in one hand.

I saw you through the window? Adam texted.

I didn't reply, and soon he came across the hall and into my apartment, looking over me with one hand still on the doorknob of my room. "What's wrong, Gertie?" he asked, and then he got in bed with me. In the familiarity of his closeness I could see myself staying. Blocking Ciarán's number, ghosting him and what I felt for him, because in the grand scheme of my past and what I'd been through— what Adam and I had been through—Ciarán didn't know me. Adam did. He had known a part of me that hadn't lived past sixteen.

There had been a plan in place. Adam was graduating but staying in Michigan for his MBA, and after next year, my last in school, I would try to stay, too, for the MFA. Adam put his hand on my back.

He thought he was soothing me against something routine, and he was warm but detached, waiting for whatever it was to pass.

I wiped my eyes, removed myself from Adam's arms, and tore up the plan.

It took weeks for us to die. Weeks of Adam trying to convince me, and me almost being convinced. And then Adam's hurt set in, his anger, his *how could you after everything?* I saw it then, or maybe I'd always known: He believed he'd saved me, when in truth I'd always been the one to save myself.

I was never going to forgive myself if I stayed with Adam. I took his face in my hands and told him that he needed to let me go.

After Adam left me in my room the last time—after years of our sleeping in his bed, our ending took place in mine—I called Ciarán and told him where I'd been those past few weeks, why I hadn't been in touch. I asked him to tell me what he was thinking.

July

THE PAST

"HOW'S YOUR DAD?" I ASKED CINDY.

"How would I know?" she said. "He disappeared from my life. Sixteen years as my father, and now he's just gone."

"Do you want to talk about it?"

"He could be anywhere," she said. "And no, not really."

"Are you worried about him?" I asked, ignoring her.

"I try not to be. What good does it do to worry and not do anything?" She paused. "But I was thinking about calling some motels. Maybe I can find out where he's staying."

"Earth to Gertie. Are you coming to the party next week?"

The question reached me on a delay, like it was first radioed into space and then beamed back to the table under the Hy-Vee pavilion.

"What party?"

"She wasn't listening to us." Willa looked offended.

"I go to all your parties," I said.

"This is a special party," Austin said. He was at the table behind us, lying across the entire bench with his hands behind his head. "Every summer we have a big blowout at my family's cabin on Lake Campbell. We shoot off enough fireworks to destroy a small town."

"Your parents don't care?" I asked.

"My dad only uses the house for hunting season," Austin said. "He thinks Adam and I just go there with Lucas to chill."

"And your mom?"

I'd met his mom once when I'd stopped by their house with Adam. She'd been reading on the couch with a blanket thrown over her lap, a glass of white wine studded with ice cubes perched on her knee, her eyes magnified behind big round glasses.

"She hates that my dad hunts," Austin said, "so she pretends the house doesn't exist."

"I can drive us." Lucas looked at me. "If you need a ride."

"Okay."

"Really?"

My answer had made him brighten. I couldn't help smiling. I got this endorphin hit whenever I made someone else happy, but when the charge faded it left a fuzzy, burned-out feeling, because the way I agreed to things was just so automatic. But I couldn't seem to stop.

I considered the idea of the party. Getting away for a day, a night, an excuse not to go home, a reason to put off calling Cindy—a calm feeling fluttered like a cool sheet settling over my body.

"Yeah," I said. "It sounds fun. I'd like to see more of South Dakota."

Austin sat up and moved to our table.

"Now we have to talk booze," he said, planting his elbows next to mine. He started discussing the stores that didn't card, and I listened, but only halfway. The ribbons of thought came back. Earlier that day, my dad had gone down to the visitors' lot to meet a guy I'd never seen before. There was a quick exchange through the man's car window. I'd been on the balcony, looking at a photo Cindy had just posted of her and Gabe lying together in the grass of a park near her house.

I'm feeling really guilty about what we did, Gabe texted not long after I'd liked the post. *Cindy deserves better. I want to tell her the truth.*

It had been a few days since I'd heard from him, but there he appeared, pulling me back into a conversation we'd had a thousand times.

Can we wait until I'm back? I asked.

He wanted me to worry about what he might do. Enemies closer—he was counting on it.

July

THE PAST

I WAS AT THE POOL, THE SUN PINNING ME DOWN TO THE DECK LIKE THE rays were tridents. My phone next to me cupped a text from Lucas in its palm: *Want to hang out?*

A new text came in and I peeled my face off my dad's threadbare towel. It was familiar, taken from the very back of the linen closet at home, a towel that had been wrapped around me when I was very young.

I was living in trepidation of a text from Gabe. I hated that sometimes he told me the truth about myself, that sometimes he was right even though he was also always wrong. But the text was another from Lucas, asking if he could come over. *I need to stash some stuff for the party at your place.*

Sure. I'm at the pool.

"I know you're at the pool."

I lifted my head; it felt heavy on my neck. Lucas stood by the pool gate, balancing a case of beer on one of the metal spikes of the fence.

"Why did you text me if you were right there?"

"I wanted to see your reaction to getting a text from me."

"And?"

"Expressionless. You can be an enigma, Gertie."

I scowled, but my sunglasses hid it. I didn't like being read by him. It didn't feel intimate. It didn't feel like understanding. It felt like a joke.

"All right." I heaved myself off the ground. "Let's go."

Lucas handed me a plastic bag. Bottles of vodka clinked together, jockeying for space. He stood close behind me as I unlocked my door. I felt his finger play with the edge of the towel wrapped around my waist. I pulled it tighter and pushed my way inside.

"You can put the beer down in the corner," I said.

I nestled the vodka next to it and threw my sun-stale towel over the pile of booze, burying it in a shallow grave.

"Your dad really doesn't give a shit, does he?" Lucas asked.

"I'll hide it better later," I said, knowing I wouldn't but feeling protective of my dad all the same.

"This is where you sleep?" Lucas pressed his palm into my mattress. "I think it has a leak."

"It's fine."

I held my elbows. My skin itched. Despite his disdain for the air mattress, Lucas flopped onto it, and a hiss of air whispered from its seams.

"Careful! You're going to pop it."

Lucas held his hand out to me. I hesitated, but I took it, and he pulled me down hard into his lap. I squirmed to get out.

"What does your dad do?" Lucas settled back against the wall, looking around the apartment. "Is he at work?"

"He worked in advertising in Michigan."

"My dad beat it to Texas years ago. Got a new family, pays shit in child support. I kinda hate the guy. I got sent home early from Christmas at his house last year because he said I was being a monster to my half brother."

"If you're a monster, he created you."

"You're so right." Lucas's eyes widened. "I'm going to tell him that."

I'd meant it as a joke. I imagined Lucas accusing his dad seriously of it, and Lucas's dad laughing in his face.

"I knew you'd be cool," he went on. "I knew as soon as you moved here."

"I mean—" I started to protest, because objectively I hadn't really done anything cool, but then Lucas kissed me, hard, and a small voice in the back of my mind told me that was what he'd meant by *cool*.

I started to feel frantic, because I wasn't pulling away. I wanted to, but I wasn't. Lucas backed off long enough to ask when my dad was getting home, and when I said I didn't know, he seemed to take that to mean *yes,* and he unbuckled his pants and took my hand and put it on him. I was a thousand miles away from Alice's guest room with its linen sheets and throw pillows, but I felt like I was back there with Gabe, the last person I'd touched.

My hand moved, and I asked myself why it was moving. Lucas leaned back on his elbows and in a breathy voice, he said, "Suck me off, Gertie," and then his hand was on my head, pushing me down on him. My mind went blank for just the right amount of time for my brain to click into thinking it was too late to stop. That, maybe, it was easier to float away. I kept my eyes closed. I got up after and spat into the sink and ran the faucet.

"I knew you'd be cool," Lucas said again.

I felt like the character in a book who, at the end, you find out was a ghost all along. Lucas lay with his eyes closed on my mattress. I straightened my bikini top and ran my hands through my hair.

"Hey," I said, twitching my fingers to tear a tangle out. "Can you maybe not tell anyone about this?"

"Don't worry, we won't slut-shame you."

"I just mean, keep it between us, please? This is private. I don't feel the need for anyone else to know."

Lucas shrugged. "You're an enigma," he said again, and again I didn't understand how something that seemed so clear to me could be a mystery to someone else.

Lucas stood up, buttoned up, dusted off his hands. The door opened, and my dad walked in. He held the doorframe as he toed off each of his shoes. Whatever anger was still left in me after that night at McNally's drained away at the sight of him, replaced by deep shame at having almost been caught.

"Oh," he said when he saw us. He looked at Lucas.

"Hey, Gertie's Dad," Lucas said cheerfully. I couldn't understand how he wasn't appalled by the close timing like I was. A few minutes' difference would've meant my dad walking in on us, and the near mortification mortified me equally.

"We were just going out, Dad," I said, throwing a sundress on over my bathing suit.

"And you're coming home when?"

"Just later."

"Is she this noncommittal with you, too?" my dad asked Lucas.

"She's an enigma," Lucas said.

"Did you just learn that word or something?" I snapped. Lucas's eyes leaped, startled.

"Sorry," I muttered. "Let's just go." I grabbed my bag from the chair where it hung and said goodbye to my dad as I slid past him. He raised his eyebrows but—mercifully—he let me leave.

"Where are we going?" Lucas asked when we were in his car.

"You pick," I said.

I closed my eyes, and I wondered how tomorrow would feel. It was like the things I did were borrowed, not mine, and they were adding up to someone else's life.

"Did you have fun with your friend?" my dad asked when I got home later.

"Yeah."

"What did you do?"

"Nothing," I said. "We just got McDonald's fries."

"He wasn't the boy who gave you the bike," my dad said.

"He was not."

"I'm just going to keep giving you windows to tell me more, you know."

"We can play this game all night," I said.

July

THE PAST

AS SOON AS I GOT TO WORK, I KNEW LUCAS HAD TOLD EVERYONE. I KNEW as soon as I keyed into my register and looked up at Jill and Willa and saw them watching me from their own lanes. Once their eyes locked on mine, they abandoned their stations and surrounded me.

"We heard you had a good time with Lucas," Jill said.

"Jill, don't be mean," Willa said. "We just want you to know he's telling people about it."

I turned away from them and yanked the almost-empty roll of receipt tape from my register.

"I didn't know," I said finally. "Please don't tell anyone else."

"I only told Austin," Lucas pleaded with me later. "I told him not to tell anyone."

"Lucas, I've known Austin two minutes, and I already know not to trust him with a secret."

"He's my best friend. I've known him since the second grade. I have a right to tell him stuff."

"It's just, this kind of thing is private for me. I don't really go around talking about it."

"Chill out," Lucas said. "They like you. *I* like you."

"You and them liking me isn't the point. I asked you not to tell. It's really fucked up you did."

"*Sorry,*" he said, but it was an aggrieved apology.

They thought I was worried they were judging me, but, really, I was worried what I thought of myself.

On my lunch hour later in the week, I sat on a bench in the break room, holding my sandwich in my hands. The rest of them were outside. I'd been eating alone the past few days, and the smirks and smiles had turned to raised eyebrows and sideways glances. Even Lucas had grown less friendly, and I mourned, just a little bit, the loss of what I could've felt for him, if I'd just given us a little more time. If he'd given us a little more time. I didn't hate him, after all. I didn't really like him either—but he was a source of attention, he filled the time, and he seemed to want to be around me. I didn't know how many people I had left who did.

Willa, Jill, Austin, Lucas—what was I willing to do to keep them as friends? Without them, what would I do for the rest of the summer? What would happen when the newness of me wore off and the gossip wasn't interesting anymore? I'd watch the pills go, the refills come in. Adam was officially dating Regina, I'd heard, and he hardly came around anymore.

I sighed, the decision made. I went out to the picnic tables. Willa and Jill and Austin and Lucas were sprawled across the benches, bathed in heat and fumes from the cars in the lot. Lucas sitting backward on the bench, his elbows on the table. Austin holding court with some joke or story. Their laughter stopped when they saw me.

"Sit down." Jill patted the bench beside her.

Lucas watched me as I rounded the table. Silence hung a low sky over us.

"So," I said quietly. "Who else wants a blow job?"

I felt sick as soon as I said it, but they erupted with laughter. Even

Austin's mocking face broke into a grin. I felt shocked and shy and all mixed up inside, but I laughed along with them.

"Great timing," Jill said. "We were starting to wonder if you didn't want to be our friend anymore."

"Of course I do." I leaned backward and tossed my sandwich into the garbage can nearby. "Can we talk about something else?"

The conversation moved on. Lucas broke off a piece of his Snickers bar and handed it to me. I pinched it, not wanting to eat it, and the chocolate melted between my fingers.

Adam pulled up on his bike just as everyone but me was stacking their trash and stepping over the benches, getting ready to go back inside. I hadn't expected him, and seeing him made my stomach flip over.

"Oh, did I miss lunch?" He watched Jill as she piled drained soy sauce packets and used napkins onto a plastic sushi tray.

Austin went up to his brother, pulled back his fist and lurched forward on his toes, stopping short just before the punch met Adam's nose. Adam flinched. "Fuck you, man," he said. Austin laughed, shook Adam's shoulders, and left without saying a word to him.

"Brotherly love," I said. "I've got a few minutes of break left."

Was it a smile or a grimace on Adam's face? Lucas glanced over his shoulder at us as he went inside. Willa had slid her leftover salad across the table toward me before she left, and I looked at it so hard, trying to think of what to say, that I thought the leaves might turn brown.

Adam sat down across from me and unwrapped a tight layer of cellophane from a sandwich he'd pulled out of his bag.

"God, you really strangled that sandwich," I said.

Adam looked at the ball of plastic in his hand. "Maybe I just don't want peanut butter to get all over my bag."

Was there an edge to his voice? I'd read so many things the wrong way since I'd been there, and they all crept out like vines and strapped my wrists to the table.

"Sorry," I said.

"Why are you apologizing?"

"I don't know. Never mind. Are you excited for this weekend?"

"The lake?" He looked surprised that I knew about it. "Oh, no. I'm not going."

"Not going?" I said. "But it's your cabin."

"I told myself after last year that I wasn't going again."

"What happened last year?"

"Nothing specific. Austin always gets super drunk, so I get stuck cleaning up and then fighting with him about it. It's just not that much fun ultimately, you know? Like, it's a letdown."

"Parties usually are. You leave disappointed either with yourself or with someone else."

Adam laughed, and the laugh startled me. I'd had this idea that we were sort of fighting.

"What kind of parties are you talking about?" he asked. "I'm just saying it's boring. If you ask me, I'd say skip it."

"Oh. I think I'm going to go. I'd like to get away for a day."

"I'm telling you honestly, it's not worth it. It's really just Austin's douchebag friends."

"And I'll be one of them," I shot back, scooping up Willa's salad and peeling my legs off the bench. "I have to clock back in. Sorry you came all the way here to eat alone."

An empty apartment met me when I got home that night, and I wasn't sure how today could possibly feel worse than the last few days, but it did, another in a series of failed tests bringing the summer's average down. And the average was pretty low to begin with.

Last payday I'd stocked the freezer with frozen dinners. I peeled back the film from a chicken alfredo, prodded a pea stuck in the frozen sauce like a buoy. Mom had always made us eat healthy, but my dad and I pretty much just injected fat and salt into our veins every day.

I daintied the meal out of the microwave and onto a plate and went out to the balcony. Going to the party wasn't going to change anything, wasn't going to clear my head, was probably going to be just as bad as Adam had warned. But I was still going to go. My food congealed, I let it, and I finally plunged into a text to Adam.

Hey. I didn't mean to snap at you earlier. I've been having a hard time triaging my emotions lately. They apparently all need urgent care.

No worries. Let it all out Gertie.

Lol. I'll try. Anyway, sorry for being rude.

Are you and Lucas like a real thing?

My heartbeat snagged on his text. It wasn't something I'd expected him to ask.

Aren't you and Regina dating?

No, that didn't last very long.

We're not. Not officially anyway. Why?

Adam didn't answer, but I watched the thread for a long time after because I really wanted to tell him—to tell someone—that I hadn't wanted to do what I'd done with Lucas. But he didn't text again, and I couldn't bring myself to say it.

July

THE PAST

ONCE AGAIN, I'D MANAGED TO PACK A LIFETIME OF ERRORS INTO A HAND-
ful of weeks, and now I felt like I had a hangover while still drunk.

"You're too young to look so haggard," my dad told me the next
evening while I was out on the balcony.

"That's really rude," I said. I crossed one knee over the other and
pulled them both toward my chest. My dad's smile revealed nicotine-
stained teeth and wrinkled his tear-glossed eyes. Small and blue, like
mine.

"But you're not wrong," I added, burying my face in my knees.

I looked out over the spread of grass and pool and apartments that
had become so familiar. I ignored a chime from my phone—every
sound it made shot me in the heart, made me afraid of whom I'd have
to face.

I finally looked at it. It was Adam.

Hey I came to Hy-Vee, Willa said you were hanging out tonight?

"Shit." I'd decided not to go because the thought of seeing everyone was ironclad dread. Everyone except Willa—and Adam. My thumbs hovered over the keyboard. I typed something—*Hey Adam, I'm sorry*—but deleted it. I prodded my forehead with the corner of my phone.

My dad laughed again. "What tangled webs we weave."

"It's nothing," I said.

"Well, you look about as serious as if you have the nuclear codes and are about to use them."

"I do not."

"Have the codes? I hope not. I was gonna drop it, but that thing you said about blowing up Mount Rushmore was a little concerning."

"Shut up."

My phone was in my lap, dead silent now, a graveyard of old texts resting in peace. Beyond the pool, the clubhouse was closed, and beyond that, two women sat at one of the picnic tables by a stand of charcoal grills, beer bottles dotting the space between them. Thousands of miles away, my mom floated through a Mediterranean night. And in Michigan, Cindy was somewhere with Gabe, his arm and the weight of his attention around her shoulders.

"How's work been?" my dad asked.

"It sucks," I said. "I hate Hy-Vee."

"Send them a telegram." He opened his book to the spot he'd been marking with his thumb. "'My employment with this company has got to stop. Stop.'"

"Pretty good for a dad joke," I said.

"Dad joke? Give me some credit."

"What? It's a joke, and you're a dad." I took in his smile. The hardest part was, sometimes he seemed so okay. "By the way, I'm going to be gone this weekend. Leaving tomorrow and staying overnight. Some friends have a place on Lake Campbell."

"What friends?"

"My friends."

"Bike-boy?"

"No. He won't be there."

"The other boy, then?"

"Please stop asking me questions."

"Will parents be there?"

"Yes," I lied. "Are you going to tell me I can't go?"

"Were you going to leave without telling me?"

"I'm telling you now."

"Leave your mom a voicemail in case she calls here wondering where you are."

"She never calls," I said.

"She hasn't had service."

"She seems to prefer not having service."

"Just call her?" my dad asked. "Please, Gertie."

"*Okay,*" I said.

Cindy told me you're dating someone.

Please Gabe leave me alone.

April

THE FUTURE

MOM IS SCRATCHING A PATCH OF ECZEMA ON HER ARM. I GRAB HER HAND to make her stop.

"Where's your cortisone?"

It's the middle of the day on a Wednesday, and Mom and I are on the couch. I turned the television on, which annoys Mom: Television during the day is lazy. Ciarán is in our bedroom, editing. I would be crowded in there alongside him, working in the blankets with my knees bunched beneath my laptop, except last Friday I was let go from my job.

"The remote arrangement isn't working," my boss said over the phone. "We need someone in the city, who can be here for events."

Today I see my job posted on their website. The listing includes several more duties than I was doing, and offers ten grand less per year. And no mention of events.

"Typical nonprofit bullshit." I shut my laptop sharply.

"What's that?" Mom asks.

"Just work."

"Not your problem anymore."

"Now there's just the problem of unemployment," I say. "And we need to follow up about that co-pay assistance program for you."

Finally, Mom agreed to the drug her doctor recommended. I've tried to help her through the paperwork for co-pay cancellation, but she quickly grew frustrated. They were asking questions, she said, that were none of their business.

"I don't know anymore if I want to take those drugs," she says now.

"Remember what Dr. Berglund said? Your disease will start to impact you cognitively. You need to take the drugs."

"Your boss was a bad boss," Mom says, taking me back to a subject she knows I won't be able to resist. It takes me only a moment to slide into a warm bath of complaints.

"She hates women," I say.

"A lot of women do."

"She was nicer to men, but she never hired any because she couldn't diminish them in the same way."

"Good rig— Good rid— Ack." Mom stretches her neck, grimacing. "Good riddance, I mean."

Sometimes words get tangled in her mouth, lost somewhere on the path from her brain, reminding me of when Dad would trail off into a fog. The memory bears down on me, and I need to escape.

"Do you want to go for a drive?" I ask. The endless road, the waste of fossil fuels, is so Midwestern that I'm brought back to the time when Cindy and I had just gotten our licenses, the freedom we felt when driving was new.

"Does Ciarán want to come?" Mom asks.

"He's working." But I slip into our room anyway, wrap my arms around his neck. He takes my wrist and squeezes it. We fought last night because I couldn't stand being both unemployed and inside the house, so I'd taken a walk and, seeing a small restaurant set cozily at garden level, three stairs deep in the ground, I'd gone in and eaten dinner alone at a candlelit table, leaving my phone in my bag as I pretended everything was fine and whims were my right.

"You can't do that without telling us," Ciarán said when I'd gotten home. "Your mom was worried."

"Oh, so now all of a sudden people want to know where I am?"

He was angry, because he's always been there for me. He softened overnight, but he was still making me live with being in trouble for a day.

In the car, Mom exclaims at every pothole, "Jesus Christ, I forgot about these goddamn roads."

We drive east out of town, a storm of early spring petals swirling around the car.

"Can we go past the old house?" I ask only because I'm driving there anyway.

"I'd like to see it again once more," she says.

"What do you mean, once more?"

She doesn't answer; a crazy driver distracts me. We pull onto our old street, and nothing about the house looks different on the outside, at least not from where I pull off onto the grass, in the same spot where Dad had parked his car, packed and ready to go, that night he'd taken me to the hospital. The green shutters still frame every window, and the angel's-trumpet vines, dead and dry for winter, wind around the copper trellis in the yard. The garage door is closed, no chair where Dad's used to be.

"I wonder if the people who bought it from us are still there," Mom says.

"We could look on Zillow."

It had taken years for the house to sell. Mom wanted so much money for it, as though it was the new buyers who owed her recompense for the misery she endured there. My freshman year of college, she moved to Florida with Vaughn and left the house on the market. Every few weeks I would borrow Adam's car and drive home to collect the mail, dust the shelves, mop the corner of the basement where rainwater leaked in. The house's three bedrooms, the large lofted ceiling in the living room, and all of it empty, radiated grief, seeming to say, *My family left and now they're dead to me.*

Mom gazes at the house, the yard that clings to a few patches of snow. The black walnut trees in the yard loom tall over it, protective, and we're the strangers now.

"Did I ever tell you the plan I proposed to Vaughn, right before you went to college?" she asks.

I bristle but let her finish.

"I suggested we keep the house and split our time between Michigan and Florida. He would help pay the mortgage, and I would add him to the deed. And you would have a place to come home to."

"He said no, presumably?" I have to look away as I tamp down the familiar anger that twitches to life.

"I remember it so vividly," Mom says. "He was standing in the kitchen, looking out the window at the woods. He was silent and his hands were clasped behind his back and then he said, 'I don't want anything to do with this house or that girl.'"

"And you're telling me this *why*?" I snap my head back to look at her, bitter and incredulous, until I see the look on her face.

"I was just trying to say that I tried," she says quietly. "I wanted security for you. That was part of why I was with him."

Even from such a distance that man could make me feel like I mattered so little.

"I'm sorry," I say.

"What was your dad's apartment like," Mom says after a pause, "in Sioux Falls? I don't think I ever asked."

A woman steps out onto the porch of our old house. With one eye on us, she tends a few dead vines that have flopped from the garden onto the steps. I turn on the engine. I've been spending so much time in Dad's apartment lately, in my mind, as I work on my book. My imagination crawls through its rooms, trying to extract what I remember and create what I don't. It was a home, sometimes; other times it was just a place to be.

"There was a balcony," I say.

August

THE PAST

I SLID INTO LUCAS'S CAR AND THREW MY OVERNIGHT BAG IN THE BACK. HE tried to kiss me, but I turned away.

"Sorry," I said. "Wasn't ready."

"It's okay," Lucas said.

He didn't try again. I fiddled with the radio knob. Lucas spun out of Rolling Prairie, and a single mammoth cloud to the west rested against a continent of sky, making my life feel small in the best way. Adam was wrong: I had no expectations of the party, so there was no way it would let me down.

A country song played on the radio. Lucas drove with his hand on the gearshift even though the car was an automatic. He noticed my hand resting on the edge of my seat, and he moved his to cover it. I was so bewitched by the landscape I didn't even think about it. The grass went on so soft and endless, the background to a dream. I was thrown awake from time to time by towering billboards plastered with a photoshopped picture of a bloody fetus. A gruesome night-mare, a bomb on a bright day. Contradicting the place but so much a part of it, like a scar from cutting yourself. And then right away the soothing gold-and-green grass returned to its waving rhythm, and I wasn't sure which place was the real place.

Lucas slowed and turned off onto a driveway that cut open a stretch of trees. The road snaked through the woods and opened into a clearing, a bonfire towering in the center of it, heat making the air wavy, and beyond that a cabin and blue shimmering water. The lake's perimeter was fortressed by trees, other houses stationed along it, but Austin's was alone in this big patch of woods.

Lucas turned toward me. "Best day of the year," he said.

He leaped from the car, leaving me alone in the trapped warmth. There was a group of people milling around the fire. I looked at them through a thin film of dead bugs on the windshield. I didn't see anyone I knew. Lucas had disappeared. I pressed his car door shut and, happy to be alone among strangers, I went over to a card table where there was a keg of beer, and all the booze Lucas had bought, and I grabbed a plastic Solo cup and poured myself a beer. The surface trembled a millimeter above the top, and I slurped to bring the level down, and then chugged the rest quickly.

A few girls were dancing by the fire, and I watched them and stood in the moss that grew near the house, the earth spongy and cool beneath my feet.

"Hey, Gertie."

I turned around. Adam was standing half in and half out of the cabin, the door propped open by his elbow.

"Oh," I said. "You're here."

He shrugged and shouldered his way outside, letting the door fall closed behind him. He wore a Lincoln High School Lacrosse T-shirt that I'd never seen before.

"I didn't know you play lacrosse."

"Oh, yeah. I don't know. I might not do it this year."

"Why not?"

"College applications, I guess. I'm tired of getting hit by sticks every day."

In my mind, I asked him which schools he was applying to, but in reality, I just stared at him dumbly as I started to understand that I was really happy to see him. I refilled my beer. If I didn't say something, we'd stand there in silence forever and die eventually, and I didn't want the last thing we ever talked about to be lacrosse.

"Can I have a tour of the cabin?"

Adam looked over his shoulder at the door. "Sure."

I offered him my beer. He looked at it but didn't take it. I moved the cup under his lips and tilted it. He sipped, smiling, laughing as he jumped backward from a splash that almost hit his feet.

"Stop," he said. "C'mon."

I was surprised by how spacious the cabin felt inside. Big picture windows looked out at the lake, filling the house with light. I spun in a circle, looking around, and came to face the giant head of a dead moose.

"Jesus Christ," I said. "You could've warned me."

On one of the walls were mounted animal heads: a deer, an elk, a mountain lion. Adam laughed behind me, and I stepped farther into the frozen menagerie of open-throated animal heads, glassy eyes that looked empty, coarse and wiry fur shooting out, still rich in color. I reached up and touched a yellow-white tooth in the open mouth of a fox.

"Which one's your favorite?" I asked.

"I don't know," Adam said. "They're my dad's. To be honest, I think they're kind of grim."

"They are," I agreed. "But also sort of gorgeous, though I feel bad saying that."

"You would think that."

"What do you mean?"

"You always see two sides of everything."

"Not always," I said, but it wasn't untrue, the way I tried to believe in everything all at once. It was also stanceless and spineless—an excuse.

"If you went vegetarian," I asked, "would your dad disown you?"

"He doesn't know what to do with me," Adam said. "Austin, he gets."

He ducked past me, spread his arms out with the rest of the cabin behind him.

"I had no idea there were lakes in South Dakota. It's so beautiful here. I came vowing to hate this place and all you people."

I stood at the window, looking out at the sloping grass lawn that led to the water.

Adam showed up at my side. "It was great to come here as a kid."

I looked at his reflection in the glass as we talked.

"You and Austin must've been pretty cute kids."

"People say that about twins even if they're ugly."

"Well, not in this case."

Adam pushed his glasses up the bridge of his nose. "I don't know."

"What's in here?" I looked into a small room with bunk beds, a lamp that looked like a carousel, and cowboy wallpaper. And it wasn't until I was inside the room that I realized it was their bedroom. A small feeling that I shouldn't be there grew in me, but when I turned around to leave Adam was in the doorway. I rocked back on my heels.

"This room is like a museum of childhood." I heard my own voice, and it sounded nervous.

Adam leaned his shoulder against the doorframe, looking at me, and to avoid looking back I moved around the room. His wristwatch rested on a small dresser beneath a mirror, and I picked it up and tilted its face back and forth, then checked my phone. The time was off by a few minutes. I nudged the crown until it was right and handed it to Adam.

"Here," I said.

He took it and held it as though it were something alive and delicate.

"Gertie," he finally said. "I know things are complicated, but you don't seem happy. And . . ."

"And what?"

I looked down at the floor and saw Adam's feet moving toward me. They stopped near my toes.

I looked up. His face was closer to mine than I'd expected, and it made me flinch. His nose brushed mine, and I didn't move away, and our lips touched and he moved his chin up, pushing my head back. His mouth was open, and my lips were hot from the beer. He guided my hand with the Solo cup down to the dresser. He put his hands on my face, and I pulled at the bottom of his shirt, and we took one step together—going nowhere, going somewhere—and then a voice broke us apart.

Jill stood in the doorway, her hand covering a drunk, astonished smile.

"Whoa," she said.

Adam looked at Jill like she was a ghost. My stomach lurched. Every nerve in my neck was electric. I grabbed my beer from the dresser, clutched Jill's arm, and dragged her from the bedroom.

"Come on," I said. "Let's talk outside."

At my side Jill was exclaiming under her breath. "Wow," she whispered, over and over, reciting her surprise.

What was wrong with me? Making the same mistakes, causing the same drama, wanting when there was so much wrong with wanting. And all the while feeling the memory of Adam's hands on my face and wanting more of that feeling.

I took Jill down to the water's edge. I didn't say anything until we were on the bank, our voices covered by the sound of water.

"Look, it was a mistake," I said. "It was stupid. Please don't tell anyone. We were just talking, and . . ."

My sentence hung unfinished, waiting for Jill. She took a long, deliberate sip from her beer.

"I know Adam," she said finally. "It makes sense to me that he'd fall for you. It's a confidence thing. He sees you with Lucas, and it's like permission to like you. He's so afraid what people think of him, he can't even have a *crush* on someone without someone else showing him how."

"Oh, no," I said. "This doesn't have anything to do with Lucas. Adam and I are friends, you know, we're close."

Jill's eyes widened.

"I mean close as friends. It's nothing, just a weird confused thing that happened."

Jill sipped her beer and looked at me over the edge of her cup with skeptical eyes.

"I'm sorry, Jill," I said, though I didn't know why I was apologizing to her. "I don't want to cause any drama."

After a long moment, she smiled. "Hold my beer," she said as she bunched her hair into a messy bun, tying it off with a hair tie. "No, you're right. We shouldn't say anything. It would only embarrass you and make Lucas angry."

I breathed a sigh of troubled relief, but it was impossible to feel completely reassured. Jill took her beer back. Laughter echoing from the bonfire pulled her gaze over my shoulder. "Let's forget it, okay?" she said.

"Thank you, Jill," I said breathlessly.

She raised her beer as she took a few backward steps. "Don't let your cup get empty!"

"Right." I forced a small laugh. Jill walked away. I had the urge to chase after her. Guilt always made me want to explain myself, but she was gone, and I picked my way over the rocks to a dock jutting out into the lake. I sat at the end and dangled my feet in the water.

In the aftermath of Adam, I thought of Cindy.

Someone was swimming in the lake. This was where Lucas had gone—right into the water. The boyishness of it almost made me smile, but Adam's kiss lingered on my lips. If Jill hadn't walked in, what would've happened? How long would it have been before we pulled apart, and what would we have said when we did?

Lucas swam over to me and pulled on my ankles.

"Get in the water," he said.

I took off my dress; my bathing suit was underneath. I slid off the dock. Lucas swam away from me, turned on his back, and beckoned with a smile. I should've told him by now, *No more of this, I don't want to be your girlfriend,* or whatever we were, but his charisma was like a tossed net. I swam toward it and got tangled in it, tangled in his arms, not meaning to. He lifted me up, and my legs wrapped around his waist. I tried to stay tangled in his net as he kissed me. I tried to be with him. I tried to shove everything else away.

So now I'm just nothing to you? Gabe had texted me yesterday. *You're a bitch, Gertie. Cindy's never going to forgive you.*

But first I'd been nothing to Gabe.

Lucas put the tips of his fingers underneath the elastic of my bikini top and pulled its string loose. The fabric fell away from my chest.

"Stop," I hissed, squirming to cover myself. "There are people around."

He dropped me. I sank beneath the surface and tied my swimsuit, fingers numb in the cold water.

"You were into it." Lucas looked annoyed.

"I didn't say you could do that." I looked over my shoulder. My cheeks burned volcanic. Adam was on the shore, sitting with Willa, and they were looking out at us.

"*Okay,*" Lucas said.

"Sorry," I muttered, and regretted it immediately, especially when Lucas softened in appreciation of the apology. I looked down and saw through my reflection to the bottom of the lake. All this—Sioux Falls, summer, Lucas—what was I supposed to be doing? Was fate a feeling of owning your life, or of belonging to it?

August

THE PAST

HOURS LATER, I STUMBLED, DRUNK, INTO THE HOUSE, LEAVING LUCAS BY the water with Austin, holding firecrackers in their hands until the last moment. I fell asleep in Adam's empty room and woke again after a short, shallow sleep, the night still deeply dark. I needed air. I almost tripped on a sleeping body on the floor by the door. There were voices by the fire still, and as quietly as I could, I slipped outside and crept down to the lake and waded through the shallows, the water rustling as I disturbed it. Ahead of me, I heard the creak of boards, and in the dark, someone sitting on the dock rose up.

Watery moonlight bobbed around my knees. It was Adam, I knew, even though I could see only his outline.

"Of course you'd be here." I meant it to be funny but it came out serious. I pushed through the water toward the dock, and Adam met me at the edge. He'd put a flannel shirt on over his lacrosse T-shirt, and he reached out with both his hands and pulled me up onto the dock, all the way into his arms, and I kissed him.

The only light was too far away to reach us, wincing from the back door of the cabin. I kissed the space where his ear met his jaw, and he inhaled sharply and pressed his hand against the small of my back until there was no space left between us. It went on and on and never stopped feeling good, until finally I buried my face in his neck, my forearms pressed into his chest, and he wrapped his arms around me.

"Hey," he said. "What's new?"

"Shut up." I pulled away from him.

His hair was sticking up from where my hands had been in it. His eyes shone, and he looked tired. He looked like he wanted me. He looked like mine.

I reached up and touched his cheek. His hand caught mine on its way down. I looked over his shoulder, toward the end of the dock.

"Can we talk?" The words were heavy coming out.

We walked the length of the dock until there was nowhere else to go. We sat down, our shoulders touched, and he put our hands in his lap. I looked up at him, and he looked out at the water.

"You couldn't sleep either?" I asked.

He shook his head. "No. I mean, also, you were sleeping in my bed."

We heard a shout and recognized the voice as Austin's; laughter followed. "Is he okay?" I asked. Adam shrugged.

I wanted to tell him how much I liked him and had since I'd met him, how I had just assumed he was dating Regina, and maybe he was for a minute, and then there was the thing with Lucas in any case—but I was afraid to say those things. Summer was more than half over. Too much of its story had already been written for it to begin again.

You're a bitch, Gertie. Cindy's never going to forgive you.

"Adam, I didn't come here to hurt people. To date someone and then exchange him for his friend. Even if it . . ."

"Even if what?" Adam asked.

"Even if it feels right."

"To be fair," Adam said, his mouth curving into a smile, "Lucas and I aren't that good of friends."

"You know what I mean. It's shitty. I'm being *shitty*. I didn't think it was possible for one person to cause so much drama."

"Tiny but mighty," Adam said.

He untangled our hands and brought both of his to his face. He rubbed his eyes.

"Every summer from now until eternity," he said, "no matter how drunk I get or how much gunpowder I light on fire or which extremities I burn off, I'll think of you."

"Please do think of me as they reattach your thumb."

It was getting light. A part in the clouds revealed a scalp of lavender sky. The air was cool and dewy.

"It's morning soon," I said.

"Nightingale not the lark or whatever."

"You're such a nerd." I tried to sound like I was making fun of him, but my heart felt like it was breaking. For so many reasons, and the worst one was that I couldn't talk to Cindy about it, because she would tell me it was okay to have feelings for Adam. That it was okay for me to make mistakes. That when we fucked up, we fucked up together because we shared a star in the sky. I couldn't let her comfort me, not when she didn't know.

"Want to get out of here?" Adam asked. "Get breakfast in Sioux Falls or something?"

I looked over my shoulder at the sleeping cabin. Lucas was there, he'd driven me, but I didn't want to go back with him.

"Yes," I said.

We stood, and Adam wrapped me in his arms. I closed my eyes against him. He kissed the top of my head, but that was all.

We usually had a lot to say to each other, but in the car we were quiet. Adam pulled into an IHOP and the waitress led us to a booth in the back by the window and we collapsed into the seats. The sun broke the horizon and landed in our eyes, and Adam unstacked and restacked the jams in the caddy so they were sorted by flavor. He moved on to the sugars, and I stared out at the parking lot and wondered how I'd ended up here.

"I've never been to an IHOP," I said, looking around.

Adam's jaw dropped. "You're joking."

I shrugged. "We always went to Big Boy. It's, like, the Michigan version of IHOP."

"Welcome," Adam said, smiling. "I'm glad I can be here for this moment."

The waitress brought hash browns for me, blueberry pancakes for Adam, and a plate of bacon that Adam set between us. He drizzled syrup over his pancakes. The diner was scattered with a handful of early risers, swirling plastic stirrers in cups of coffee.

"What are you thinking about?" Adam asked.

"Where to start?" Getting my thoughts out was like trying to work a jammed sewing machine. "I've messed up a lot this summer. I imagine I'm a real pain to be around."

"What are you talking about? You're a ray of fucking sunshine."

"Ha ha," I said. "Is that sarcasm I detect? Really, though, you don't know anything. I'm a monster. I make everything harder for everyone."

"That's probably not true."

"I love how pragmatic you are. *Probably* not true. It's good to hedge your bets. You don't know me that well."

"I know you." He put his fork down, reached across the table, and put his hands on mine.

The waitress zoomed by and stopped abruptly to refill our coffees. Our hands flew apart.

"You two are so cute," she said.

I put my hands underneath the table when she left.

"See?" I said. "Proof. I'm a monster."

"What do you mean?"

I gestured from him to me and back. "This. Us. I'm a bad friend to you and everyone else. I have to stop betraying everyone."

Adam laughed, but I didn't.

"I'm *serious*." Heat brewed on the back of my neck.

"What do you mean, betraying everyone?" His eyes wrinkled behind his glasses.

"I don't know," I sighed.

Of course I knew, though.

"I just owe someone back home an apology," I said.

Adam smiled and tilted his head to the side. "An apology? That's not so bad."

"I guess not."

"So. Back home. When will that be?"

"I'm not sure," I said. "End of the month, I guess."

"It's only the beginning of August. We have time."

"A little time."

Adam got a text that took him to his phone. We drifted away from the moment our hands had touched, and I didn't know how he felt, but I scolded myself for kissing him again on the dock, like I was a fool for believing, for a second, or, if not believing, then ignoring what I already knew. It was hard to sit there feeling mutually rejected—not by each other, not really, but by chance.

I thought of Jamie and Hayden. Jamie will want so badly to trust him, to tell him the truth, but she'd be putting everyone in danger. Commitment is new to her. Back home she couldn't even commit to her own feelings. But in the Underworld, she has a purpose. Her purpose—could I make that my purpose? Maybe I couldn't write convincing physics or epic battles or basically any scene where people weren't just sitting and talking or thinking, but maybe, at least, I could write about a commitment someone had made.

"Gertie?"

"What?"

"What are you thinking about?"

"I already told you." The book was as much of a secret as anything else.

"I had to say your name, like, three times."

"Actually, do you have a pen?"

Adam reached into his pocket and pulled out a Pilot gel roller.

"Oh, my favorite kind," I said.

He grinned at me.

"What?"

"You're just so genuinely excited about the pen. It's cute."

"Well, it's a nice pen." I tugged a napkin free from the dispenser on the table. I wrote down the line: *At home she couldn't even commit to her own feelings.*

I covered the napkin with my hand as I wrote, then folded it and shoved it in my pocket. I handed the pen back to Adam, but he shook his head.

"Are you going to tell me what you wrote down?"

"Nope," I said.

I finished my hash browns. The diner was filling up with the morning rush.

"So, what do we do?" Adam asked.

"Do we have to decide right now? Can we just put a pin in things, I don't know, take a step back?"

Adam nodded. He looked disappointed.

"Should we go?" he asked.

"Oh, Gertie," Cindy said, after I'd told her.

April

THE FUTURE

MORE THAN TEN YEARS AGO NOW, CIARÁN SAID, WHEN I ASKED HIM WHAT he was thinking, "I want to see you this summer."

I laughed at first, the idea of someone traveling that far to be with me so ludicrous in my mind, but Ciarán started talking about finding a job. He had citizenship through his father; he wouldn't need a visa to work. I realized he was serious, and I remember falling silent, stunned and unbelieving, though I'd done similar once, giving up on the dream of New York with Cindy so I could be with Adam.

"Are you sure?" I asked.

I picked Ciarán up from the airport the first week of June. Earlier that spring, without Adam's car to borrow, I'd used some of my savings to buy a friend's ancient Sunfire. Something loose rattled in the undercarriage, drowning out the other engines as I reached the pickup zone where Ciarán waited outside with his bags. Through the open window I could hear his laugh, blooming beautifully, as the noisiest car in the lineup stopped beside him. He dropped his bags and came around to the driver's side, pulling me up out of the car. We embraced until the airport police barked at us to move on.

"I can drive if you'd like," he said. "Just make sure I don't go on the wrong side."

It seems to me now as though Ciarán has driven us everywhere since.

He'd arranged his own housing, a room in a Classical Revival belonging to a frat that had been kicked out of Greek life after a girl fell from a second-story window. I directed him there, pointing out places on campus where I'd lived or taken classes. We went through the unlocked door and searched for someone named Josh, who was nowhere to be found. What we did find was chaos: Cockroaches skittered across the kitchen floor. Mold spread lusciously from the corners of the ceiling. The smell of beers and boys and vomit crept oppressively throughout the house. A few loose residents were passed out across furniture in the living room, the start screen of an abandoned game pulsing impatiently on the TV.

"You didn't give them any money yet, did you?" I asked.

Ciarán shook his head.

I weighed whether I had the courage.

"Why don't you just stay with me?"

The possibility had been simmering in me. It seemed to be the point of the whole summer. I would need to be the one to bring it up, and until that moment I'd cowered before the chance he'd tell me I was moving too fast.

"Thank God for you, Gertie," he replied quickly, and I burst out laughing, full of relief.

"We'll have to look at that," he said, bending to peer beneath my car when we parked in the lot of my apartment building. My eyes grazed the railroad tracks where, two years earlier, I'd closed myself off to him, shutting down the idea that we'd ever see each other again.

Adam still lived across the hall from me, and as I led Ciarán inside I glanced quickly at Adam's door, his apartment quiet behind it. My roommates greeted Ciarán with anxious delight; they'd been waiting for us to get home. The drama of the past few months had been thrilling, and they insisted on a trip to the bar.

That Ciarán hardly touched me the whole evening felt designed, like he wanted to wait for us to be alone. Just the tips of his fingers on my back when he held the door or two hands gripping my shoulders in apology when he kicked my foot beneath the table. We all came home a little drunk, and though my roommates wanted to keep going, I saw the warm-blue dark circles beneath Ciarán's eyes as his body pulled him toward the time of night in Dublin. "Should we go to bed?" I asked, and when he nodded I shot my roommates a begging glance, silently asking them to behave.

Ciarán followed me into my room and closed the door behind him and then closed the space between us. He was only a little taller than me, his lips almost even with mine, and he moved closer and asked, "Is this okay?"

"Yes."

I kept saying yes. I was wearing a red dress that landed above the knee, with buttons that went all the way down the front, and as we kissed Ciarán undid them. We'd gambled so much on this, and I remember thinking, as he unfolded me from the fabric, that we might still come up with nothing. He knelt and kissed me through my panties, tugged them down and nudged me back until my legs met the bed and I fell onto it. His tongue traced me in a circle; my hands messed up his hair.

He laughed, embarrassed, when I asked if he'd brought condoms. "I didn't want to assume, you know, but I did, yes . . ."

He put one on and touched his forehead to mine. He was slow and careful and he kissed me down to my jawline, his breath hot on my neck. He put his tongue tentatively in my ear and when he saw that I liked it he shoved it deeper.

"God, you're tight," he said. "I don't know how long I can last."

I told him to hold still inside me. He shuddered and gasped into my shoulder. I held him, and he lay with his head on my chest. His fingers traced my body, stopping on my right thigh, where the scar from the aerosol can was a shiny silver memory burned on my skin. Adam, who'd seen the wound before it became a scar, had always avoided it, never looked at it or touched that part of me, maybe wished the scar wasn't there at all.

Ciarán ran his thumb over it, back and forth, lifting his chin to look up at me with lightly warm eyes.

"What happened here?" he asked.

August

THE PAST

ADAM STOPPED COMING AROUND ON HIS LUNCH BREAKS. I THOUGHT HE'D understood what I'd told him, the problem we faced. He hadn't *seemed* angry in the diner. But it turned out he was.

I really can't believe you're still with him, he texted me.

Once again, I thought, *Maybe I could be with Adam* . . . But after I'd made such a big deal about my choice, putting a pin in it, doing the right thing, my decision was like a lost library book. I couldn't return it. I just had to suck it up and pay for it.

"Things still good with Lucas?"

The voice was Jill's. I turned around and saw her leaning over my conveyor belt, her eyes wide and wild. She glanced over her shoulder at Lucas, who slouched against his register. A smile eager for gossip grew on her face.

"He was annoyed you left the lake early," she prodded.

"Nothing's changing," I said. "I told him my dad needed me for something. *Please* don't say anything to anyone."

She nodded, but her eyes darted to Willa, who watched us from the coffee aisle, where she was cleaning the grinders. Willa already knew. Of course she did. It was stupid of me to think Jill wouldn't tell her. Any promise to me was immediately vanquished by what must have been their eternal promise to each other never to hide a single piece of gossip. I couldn't blame them. I would have told Cindy.

Without Adam to hang out with, and avoiding Lucas as much as I could, I had more time to rewrite the pages in my novel I'd torn up. I'd thought about Jamie and Hayden since then, but when I tried to write, I felt I couldn't reach them—they were gone, like they'd never been real. I tried to call them back. I imagined it was time, finally, for something to happen in this so far incredibly relaxed war I'd written.

A battle to save the last free city, a fortress built on a tidal island, accessible only at low tide. The rebels arrive at night, and lights crawl up the tiers of the city, a church at the top glowing bright. A heavy wood-and-iron portcullis rises as they draw nearer, and Jamie can feel its gears grind in her ears. Beyond the gate a courtyard spreads out, burdened with refugees, people with nowhere to go, all civilians, not nearly enough soldiers. Their enemy will be there in two days, two days they spend caking the ramparts with broken glass and anchoring chevaux-de-frise into the sand, unspooling barbed wire between each barricade at low tide.

The night before the battle, Jamie looks through the things from her old life she keeps squirreled away. For one last night, she'll be that girl. She puts on the clothes she was wearing when she first arrived in the Underworld, a yellow dress and gold bracelet. She applies pressed highlighter that had been in her pocket to her nose and cheeks and pulls at her hair. Then she goes to a tavern near the top of the city where everyone has gone to drink. She finds Hayden sitting in the back, and he smiles when he sees her. "Just like the day I met you," he says.

He drinks quickly, and she tries to match his pace. Her mind enters a blissful, light space, floating almost, and when the dead eyes of the man she killed burn her memory, she takes another drink. She clasps Hayden's shoulder and laughs at something he says, though by the time the laughter escapes her she can no longer remember why she's laughing. A lantern swinging from a wall sconce is knocked free and a small fire blooms in a puddle of spilled liquor. A stampede of people rush at it with their boots. In those flames, Jamie sees the city burning, a swell of bodies colliding in blood, and she feels trapped and hot and like she's going to throw up, so she tears herself from Hayden and stumbles through the crowd and out the door.

Fresh water runs from a spigot on the city wall, and Jamie brings a palmful to her lips. She wipes her face and pushes water through her hair. She can breathe again. Hayden stands a few feet away, his hands in his pockets.

"Are you okay?" he asks.

She doesn't answer.

Hayden pulls two cigarettes from his pocket. He holds them to the torch blazing outside the tavern and takes a long drag on both at the same time. He hands one to Jamie. "This will make you feel better," he says.

She inhales, lets the smoke strike her lungs with a cool, uplifting feeling.

"These things are bad for you." She flicks her thumb against the butt.

"I know." One thing their worlds agree on.

Jamie remembers Dove telling her she has to guard her secret. Take it to the grave if she has to. But standing before her is someone who cares about her. And her grave is already dug, the turned earth fresh. She can hear tomorrow's bayonet tearing through her stomach. She doesn't want to die having lied to him for the whole time she knew him.

"I have to tell you something," she says.

At first his face is as still as a portrait—lips slightly parted in the frozen moment of having just heard something strange. Then his smile—a little drunk, a little mocking—slackens, disappears.

"You shouldn't have told me," he says darkly.

He looks at her from the new distance where he finds himself.

"Hayden, I couldn't *not* tell you. Not after—"

"Not after what?"

"Not after I realized I loved you."

Hayden's face grows darker. "Go get some sleep," he says after a long silence.

He leaves her at the top of the city, her dropped cigarette glowing at her feet. Was it wrong to have told him? Or had it just been hard to hear? Was it selfish, all about her? Was the truth really always so valuable?

My dad's voice broke into my thoughts. He was looking over my shoulder, reading what I'd written.

"Hayden's right, you know," he said. "About sleep. Can you imagine being hungover and tired and having to fight a *battle*? Jesus Christ, I'd just speed things up and kill myself."

August

THE PAST

MY TEXT THREAD WITH ADAM WAS DEAD; HE'D NEVER RESPONDED TO A message I'd sent asking if we could talk, saying I didn't realize staying with Lucas meant I wouldn't have him as a friend anymore.

I was thinking about Adam the day I came home and saw my dad sitting on his bed with his arm tied off, a needle poised over a vein in his inner elbow. I shouldn't have been home yet, but I was let go early because Anthony had made a mistake in the schedule. The only sound was screaming inside my head and the soft thud of my bag as it landed on the floor.

"Nothing's changed," my dad said later. "I've been doing this awhile."

"It changes everything," I said quietly.

It changed who I was, knowing.

"What was that?"

"Nothing," I said.

.   .   .

Anthony was cracking down on phones on the floor; he told us we needed to keep them in our lockers. After my shift one afternoon, I saw four missed calls from Cindy. Panicked, I called her back.

"Never mind," she said. "It's all okay."

"What happened?"

"My dad left me this completely garbled voicemail," she said. "He was *not* okay. I think he was asking for help, but when I called back he didn't answer."

"Did you ever reach him?"

"No, but my mom heard from his sponsor that he's okay. So he's alive, I guess."

"I'm so sorry, Cindy. What can we do? Do you have his sponsor's number?"

"I don't think we can do anything. I only called you so many times because I wanted someone to talk to, someone who understood."

A pang. I hadn't been there.

"Fuck my manager's rules," I said. "I'm never letting my phone out of my sight again."

"Let's not talk about it," Cindy said. "Tell me about Gertie in Boyland. Gabe ditched me again. I'm worried he found someone new."

May

THE FUTURE

THE MONTH OF MAY FALLS BEAUTIFULLY ON ANN ARBOR. IT'S BEEN A LONG
time since I was here this time of year. The big waxy blooms of the
magnolias have already come and gone, the watery greens of spring
deepening into emerald summer. I look for joy in Mom, warm
weather has always improved her mood, but she seems doubtful it will
last.

There's an Irish bar on Main Street. One night Ciarán and I go to
it. He shakes his head, smiling, looking around at how it hasn't
changed.

"Our old usual?" he asks, meaning a pint and a shot.

He worked there the summer he visited me. The manager had
hired Ciarán on the spot; he was good for business, and so he spent
those months elbow-deep in Guinness and Jameson while I worked
my campus jobs—one in the study abroad office, the other behind
the counter of a Wendy's in the student union—and at the end of the
day I took the long walk from campus to the bar, where Ciarán's shift

was just getting started. The owner of the pub liked me because his grandma was a McMahon, and he liked Ciarán because, I was learning, it was impossible not to.

He even charmed Cindy, who came to visit in July. I brought her to meet him one afternoon. She walked into the bar scowling, full of skepticism. She'd liked Ciarán as a hypothetical alternative to Adam, but, as usual, she felt I was moving too fast.

"I told Gertie she should play the field," she said, shaking Ciarán's hand.

"Is that not what I am?" Ciarán winked at me. "A player on Gertie's field, on my knees begging her for mercy?"

A smile touched Cindy's lips. She took the pint Ciarán handed her.

It was late in the afternoon. The sun was bright outside, but the bar was dark and cool and mostly empty, so Ciarán could linger near us.

I hadn't seen Cindy since Christmas, and we finally felt, she and I, like we'd been born into an adulthood of our choosing. "I told Willa," she said, "I'm, like, becoming a person."

For years I'd been trying to get Cindy and Willa to connect in New York, and now I grasped Cindy's arm and exclaimed how wonderful it was that they were friends. Our laughter filled the whole bar; we were obnoxious, but happy. Cindy bought three shots of whiskey. "One for you, Ciarán," she said, pushing it toward him.

"All right, but only one for me, girls," he said.

Gorgeous burning in my throat, and as soon as the glasses landed back on the counter, Cindy and I were laughing through the triumph of the shot, how it hit our blood immediately, but our laughter slipped when the door opened and sunlight came in so bright it could crack glass. Adam's roommate, Doruk, walked in, followed by Adam, who had his arm around a girl. My eyes adjusted. It was Rachel, whom he'd always gone to every time we broke up. She was nice, and smart, and I'd always felt bad for the way Adam treated her.

Adam saw us. His eyes flickered between me and Cindy, his expression frozen on his face—bewilderment, and hatred. We watched as the three of them claimed a table in the far corner. Adam faced so stiffly away from us that Doruk turned to look, then Rachel. They said nothing, but I could tell from the way they shuffled their chairs, so deliberately, that they were wrestling their discomfort, avoiding eye contact as Cindy and I stared at them openly.

"Ciarán." Cindy beckoned him frantically. He was bent over the dishwasher, steam rising religiously around him, and he emerged from it smiling, wiping his hands on a towel.

"Another?" he asked.

"Kiss Gertie," Cindy demanded.

"You're quite pushy," he said.

"Do it."

Ciarán looked at me. I tossed my head to one side to indicate Adam, who had come to stand at the far end of the counter.

"That's Adam," I said quietly.

Ciarán's eyes widened. "Oh, hell," he said.

"*Ciarán*. Kiss her. Right now."

"Do we have to do that to the poor man?" Ciarán asked, still drying his hands, but he couldn't hide his smile. "Only if Gertie wants me to."

"You're *never* petty, Gertie," Cindy urged, gripping my arm. "Be petty this once."

I shrugged. Ciarán leaned over the bar but his lips stopped just short of mine, his face so close I could feel the laughter on my skin, and he ruffled my hair. Throwing the dish towel over his shoulder, he went over to Adam, smiling as though they were old friends. Ciarán jutted his thumb casually in our direction and then rounded his hand to shake Adam's. Adam, who had steeled himself against me ever since we broke up, looked disarmed.

Ciarán filled a few pints, talking as he did, and by the time Adam was carrying the beer back to his friends the darkness in his face had lifted, if only a little.

"Oh, he's good," Cindy said.

"Still want me to play the field?" I asked.

. . .

Midway through the summer, the study abroad office lost its administrative assistant, and I took her place and went full time, which allowed me to quit my other job ringing up burgers at Wendy's. I
opened the office at eight each morning to take calls from parents
who wanted to complain about their children's troubles abroad. At
five every evening I left to go to the bar, where I stayed until I couldn't
any longer, and I'd go home and sleep for a few hours until Ciarán
crept into the room in the middle of the night and I opened my arms
to him and took him inside me. He always asked what I wanted, and
I always wanted it.

The shame was lifting slowly, vines burned back in a garden. I'd
been seen as a slut before—and not even a deserving one; "she's not
hot enough to cause so much drama," Austin said once—and I'd also
been seen as frigid, only halfway present, and withholding. But I'd
never been appreciated for what could be given to me.

It wasn't just boys my age. Vaughn had looked at me and seen my
body. Early on, when he hadn't been around long, and my goodwill
toward him was starting to shrivel, he put a snide smile on his face
and said to my mom, "Does Gertie have a boyfriend?"

"I don't think so," she said.

"Maybe she needs sex," Vaughn said, his eyes on me. "It would
loosen her up a little."

I was putting my shoes on, getting ready to flee. What Vaughn
said lashed my wrist to the wall, where I'd been holding on for balance. His voice was slim, snakelike; he knew how he was making me
feel, and he was doing it on purpose. My body was without prove-
nance, he seemed to say. I was nothing on my own.

I told Ciarán this story one night that years-ago summer. He'd sat
up abruptly in bed, the sheet falling from his chest as he twisted to
look at me.

"You're not serious?" he said.

I hesitated. Talking about sex was as risky as doing it, opening myself up to the judgment that had depleted me and would continue to until one day there would be nothing left. But I was starting to feel, even in those early days, that Ciarán and I could imagine something different.

"It made me think sex was something other people would always use to change me. It was always about them, not me."

"God, I'm sorry. You deserve better."

I reached up, let the back of my hand fall against his arm. "I think I found better. If it's okay to say that."

Ciarán placed a hand on either side of me and kissed me between my eyes.

"I keep saying crazy things to you," he whispered, "but I want to marry you one day."

Ciarán fell asleep soon after, but I couldn't. I turned on the bedside lamp. He'd scared me. The days were numbered until he had to go back to Dublin. The hours were numbered until I had to be at work. But my pulse was shredding sleep apart, leaving it in a pile on the bedroom floor.

I'd been reading a book of stories by Pam Houston, who wrote about life in a way that made me see how much I'd been missing. The spine of the old paperback groaned as I folded the book over on itself. I'd read *Waltzing the Cat* before, but this time I was searching for something. I shifted the book within the perimeter of the lamplight and started from the beginning. And when I reached the end of the first story, I found what I was looking for. I felt like this was it, like I was taking a step into my future, too.

Six years later, Ciarán and I got married. I hurt everyone by walking down the aisle alone. It was at the wedding, for the first time, that I noticed Mom limping.

"I understand," she whispered during the reception. "You wouldn't want an old lady falling while she's walking you down the aisle."

"That's not it," I said, but I couldn't offer a reason.

I asked Cindy to do a reading from *Middlemarch,* the passage about how Fred and Mary didn't have the "glorious equipment of hope and enthusiasm" but instead achieved a "solid mutual happiness."

"Kind of sober for a wedding," Cindy said.

That's what I'd liked about it.

August

THE PAST

HOME WAS CONTAMINATED WITH THOUGHTS OF SYRINGES. AT NIGHT THEY hovered in my dreams, pricking me, and when I threw back the blankets and put my feet on the ground I sometimes jumped, thinking I'd stepped on one.

I got home from work early just as my dad was waking up from a nap, coming out of his bedroom scratching the skin beneath the elastic band of his sweatpants. He looked happy, refreshed even.

In the kitchen he fixed a bowl of strawberry yogurt, Cheerios tossed on top. When he plucked his pack of cigarettes from the counter and went out to the balcony, I followed. Like always.

The balcony was in the shade and the chairs were cool. I lifted my face to the sky. My eyes felt cold behind closed lids. I didn't say anything. I would rather have silence than a conversation clinging to life on a ventilator. I couldn't stop seeing syringes and that reddish-brown liquid plunging into my dad's arm.

My dad opened a book about World War II, and his nose whistled softly as he breathed.

"Did I ever tell you much about when I lived in New York?" he said a few minutes later.

I shook my head and picked at chipped polish on my toenail. "Not really. In the eighties?"

"Late eighties, early nineties. Ansel went to Columbia for his MFA."

I looked at my father's deep scowl and small mouth. His eyebrows moved up and down with his thoughts. Sometimes, when I looked at him, I saw the empty space next to him where his brother should be.

"I always looked up to Ansel, so I followed him to New York when I got kicked out of Michigan State."

"Kicked out for drinking too much?"

"Your mom exaggerates that part."

"Fair enough," I said. "What was New York like when you lived there?"

"I lived with Ansel in Morningside Heights, and Michael Fellows used to come down from Boston for visits. I know you're thinking about New York for college—the New York we lived in doesn't exist anymore, it's all gentrified, but back then it was great. He worked on a novel, and I wrote songs. It probably sounds cliché, but all dreams do when you say them out loud. That's the real test, Gertie. You have to do it even if it sounds stupid."

My knees cradled my chin, and around me a New York City I could only vaguely imagine rose up—all its bridges and buildings, with people filling the streets, my dad among them, a much younger version of himself with a neat mustache I'd seen in photographs. He walked alongside his brother, the man who stayed frozen at thirty-seven.

"Do you remember any of the songs you wrote?" I asked.

My dad tapped his thumb on his book, beating out a rhythm. "Probably. My guitar is still in the basement in Michigan, though."

"You should've told me to bring it," I said. "I can't believe you left it at Mom's."

My dad had the perfect folk voice, fed by his love of Gordon Lightfoot and Cat Stevens, low and a little grainy. It cracked on the high notes, and I'd missed it.

"That's okay," my dad said. "I'll get it one day."

"When Cindy and I talk about moving to New York, we wonder who we'll meet there. I wonder what they're doing this exact minute."

"That's the best part about people you haven't met yet," he said.

"What? The not-knowing-them part?"

He laughed. "No. The one-day-coming-together part. How it happens. It's fun to think about."

A blurry face crossed into my mind. Someone I would know someday.

"Did Uncle Ansel ever finish his novel?"

My dad's expression turned thoughtful. "You know, everything I have that's his is in the basement at your mom's. I don't remember seeing a manuscript, but I never could look through all those boxes. I couldn't even pack them up in the first place—Michael did it for me. If Ansel did ever finish his book, the boxes are where it would be. When you go home you should see if it's there."

"Wow," I said. "I don't know. Maybe."

"Anyway," my dad said. "I met a woman there who thought I was the one. Stayed for years after your uncle Ansel died because I couldn't leave the place where he'd last been alive. But then it got to be too much."

"You went to rehab in Michigan?" I knew this part of the story.

"Where I met your mom," he finished. "And then five years later we had you."

I wondered who the woman was, the person who thought my dad was the one. The feeling returned, the involuntary twitch of knowing that it wouldn't have taken much for the world to have rearranged itself and everything to be different.

The conversation seemed to stop there, but it didn't feel like we needed to resuscitate it. We could let it rest. They were almost too much to stomach, these unlived dreams.

May

THE FUTURE

THESE UNLIVED DREAMS. IT'S A HARD PART OF THE BOOK TO WRITE, TEMPT-
ing to deus ex machina the shit out of everything, since those versions of myself and my dad can't seem to help themselves.

I've started going to the library during the day to work on job applications. The two-month break I took to write is clearly over, de-
clares our bank account.

One evening, I come home to what feels like an empty house.
Through Mom's bedroom, her bathroom door is closed. I unpack the
groceries I picked up on the way home. There's still silence from
Mom's room. I peek in again.

"Hello?" I call.

"Is that you, Gertie?"

"It's me." I touch the doorknob to her bathroom gently. "Can I
come in?"

"You can, but I'm in my birthday suit."

"Mom!" I cry when I open the door to find her on the floor, a towel she pulled from the rack covering half her body. I wrap her in another and help her to sitting.

"Didn't you hear me come in? Why didn't you call out?"

"I didn't know it was you. Ciarán can't see me like this."

"Oh, Mom," I say. "We're getting you a Life Alert."

"I'm not wearing one of those."

"An Apple Watch, then."

"Stop, Gertie. I can shower on my own without a robot to help me."

I wrap my arms around her middle; she puts hers around my neck. I lift her onto her scooter. "Let me get your clothes," I say.

She dresses herself while I wait in the kitchen. "That was embarrassing," she says when she emerges, shaking her head as I watch her from behind the island.

"We *have* to think about getting you on Medicaid one day," I say.

"I swear, if you're trying to put me in a home, I'm going back to Florida." Her face is set in a grimace. "I could live just fine on my own."

"We're not going to put you in a home, but you need an aide, Mom. Ciarán and I need to be able to go to work and go out or whatever without worrying you're lying naked on the floor!"

"Oh, stop," she says. "I have my plan."

"Your plan," I say, "is bullshit. You don't qualify for die with dignity."

"I don't *qualify* for a dignified death?"

"You know what I mean. Ciarán and I can't plan our lives around that. We can't say, 'Oh, we don't need to think about the future because Mom's just going to kill herself.'"

"And then you two can go back to New York if you want."

"You're alive and well and lucky," I say. "Please remember that."

"I don't know about well," she says, struggling off her scooter and onto the couch.

"I can't believe I'm even entertaining this conversation."

I tell Ciarán about her fall, and our conversation, later. "Did I say the right thing when I scolded her?"

"I think you can trust your gut there, Gertie." He's just kicked his shoes off and collapsed on the bed, home from the coworking space he broke down and rented after months of me and Mom piled on top of him.

"I don't know what to do to get her to stop thinking like that. Maybe she should go to therapy."

"We should all be in therapy." Ciarán closes his eyes, arms crossed over his chest.

"I'm worried boredom is an accelerant for this awful death drive she seems to have." I move the latest load of laundry around the room. "Why is it impossible for us to fold laundry once it's clean? Remember the Camino, when we had one pair of pants?"

"Gertie," Ciarán says, opening his arms without opening his eyes. "Come over here. She's not going to kill herself. One day she'll concede about Medicaid."

His voice makes me go limp. I crawl across the bed and fall on top of him. His arm folds over my back.

"I'm happy," I say into his shoulder. "I want her to be, too. She's had such a hard time being happy in this life."

This life. As though there's one coming after, too.

August

CINDY WAS STRUGGLING. SHE THOUGHT HER DAD WOULD'VE RESURFACED by now—gotten in touch with her, especially after he'd scared her with his desperate voicemail, but he hadn't. I was thinking of her one afternoon as I walked into Hy-Vee, my head down, and then I looked up and saw Adam.

"Hey," he said.

"I'm surprised you didn't run away when you saw me." I tried to smile.

"You don't get it," Adam said, his voice harsh but quiet. "Do you?"

"Apparently not," I replied, "but I have a feeling you're going to tell me."

"I'm afraid you're going to turn out miserable."

"It's too late," I said. "I already am."

When I got home later, the lights were off, no one home, and I hung my keys on the hook by the door and went into my dad's room, looking around. With a glance back at the door, I crawled on my knees and reached under his bed and found a Tupperware the size of a Bible, the kind meant for cereal. I popped the lid open; inside, a few needles leaned against one another, all plastic and poison and points. I already knew about them, just as I'd known, in some ways, that my dad was taking pills before I found his stash in my closet in Michigan. But seeing, being so near—it changed the perspective. It made me a part of things—made me, in a way, want to see them, count them, know if any disappeared. The closest I could come to control.

I returned them beneath the bed and sat on the balcony. I looked out at the same things and tried to see them in a different way. The sky, the pool, the clubhouse, the grills on iron poles cemented into the grass—all of it looked back at me like it didn't remember me.

I took out my phone and dialed Cindy's number.

"My love," she answered. "You didn't text me today. Where have you been?"

"Nowhere," I said, truthfully. "Sorry I didn't call. I ran into Adam earlier, and it was awkward."

"I'm so mad I'm not there for all the drama."

"Well, that's good, right? Haven't we had enough drama for a while?"

"I guess so. Still, though, I miss you."

"I'm sorry," I said. "I should've tried harder to stay."

"Don't be silly," she said. "It's not your fault. Tell me what's going on with you."

Each phone call to her felt like pulling a petal off a flower—and once all the petals were gone, I'd have no more chances to tell her the truth, and our friendship would disappear, and I'd be a beast forever.

Abruptly, Cindy swore under her breath. "What?" Her voice sounded like she'd thrown it into another room. "*Okay*, fine!"

"Shit," she said to me. "My mom needs me. Hold on. Talk to Gabe for a sec."

"Gabe's there?"

But Cindy was already gone, and it was Gabe's voice I heard.

"Yeah. I'm here."

"Oh," I said. "Hey. What's going on?"

"I saw photos from the lake party on Instagram. Looks like you had a good time."

"I didn't post anything."

"You were tagged in a lot."

"Oh," I said.

"Cindy said you've been hanging out with your boyfriend's best friend. It's like the inverse of what you did to me."

"So, what, Gabe—are you going to call me a bitch again? Cindy could walk back in and wonder what the fuck you're talking about."

"That's exactly it. Things stayed weird with us because you wouldn't tell Cindy. We could've figured it out."

"*You* didn't want to tell her. How many times do I have to say that? God, with *everyone,* it's like I'm living in an alternate timeline. Gabe, I'm saying it now and I'm not going to say it again. This is over. It's *finally* over."

Gabe inhaled, the line rustled, and Cindy returned.

"I'm back," she said. Then, "What did you say to Gabe? He just walked out in a huff."

"Oh." My blood was ice. "I don't know."

"He's a weirdo," she said. "So, you don't like Lucas, and you like Adam, but you're with Lucas, and Adam hates you, and honestly the more I know about this alleged nice boy the less I like him. Do I have that right?"

"Hey, Cindy, do you need to see if Gabe's okay?"

"Yeah." She sighed. "I probably should. But I'm calling you later, and you better answer my questions about what the heck is going on over there in the Great Plains."

"I will."

I didn't want to, though. I was sick of me. I was sort of sick of seeing myself in Jamie, too, but for some reason I couldn't give up on her—if I did, I'd truly have nothing. I'd been thinking I could just kill her in the battle scene, and the book would be over, and I'd put it away, because writing had become a way of reliving my life, and it had been hard enough the first time.

I tried to imagine: The sky will be gloom and steel the morning of the battle. Soldiers sit against low walls, hands clasped behind their heads, waiting with their guns quiet in their laps. A few finicky, precious machine guns are mounted on the ramparts. Hayden stands far away from Jamie, silent as though they'd never met.

Jamie looks across the water at the army on the other side of it, columns of soldiers framed by grassy dunes. Their guns find what little sunlight there is and reflect it. Shivers spread through the lines of their cavalry as the horses respond to the small, restless movements of their riders. The tide pulls away from the shore, and with each wave that rolls past the city, the water surges one step forward and two steps back. Everyone is lost to the shadow of their future selves, the ones they can already see in the battle. The ocean pulls back a little more, and then, as though the sea draws the enemy army on a string, the soldiers take their first steps off the dunes. As simple and inexorable as a quarter falling into a coin slot. They spread out like a sheet across the damp sands, horses now and then sending up sprays of water from tidal pools. Their standards forced sideways in the wind. Behind the cavalry, soldiers on foot carry their rifles or drag mortars and machine guns. A few shots, fired alone, spit from farther down the wall. Jamie's gun holds a cartridge of bullets, each one the size of a rabbit's foot. She shouldn't be here, but it doesn't matter anymore. Today's the end.

But I found I couldn't kill her. She refuses to let go, as easy as it would be to stop and wait for a bullet. She admires, or maybe I admire, that determination—human, prehuman—that makes her want to see this through.

The battle won't last long. Jamie is captured. As desperately as she looks for him, there's no sign of Hayden.

June

THE FUTURE

AFTER MONTHS OF INSURANCE APPEALS AND APPLICATIONS TO CO-PAY programs, which Mom works through with increasing frustration and confusion, medication arrives, a small box of slim auto-injectors housed in a refrigerated case of ice packs. She turns them out of the box, grimacing as they land on her lap.

"Careful," I say. "You're not supposed to shake them."

From the look on her face, I can tell she's getting cold feet.

"I want to do it in my calf, where my leg is already numb," she says.

"The box says thigh or stomach."

"No, I don't think so."

"Mom, you have to."

"I don't have to," she says. "I might have changed my mind."

"Mom!" I stand up, huffing over her. "Come on!"

My voice brings Ciarán into the living room. "What's going on?"

"She won't take her drugs," I say to him out of the side of my mouth. "Mom, it's not okay for you to get worse. There's only so much care Ciarán and I are qualified to give."

"You know I'm not going to let it get to the point where someone has to spoon-feed me and wipe my ass." She looks away from me, out the window. "I won't live without dignity."

"Jesus *Christ*. You don't have a choice."

"I have a choice."

"Mom, you can't just walk up to the right-to-die drive-through. It doesn't work like that."

"I can't walk at all." Her voice goes high, strained and offended. "Fuck!"

"Okay, you two," Ciarán says.

I soften. "Please just try it."

She looks at me. Her face falls. "Let me put on my shorts."

I read the instructions. I wipe her thigh with alcohol, wave the vapors away. "You're doing great," I say, though I haven't even torn the plastic backing off the auto-injector. She's already closing her eyes, looking miserable, and I hesitate briefly before driving the needle into her thigh.

"Almost there, almost there," I say to comfort her.

"Fuck, that hurt," she says.

"Was it really that bad?" I say, dropping the needle in the sharps box.

"Gertie," Ciarán warns.

"I'm sorry. You did great, Mom."

"You have to go easy on her," Ciarán says to me later. "That drug is scary for her."

"I just hope we can get her to take it again next week. Will you talk to her?"

"You're making me feel like the umpire between you and your mother."

"If she would just listen to me for once in my life, we wouldn't be in this position."

Ciarán sinks onto the bed, shaking his head. Recently, he hung hooks on the back of our bedroom door, and I survey the clean robes and towels I've spread across the floor.

"Which hook should I use for my robe?" I ask.

"Whichever," he says. His voice is cheerless. He looks like he does sometimes when he works so hard he makes himself sick, long headaches that keep him in bed for a day. Pain shows on his face even through deep sleep, and his breath slows in a way that chills me and briefly takes everything from me, and then everything comes back as soon as he stirs.

I sit down next to him.

"I'm sorry." I scratch my scalp aggressively, a new outlet I've found for my anxiety. "There's a lot in the past that you weren't here for."

His head falls over on his shoulder; his eyes lift to mine, and he grabs my hands and pulls them away from my head.

"I've been here a long time," he says. "And I'm here now, you know?"

We wake in the middle of the night to knocking on our bedroom door. Ciarán stumbles into pants. I hear Mom's voice and untwist myself from blankets.

"I can't move my legs. At all. Not even the little I usually can."

My phone says it's three in the morning. "Do you want to go to the ER?" I ask.

"I think it was that drug."

"It probably wasn't the drug," I say.

"What else would it be?"

"Let's not argue about that now," Ciarán says. "Get your shoes on, girls."

At the hospital I go in with Mom while Ciarán finds parking. It's quiet inside, only a few patients sitting in the brightly lit waiting room; beyond the swinging doors the lights are dimmed for the night so patients can sleep. Soon Mom is in a gown and resting on an ER bed as a doctor pokes her feet. He's red-haired, tired, and I'm about to make note of his weight, heavy for a doctor, when I catch myself and reverse—living with Mom has undone years of body positivity work.

"Can I have IV steroids?" she asks. "That's helped before. One thousand milligrams."

"This happened before?" I ask.

"If it's a reaction to the drug," the doctor says, "steroids probably won't do anything."

"Can I have them anyway?"

The doctor looks taken aback. He pulls back the curtain, saying he's going to leave a message for the neurologist on call. Mom shifts her weight forward and slaps her legs. "What in the hell," she says. "Move, goddamn it."

"Come on, Mom," I say. "Act natural. If you get bruises they're going to think we're elder-abusing you."

She laughs, and I do, too. Our laughter is interrupted by voices talking over one another, the sound of running, a bundle of nurses and doctors convening in the cubicle next to ours. In the time it takes me to understand what's happening, they're saying the patient is dead.

Everyone seems to be angry.

She wasn't responsive, that's why I was giving her oxygen.

Did you know she had a fentanyl patch?

Did anyone give her Narcan?

Should we take off the patch?

Let the morgue do it.

She's been in here before. I'll call the family.

Mom and I look at each other. "Let's get out of here," she says.

I put my hand gently on her shoulder. "Wait until the doctor comes back."

"He's clearly busy with the patient he just killed."

"*Mom*," I say. "You make me say your name so much. *Mom, Mom, Mom, Mom, Mom.*"

As we gently argue, the doctor returns—nothing left for him to do next door, for now, anyway—and says, "I'm of the mind to admit you."

"I'm of the mind to not," Mom says, pulling at the IV in her arm.

"Stop, stop, stop." I paw at her frantically. "If you stay, maybe they'll give you steroids."

"Forget it," she says. "I want to go home."

The doctor, whose shift must be almost over, doesn't protest. "I'll just need her to sign the AMA," he says.

I close my eyes, breathe in plastic and saline and disinfectant, the sweat of adrenaline coming off the doctor, listen to the texts dinging, Ciarán wondering where we are, and I say, "Fine."

August

THE PAST

MY DAD TOLD ME TO STOP ASKING IF HE WAS OKAY. THEN HE DISAPPEARED. Two nights passed, and I heard nothing from him. The number to my mom's satellite phone was pinned to the bulletin board. I could read the numbers from my air mattress, but what was she going to do from the middle of the Mediterranean?

Earlier in the summer Adam and I had downloaded a night sky app on our phones. After work one night, I opened mine and held it above my head. I'd hoped to find the star Cindy bought for us, but the technology wasn't that advanced. Instead, Jupiter appeared on the screen, a misty orb swirling with orange gases, and I lowered my phone to look at the real thing, a small dot of stilled red light. When I got cold, I went inside. I took my dad's ashtray with me and knocked it against the inside of the garbage can. A bouquet of dead nicotine rose up to meet my nose. The ringing landline made me jump; hardly anyone used it.

"Hello?"

A woman's voice was on the other end, low, tinged with strange emotion. "Do you know someone named Mark McMahon?"

"Is this a hospital?" I didn't wait to panic. "Is he okay?"

"I'm not a hospital. But you need to come get him."

"Is he okay?" I asked again.

"Here's the address."

She was calling from Vermillion, a place I only vaguely recognized. When I didn't respond, she asked, "Did you get that?"

"I'm sorry," I said. "I'm confused. What's going on?"

"Look," she said. "He can't stay here anymore, but he can't drive himself. So come get him. You need the address again?"

I scribbled the address beneath the number to my mom's satellite phone. Once I said I'd gotten it down, the woman hung up on me.

I put the address into my phone and a pin popped up, seventy miles away.

"Shit," I said. I riffled through my wallet, but I knew before looking there wasn't enough for a cab.

I went back outside to where at least there was more air than ash and I opened my contacts, sliding down the short, slippery slope to Adam's name. My thumb hovered over it. Pressing it felt like I'd detonate a bomb somewhere. I held the phone away from me, where it would be far enough that the sound of his voicemail, if he didn't answer, wouldn't hurt as badly.

"It's late." He was annoyed.

"Hi, Adam. I'm really sorry to call, but . . . I need help. It's my dad."

"Your dad? What's going on?"

"I got a call from this woman. There's something you don't know. He's a . . . I think he took too much of something. I need to go get him."

There was a long pause and in it seemed to live all the reasons I shouldn't have called. My pulse accelerated faster and faster, until, finally, it collided with Adam's voice.

"Where are you? I'll come get you."

"Wait," I said. "Before you agree to help, he's in Vermillion. It's far, it's a lot to ask, and everything is so messed up—you can say no. Please tell me you know you can say no."

"I'm coming. Are you at home?"

He didn't say goodbye.

A mosquito buzzed, unseen, close to my ear. I closed the balcony door, leaving Jupiter where it was, but I froze there for a moment, and a chill washed over me at the memory, or the many memories converged into one image, of my father in his chair, smoking, socks pulled up over his calves. Looking over his shoulder as I came home, waving to me with his cigarette hand.

I sat on the curb outside our building and tried to guess the minutes it would take for Adam to arrive.

A gold SUV pulled up, not Adam and Austin's car. But it stopped near me. I couldn't see through the tinted glass, but the window rolled down, and Adam was behind the wheel.

"Hey." He reached over and opened the door. "Get in."

I slipped into the smooth leather seat. The AC was on, making the night cold and dewy. I held my phone between the two of us, and Adam punched the address into the car's GPS. One hour and fourteen minutes.

"Don't worry," Adam said. "I can shave a little time off that."

As he pulled out of Rolling Prairie, he lifted a thermos of coffee from the cupholder and held it out to me.

"My mom made me take it with me," he said, "so I don't fall asleep. She had me wait while she brewed it."

"This is your mom's car?" I drank the coffee and handed it back to him. He took a sip and rested the mug between his knees.

"Austin has ours tonight."

"Did you tell your mom the truth? About what we're doing?"

Adam was quiet for a moment. "Yes."

"I'm surprised she let you help me."

He shrugged. "I don't know, she and I are close. She trusts me."

The radio was off. The map showed a straight line south. Everything was dark and Jupiter followed us, unblinking, as we drove.

"You know . . ." Adam hesitated for a long time before going on. "Austin gets scary drunk sometimes. Like once in a while. It kind of freaks me out."

"Does your mom know?"

He shook his head.

"Maybe you should tell her."

I waited for a reply, but he didn't give me one. I understood. It was easier said than done.

"Jupiter." I pointed. "Did you see?"

"I did."

He didn't say anything more. My knuckles were white from clenching my fists, and the skin on the side of my index finger had broken because I'd been digging my thumbnail into it. We rode most of the way in silence, and eventually Adam veered from the highway, passing signs for the University of South Dakota.

"This is probably where I'll go to college," he said.

"It's your first choice?"

He shrugged. "I don't know. But it's close. It's funny, I never told you this, but for a long time now I've wanted to go to the University of Michigan. There's a really good econ program there. But it's so much more expensive to go out of state."

"I want to go to New York City. My dad lived there when he was younger. But I'll probably end up in-state, too. There are a lot of good schools in Michigan, I'm not trying to be a snob. But, you know, dreams."

"Yeah. Dreams."

He turned through a dark neighborhood and in to the parking lot of a small apartment building with four floors and exterior hallways. USD flags hung from the railings, and the parking lot was full of cars with USD bumper stickers. Music spilled from the open door of an apartment, inside of which I could see a ponytailed girl at the sink in the kitchen, soft string lights glowing all around her.

"I didn't know it was an apartment building," I said. "The woman didn't give me a number."

I felt like I'd never find him.

Adam turned off the headlights, and just as he did, they were replaced by light from an open door on the second floor. A woman emerged, looking searchingly over the railing. Her hair was long and gray, curly, and she wore glasses with dark frames. She beckoned with one hand, waving us toward her with a stern, impatient expression.

"You can stay here," I said at the same moment Adam said, "I'll come in."

"Hey, guys," she said calmly as we climbed the concrete stairs up to her floor. "He's in here."

We stepped into her apartment. She looked at me and said, "I didn't realize you were a kid."

She had every light turned on, even the bathroom light and fan, as if warding off something evil. Her apartment was neat, organized, with furniture that matched, just as out of place in a building full of students as she was. As she passed the kitchen, she picked up a mug with the string of a tea bag dangling over its lip, curly font proclaiming WORLD'S BEST PROF. And then there was my dad, asleep on an overstuffed orange couch, his body in the pose of patient waiting.

I rushed over to him and took his wrist in my hand.

"Dad," I said. "Hey, Dad."

His pulse pushed weakly against my fingers. At the sound of my voice, his head tilted toward me and his eyes opened, revealing small slits of iris, but then an invisible chain pulled him back, and his head fell again.

I touched his forehead and felt its heat in my palm. I looked up at the woman whose apartment this was, the woman who stood sternly drinking tea, surveying us. Adam stood behind her, beneath a large framed black-and-white photograph of two children hugging each other, taken at Sears, maybe during better days.

"What happened?" I asked. "Should we call 911?"

The woman's face sank into a scowl. "He's already better. Don't you dare call 911."

"Better?" I cried. "What do you mean, better?"

She set her tea down roughly and held up her palms. "Look, he just took a little too much."

"Did you give him Narcan?"

"He had some water, we walked around a little bit. He's fine. He just needs to sleep it off."

"Why didn't you stop him?" I said, trying to keep my voice from turning thunderous. "Why didn't you do something?"

"Look." Her voice was laced with sudden fire. "I got home from class, he was supposed to have left already. Tomorrow morning my ex is showing up with my kids, and my part in this ends *now*. You've got to get him out of here."

She jutted the heel of her hand in my dad's direction.

I looked at Adam. He stood completely still, breezeless. I could tell from his face he'd never seen anything like this before.

"Can you help me, Adam?"

At his name, he crossed the room.

"Dad," I say. "Can you stand? We need to go."

He blinked and said my name.

"Put your arm around me," I said. It rested with dead weight on my shoulder, and Adam took his other side. We took a few swaying steps, and at the door, I turned to the woman.

"Thank you for calling me."

She was fluffing the cushions where my dad had been, and she waved without turning around. "Tell him to call me, okay?" she said as Adam opened the door and we squeezed through it, down the hallway, down the stairs. One by one her lights went off, as though the apartment was erasing its memory of us.

My dad's car was parked a few spots away from Adam's, shiny beneath a floodlight.

"Will you help me get him in?"

We eased my dad into the passenger seat, and I fished his keys out of his pocket before closing the door against him. I didn't want to cry. Not here, not when I had to drive. Not in front of Adam.

"Your dad's been gone for a few days?" Adam asked.

"I guess it has been."

"Why didn't you say anything to anyone?"

"I don't know," I said. "He goes places sometimes."

"Do you think we should take him to the hospital?" Adam looked warily through the car window.

The hospital, where they'd ask questions, and where a social worker would appear, acting sweet to me, acting like nothing was going to change. I shook my head.

"That lady's right," I said. "He's coming out of it."

Adam looked like he was struggling to find a way to disagree with me. Before he could say anything, I added quickly, "Thank you. So much. I know you probably have questions, but you should get home. I've got GPS, I can find my way back."

Adam took out his keys.

"I'll pull out first, if you want to follow me back to your place," he said.

For once, I was relieved he saw through me.

Our engines started with the same breath. His taillights pulled me forward, and he slowed at intersections to make sure he didn't leave me behind at a yellow. And then we got into the country, and Sioux Falls was a straight shot north. Next to me my dad's breath left orbs of fog on the window.

At Rolling Prairie, Adam parked outside my building, and I pulled into the spot next to him. My dad waved us off and climbed the stairs himself, sank into his armchair. I put a glass of water next to him, and he took a few sips on his own. He noticed Adam, but he didn't say anything, and his steady breath pulled him into sleep. Without looking at Adam, I said, "You saved my life tonight. And my dad's. I think that lady was going to murder him."

"What are you going to do?"

"Right now?" I looked through the balcony door at the empty green lawn and the road beyond. "I'm going to sit outside for a while."

"Okay," Adam said. "I'll stay, too."

"No, that's crazy."

"I'm going to stay. If you'll let me."

We held on to each other's eyes. He looked away first. I wanted to push him out the door, because he'd seen so much. But he'd already seen everything, so what else was there?

"Okay," I said.

"Okay?"

"Okay."

He went to the balcony without waiting for me to lead the way.

"Oh my God, your chair!" he said. "They match."

I looked at the chair like it contained everything sad about my life, and I felt very sorry for myself.

"Do you want to talk?" he asked.

"You sort of saw all you need to know."

"There's always more to it."

I held back tears; it might have been the kindest and truest thing anyone could've said to me that night. The thing I needed to hear the most—that you're always more than the worst parts of your life. I sat down in one chair, and Adam took the other.

"That was pretty incredible," Adam said. "That you knew what to do."

"I didn't know. Not really."

Adam shook his head. "You did, though."

"I've read about it."

"Have you had to do this before? I mean, is this a new thing with your dad?"

As much as I searched, I couldn't find a point in hiding it any longer. "It's been my whole life, and why he moved out here. It's getting worse, and now my mom's not around. I never realized until this summer how much she shielded me from the bad stuff."

"I won't tell anyone." Adam looked through the gaps in the railing. But I hadn't asked him not to tell, and his anticipation of my shame fell like hot ash.

"Thanks," I said.

"Does Lucas know?"

"No."

He met my eyes. In the parking lot a car started, and my heart turned over, too, burning some kind of fuel, but I didn't know what, or who.

"Do you really like him?" Adam asked, but his voice wasn't sad or bitter. It was the voice of a friend.

"No," I said quietly.

"Then why are you with him?"

"I . . ." I started to say, but my dad let out a gasp, like the first breath after not breathing, and I jumped up to check his pulse, his temperature. His fingers in case they were blue. He was fine.

I went back outside, but I didn't sit back down. I leaned my elbows on the railing next to where Adam was sitting. He reached out and rapped his knuckles gently against my shin.

"Why, Gertie?"

The truth was right there in the back of my throat: I was punishing myself here in South Dakota for something I couldn't admit I'd done in Michigan. I'd never imagined telling anyone here my secret—it belonged to another world—but tonight the gate was lifted like saline solution clearing out a vein and, finally, I had no energy left to guard it.

"I'm going to tell you something, and it's not going to make you want to nominate me for person of the year."

Adam laughed. "Go on."

I took a deep breath. "Back in Michigan, my best friend, Cindy. I told you about her—"

"You did."

"She was—she is—seeing this guy named Gabe. They broke up for a bit last December, and that was when everything was falling apart with my family. Cindy was out of town, and I was a mess. I ran into Gabe at a party, and I was so depressed I didn't think I'd wake up the next morning. I didn't think anything mattered. I hooked up with him that night."

A sob caught me off guard. My hands flew to my face, and I shuddered against them, but after a minute I could breathe again, a little bit exorcised.

"You don't have to tell me more," Adam said.

"No, I do." I wiped a tear away. "When I met you, I was so happy to have a real friend, because I missed Cindy so much. And I just didn't know how to say no to Lucas, it felt so hard to say no and then have to live with saying no. Because I was lonely and wanted everyone to like me. And then when I kissed you, it reminded me so much of what I did to Cindy. I think staying with Lucas—deep down it gave me this hope that I knew how to do the right thing. That I wasn't unforgivable."

Adam was looking at his shoes. I'd blurted it all out without thinking, but in the quiet that followed I wondered if I'd made a mistake.

"Anyway. I came here and had a new chance and acted the same way I did before. And I'm sorry you got caught up in it."

"Gertie," Adam said.

I braced myself.

"I think Cindy will understand. If you tell her."

"Oh, Adam," I said. "I don't think it's true. Especially not after so much time has passed."

"I would."

"It's easy to *say* that."

"I mean it. Look at everything you're going through." He gestured inside.

"I blame my parents for *everything*. That time it was all me."

"Calm down. I'm just trying to say you're not a terrible person. You made a mistake. Join the club. I kissed you, remember? And I knew what I was doing."

"You're a nice person."

"I don't know. On my tombstone, they'll probably write, 'Not as nice as he seemed.'"

"No," I said. "But they might write that your modesty was fake."

The moon's soundless light broke into millions of waves around us.

"I guess I'm worried," Adam said finally. "About you."

His phone chimed with a text message before I could answer.

"Shit," he muttered. "It's my mom."

"I must have stretched the limits of her goodwill tonight. Thank her for me?"

"She's just worried." Adam's fingers raced across the keys.

"You should go."

He checked his watch, then he stood and joined me at the railing, our arms braced against it. He looked like he was struggling with the decision.

"You should go," I said again, but I put my hand on his arm. He looked down at it, then at me, and how much he'd helped me made me want him again. A decision seemed to pass over his face, and I projected onto it what I was feeling, and I kissed him.

He pulled away.

I drew back, radiating embarrassment.

"You should go," I said, putting him out of his misery.

"I guess so."

Adam checked his pocket for his keys.

"Call me," he said. "And, maybe, I don't know, let your dad know this isn't okay."

I looked down, and my shame grew. We walked past my dad— I tried not to look at him—and paused in the doorway with the light from the hall bright in our faces.

"I don't want you to think I only call you when I need something. What you did means a lot."

Adam rested his hands gently on my shoulders.

"We're friends, right?"

. . .

After Adam left, I unearthed the Narcan from where I'd hidden it in my suitcase, to remind myself it was there. My hands trembled around the stern box. Drugs to treat drugs. It made my head spin, like the world resisted making sense on purpose. Still, I felt its big power, so big it was almost threatening. A tincture to stop death, a rope to pull someone back across the River Styx, the lantern on the bow of Charon's boat glowing red.

I sat in the dark for a long time, watching my dad sleep. His water glass was half empty, and I went to fill it. When I set it back down, I noticed a notebook I hadn't seen before. I picked it up and the pages fell open. It was a journal, written in my dad's nearly illegible script.

We probably wouldn't have gotten married if not for the baby. I remember those early years of her life fondly, when she was a happy angel who required nothing in exchange for her love.

I closed the journal, not wanting to read more about myself and why I was the reason so many people had become unhappy.

June

"I'M DONE WITH THAT DRUG," MOM SAYS THE DAY AFTER SHE SIGNS HERSELF
out of the ER.

"Dr. Berglund said to try it again. To take Benadryl beforehand."

"I am done," Mom says flatly, a pause between each of the words.

She sits in her spot on the couch, where she always is, where she
spends most of her time despite my suggestions of chair yoga, AA
meetings, computer classes at the library, TikTok.

I was on my way to her with a basket of laundry, but I've stopped
as though I have to be still to prove how firm I am about this.

"Dr. Berglund is optimistic you won't have another reaction," I
say.

"Dr. Berglund doesn't care about me," she says. "Give me some of
that laundry."

"I'm asking you to try it one more time." I set the laundry basket
next to her on the couch. "If you have a reaction again, we'll stop."

She doesn't say anything. I flinch when she picks up a pair of my clean underwear. My instinct has always been to make her believe I don't have a body. Ciarán's noticed. "You don't eat much in front of her," he told me recently, when I'd snuck a plate of leftover pasta into our room after she'd gone to bed. The lemon cream sauce and tangy Parmesan I'd piled on top turned gluey in my mouth, and I was suddenly aware of how much eating is an act of existence.

There were times when I was younger I admit to being disgusted by bodies. Watching Dad so high he drooled. Mom pouncing on every lapse in table manners as though a dribble of milk on my chin made me revolting to my core. I stood sideways in front of the mirror to assess the roundness of my stomach. Mom always seemed perfect, quiet and sharp as a statue, irreproachable. I remember the day that sense of her sanctity broke for me. I was doing homework on the floor of the living room, and I could hear her on the phone in the kitchen with a friend from AA. They were talking about Vaughn.

"I know, June, I know," she said. "He's not perfect, but look, the guy is hung like a moose."

My shock was torrential; it blew me apart. She knew I was in the other room, or I believed she did. Maybe she thought I wouldn't know what it meant, because we'd never talked about sex. "You probably know enough," she'd conceded the only time she tried, when my shame was so total I'd backed out of the room.

How could she suddenly be so vulgar? How could she move on so quickly, not just from Dad, but from me? I couldn't accept that she and I were having different experiences. But the more I pushed her to leave Vaughn, the more she clung to him.

If you ruin this for me, I'll never forgive you.

I wanted to rebel, and I did: parties, booze, Gabe, Lucas, Adam. But I had no respect for myself. I was something frozen dropped into boiling water, still cold at the center after a long time in the pot.

I worry sometimes that girl is still asleep inside me. I wish I could say I no longer see myself in her. But there are times when all my thoughts scatter from my brain and I make no effort to pick them up;

I walk around disassociated, as I had when the aerosol can spread poison through my veins. Only two years ago I ignored a cough until I woke in the middle of the night with a 104-degree fever. And last summer, when Mom's illness was weighing heavily on me, I went to the bar after work instead of going home. Just a cocktail before dinner, I thought, but I drank so much I stopped feeling drunk. A stranger's hand on the small of my back jolted me enough to realize what I was doing would kill me. I didn't cross a line. I hadn't gone there to cross a line. But I was there, which was bad enough.

I went home to Ciarán and cried. In the morning I thought I'd never love myself again. "You've just got the fear in you," Ciarán said, bringing me coffee in bed.

Mom and I fold clothes quietly. When Ciarán's with us, there's always something to talk about; he can spin conversation out of air. But I've kept so many secrets from her, I no longer remember what she knows and what she doesn't.

"Do you remember a few weeks ago, when you wanted to hear about Sioux Falls?" I ask. "I remembered something the other day. Did you know Dad kept a journal?"

"I didn't," she says.

"He wrote in one that you wouldn't have gotten married if not for the baby. That was me, I assume?"

Mom's hands tighten around the shirt she's folding.

"Are you going to put that in your next book?" she asks.

"No, God, Mom," I say. "I just wondered if you felt the same way he did. It must have been complicated."

"I didn't want to get an abortion, if that's what you're asking."

"That is *not* what I'm asking."

Her folding is getting sloppier; mine is, too. Outside, day has turned to see-through silk, night visible through it, and I feel like I've achieved nothing but drive the wedge between us deeper.

"I imagine some writers wait until their parents are dead to write about them," she says.

It's something I would say, and I laugh and reach out to touch her shoulder.

Her scowl is broken by a smile. "As I've been trying to tell you, you might not have to wait too much longer."

"Goddamn it, Mom." I pull my hand away. "Will you please quit it with that? The medication is going to help you."

"Whose side are you on? I trust what my body is telling me more than I trust pharmaceuticals."

"Your choices are to take the drug, or to get on Medicaid so the government will pay for the care you need. I'm serious."

"I am, too."

Our silence extends, my frustration grows, until I stand up and tell her I'll be right back, knowing I'm going to stay in our bedroom until Ciarán gets home.

Whenever Mom talks about dying, I scramble to find something I might have done to make her think of her life as already over, the rest of it not worth living. Could I have tried harder to convince her to get treatment earlier, no matter the cost? If I had been nicer to Vaughn, would he have loved her? If I hadn't learned so quickly to live without her in the years after she moved to Florida, would she feel her life mattered more?

Ciarán sighs when I tell him about my fight with her. I've been closed in the bedroom, in bed like a child, with my laptop open to job listings.

"You're both so stubborn," he says.

"*She's* stubborn. I'm just trying to help her without constantly hearing that she's going to die soon."

He shakes his head and laughs a little, but the laugh is tired.

"She just has a dark sense of humor, Gertie, that's all. I might go so far as to say you do, too."

"How can you stand to live with the two of us?" Anxiety grasps me by the neck. "Are you lying to me when you say you're okay with this? Tell me the truth. Every one of my friends has said the same thing to me: Their partners would never agree to live with their mother-in-law."

"I'm not lying, Gertie, I told you that. This is what family does." His voice has gotten thin the way it does when he doesn't want to talk anymore.

"I'm sorry," I say.

He sits on the bed and puts his hand on my leg to let me know he's forgiven me. I turn back to my work. I've been looking at postings at the university, though I've lost all my connections there. "The residential college is looking for an admin," I say. "Do you think any of my old professors would remember me?"

"Maybe," Ciarán says.

"How does this email sound?" I turn my computer toward him.

The switch in Ciarán is sudden. He squeezes his eyes shut, pinching the bridge of his nose, and sighs heavily.

"You have a master's degree in writing, Gertie, I think you can write an email."

"What's wrong with you?"

"You're always doing this. Asking me to confirm every little thing you do. It makes me feel awful, Gertie, like you can't do anything by yourself."

"I'm just—"

"You need to be able to trust yourself. What if I get hit by a bus tomorrow?"

I feel the impact. He fades, gone. I'm alone again until the shock retreats and he returns, sitting frustratedly beside me. His lips move, but my ears are ringing. I might have more easily accepted what he was saying had he not killed himself to make his point.

"How *dare* you say that to me."

His face twitches with surprise, like he's not sure which part I'm referring to. He puts his hand back on my leg but I stand up, throwing it off.

"I'm going for a walk."

"Gertie," he says.

"Don't worry. I'll try to make all my own decisions while I'm out."

The walk brings up the past. I can't be blamed for that. As I travel from our house on the Old West Side toward, almost by instinct, the building where I'd lived when I was with Adam, the memories are so thick they almost come back to me as a smell. Fresh damp air and old wood and the Indian restaurant I walked past every day on my way to campus.

At some point in recent years the apartment building was painted blue. It had been the color of butter when I lived there. Those concrete barriers still separate the parking lot from the train tracks, but the graffiti that once covered them has been scrubbed away. I try to remember which one I sat on that night I spoke to Ciarán all those years ago, the first time he asked to come see me, but I find I can't recall. I choose one and sit in the dark and look into the window of the room that had been Adam's.

Tonight wasn't the first time I'd accused Ciarán of regretting me. As our summer together ended, I worried what would happen once he was gone. To prepare myself for his leaving I started to imagine what would've happened if he'd never come in the first place.

"You could've done an internship at, like, *Wired* or *MIT Tech Review*," I said. "Instead you came here and worked at a bar."

"I did an internship in having sex with you," he said. "That's got to be worth something."

He was packing his suitcase, and with each possession he folded into its darkness the more certain I became he would come to regret this summer.

"I'm not sure how good I look on a résumé," I said.

Ciarán grew more and more agitated, each word I spoke a needle prodding him as he worked.

"You're hard to be around when you get going about how you repulse people. I'm sorry to be blunt, but it's not attractive."

He came over to me, nudging my legs open with his knee. There was a smile on his face, one about to bloom into laughter.

"Shut up," I said, shoving his chest.

"I didn't say anything!"

"You were going to."

I agreed we could see other people during the year that followed; in fact I'd been the one to bring it up, because I hadn't been single in years, except for the brief periods Adam and I had spent apart, and I needed to see if I preferred it that way. Cindy, as usual, was right about that. I went on dates, but with half a heart. I thought of Ciarán when I was in bed with other men, some of whom touched my scar in the same way he had. Over video call I told Ciarán I wished he was the one making me come at night, and I watched desire win out over jealousy on his face.

Whenever I ran into Adam, he acted smug. We still lived in the same building, still knew the same people, and he'd heard that Ciarán had gone home. Adam never failed to ask if it was hard to be apart, rubbing proximity, which I'd had with him in spades, in my face. But the more Adam exploited the idea of this distance, the more I felt what Ciarán and I had was real. Adam must have seen it the few times he saw me and Ciarán together. He wouldn't be trying to whittle us down if he hadn't.

The car I'd bought from my friend died, but instead of fixing it I used my savings to fly to Dublin over spring break, leaving the Sunfire to rot further in the parking lot. Ciarán had class but I stayed at his apartment, wrote my midterm papers, used the soap in his shower, took walks in Dublin's changeable weather, and at the end of the week I told him that since we were both graduating soon, we could be together, or not, but nowhere in between. He regarded me with amusement, and at first I thought he was going to laugh at me, but then he said, "Where do you want to live?"

"Here?" I offered.

"Not here. The food is bad and the people are repressed."

"New York, then."

"Ma'd be furious if I chose America. She'll think of it as my father winning." Ciarán smiled. "Let's do it."

Ciarán isn't wrong that ever since we moved in together, I *have* relied on him, maybe too much. But there was never anyone for me to rely on before him, with one exception.

Still gazing into the old apartment's windows, I call Cindy. When she answers, I hear her in the kitchen of her Fort Greene brownstone, the running water a muffled stream of conversation beneath ours.

"I guess I'm supposed to be more independent," I say, "since Mom and Ciarán are both certain of their imminent demise."

"Death is imminent for all of us, Gertie."

"Thanks for being on my side."

"I'm just saying it's all okay."

"Am I a burden on Ciarán?" I ask. "I hate the idea that I'm insufferable. Maybe I burned through adulthood as a child and now I'm regressing."

Cindy turns off the water. I can imagine being there with her, sitting on the countertop while she works in the kitchen, accepting the occasional task she gives me, as I have so many times before.

"It sounds like you need a break," she says.

"I'm unemployed. My whole life is a break."

"You're the hardest-working unemployed person I've ever met," Cindy says. "Look, I was going to call you anyway. We both have some time off, so we're going to the Bahamas for two weeks next month. We need someone to look after the house and pet sit Charles Wallace and Frankie while we're gone. Will you come to New York?"

"Can I go to the Bahamas with you guys instead?"

Cindy laughs. "No."

Her house is one of my favorite places, a glut of vertical space tucked off to the side of Downtown Brooklyn. Old-growth trees shade the neighborhood, the dark blown apart by the richly lit curtainless windows of the expensive houses on one of New York's most desirable streets. I feel the luxurious safety of money when I'm there.

"Ciarán would have to stay alone with Mom. That's asking a lot."

"Do you want me to call him?"

"That's okay."

"Tell him I'm going to call him," she says. "You can work on your book. It's not an accident you've been writing again. I'll be mad at you if you don't take this project seriously."

I laugh. "So pushy. Let me think about it."

I sit by the train tracks for a few minutes more. Then I start for home, refusing to be captured by a fugue state that would have me go wandering farther. Ciarán's in the kitchen when I walk in. I take my place at the cutting board, chop off the end of an onion, and then point the tip of the knife back and forth between him and Mom.

"No more talking about dying from either of you," I say, "or there will be consequences."

Ciarán trades a look with Mom, who laughs at the knife in my hand.

"Very well, love," Ciarán replies. "We'll live forever."

"It's not fair," I say to Ciarán later that night. "You always stay mad at me a whole day, but I'm never mad at you more than a minute."

He moves inside of me. "You have a forgiving heart," he whispers. "Lucky for me."

He'd gotten into bed and asked if he could kiss me, and then kissed me in that hungry way that's the banishment of an argument. I let him make me wet with his mouth but stopped him. "I want to come around you," I said, pulling him up my body until his face was over mine.

In the moments after, we lie next to each other, entwined, and I shiver with what feels like the improbability of our happiness, where there's only enough for the two of us. I'm almost asleep when Ciarán, his chin on my head, says, "Cindy texted me."

"I told her not to," I murmur.

"I think you should go."

"It's asking a lot of you," I say. "What if I go and don't write?"

"Then you spend two weeks in Cindy's swank brownstone with that funny-looking dog of theirs."

"Your mom texted me and asked when we're visiting," I say. "If I travel, shouldn't it be for that?"

"She'll be wondering, yeah."

"What about the carbon emissions? Someone already in New York should do it." I slip my arm around his middle.

"Don't talk yourself out of it. Just go." He scrunches his fingers through my hair. "We need to keep our rich friends happy in case we fall on hard times."

"Maybe if we get rich enough ourselves we can convince Mom to want to live."

"How?"

"I don't know. Pay off God or something."

August

THE PAST

ADAM DIDN'T TEXT ME, AND I DIDN'T TEXT HIM. I WASN'T GOING TO PRETEND any longer that anything could happen between us, but I knew regardless I had to end things with Lucas, who had started to corner me about hanging out, guilting me when I didn't. Name any wrong reason under the sun: that's why I'd been with Lucas this summer. It was time for it to be over.

Are you home? I asked him.

Ellipses popped up, but nothing appeared. Then, finally: *Want to come over?*

Lucas was standing in the window when I walked up to his building. I waved, but he didn't wave back. The curtain swished, and by the time I'd climbed the stairs he was waiting at his open door.

His mom had hung beads in the doorway of the kitchen; soft patterned quilts were thrown over the furniture; and plastic horses, his little sister's, were a tangle of hooves and heads in a box in the corner of the living room. I followed him to his room, he shut the door behind us, and I sat down on the floor with my back against his bed.

"I need to tell you something."

He rolled his eyes at me. He hadn't said a word.

"What's going on?" I asked. "You're acting weird."

At that moment I realized how tired I was. I should've made it easy on myself. I should've just texted him that we were over.

"You've been going home after work the past few days."

"I've been exhausted."

"Bullshit," Lucas said. "Austin told me you and Adam stayed out until three the other night. What the fuck is going on with you and him?"

I turned away. "I just needed a ride somewhere. Forget it."

"You couldn't ask me for a ride?"

"You were out drinking with Austin."

"Why didn't you tell me about it?"

"I have to tell you about my every move?"

My palms were hot. The room felt sweltering, and I raked my hands through my stupid pink hair, faded to peach. All summer I had thought getting Lucas and his friends to like me would give me a world outside of my dad's apartment. But they'd turned out to be just another struggle.

"Look." I rubbed my hands on my thighs. "I'm not here to fight. This isn't working, whatever it is."

"What are you talking about?"

"I'm sorry, Lucas."

I stood up, but Lucas grabbed my arm and pulled me down onto his bed. He pulled my hoodie away from my shoulder and started kissing my neck.

"Wait," I said, twisting away as he put his whole body over mine. "I don't want to."

He kissed me again, the whole length of his forearm pinning my chest, his other hand groping to unbutton my shorts. I felt the first ice of paralysis start to harden, and I sank into the sense I was trapped, this was it, until a twitch of neurons fired and I pushed him away as hard as I could.

"This is such bullshit," he said, shooting up from the bed.

"*What's* bullshit?"

"You wanted it. You *always* want it. Don't act like you don't know what I mean."

"I *don't* know what you mean."

"I know you hooked up with Adam at the lake party."

My mind was racing, part of me still trapped beneath him. The door was there, but my feet wouldn't move. "What?" I gasped, unable to understand how this had become about something I'd done wrong.

"I was right there, Gertie," he said. "I was right there telling you how much I liked you. And then Jill finds you in his bedroom and you make her promise not to tell."

"She's telling the truth." I choked on the fact that I was explaining myself to him. "And I kissed him again the other night. I'm not sorry, because I never should have been with you in the first place."

"You know," Lucas said. "You're a slut."

"Fuck you," I said.

I grabbed my phone and threw his door open. It slapped the wall. I rushed out as fast as I could, leaving his apartment door open behind me.

At home, I shut myself in the bathroom.

I ran the shower and stood beneath the stream of water and ground my knuckles into my eyes, waiting to feel like the word *slut* had washed away. Waiting to wash away the feeling of being pinned, the moment my body had thought the best chance for survival was to let it happen. None of it washed away. Maybe I was a slut.

I turned off the water and stood there dripping and cold. I twisted my hair around my fist and squeezed the water out. I didn't towel off, shivering myself dry instead. A knock on the door made me jump. I felt Lucas's body over mine.

"Everything okay, hon?"

It was my dad. His voice was a stranger in the house. I hadn't real-ized he was home; he'd avoided me since the night I picked him up in Vermillion.

"I'm fine."

"I'm running out real quick."

"Okay," I said quietly. I heard the door close behind him.

I wrapped a towel around my head and pulled on my pajamas. I unlocked my phone, and my thumb hovered over Cindy's name. A small self-loathing part of me agreed with what Lucas had said, and the secret was feeding that part, a mushroom growing in moonlight.

But before I could call Cindy, she called me.

"Were your ears itching?" I said. "I was just going to call you."

"Gertie," she said, her voice full of tears.

"What's wrong?"

"I found him at the motel where he was staying."

"Your dad?"

Her voice broke with a sob. "He was dead."

Cindy, the phone, the night outside that was sweating with heat, all waited for me to say something more. But all I could think of, over and over, was Cindy opening the motel door, the slow reveal of car-pet, the TV, the edge of the bed, and then her father's feet. Her father not responding when she shook him. The moment after the shock when she first realized he wasn't sleeping.

"Cindy. I don't believe it."

She started to cry. "We *can* believe it, though. You and I—we knew. I should've found him sooner. And now he's gone."

"Please believe me when I tell you it's not your fault."

"It was just his body there, *alone*. No one had checked on him." Her sobs were so deep it was as though they contained her whole life so far. "For *days* . . ."

"It's terrible, but you're going to be okay. I promise. I'll make sure you're okay. I'm so sorry."

"Come home, Gertie," she said.

I looked around. My mind ran through how much a plane ticket might cost, if my dad might have the money or if my mom could book a ticket with her credit card from where she lounged in Saint-Tropez—if that was still where she was. The postcard pinned to the bulletin board was from weeks ago.

"Please," Cindy said. "I broke up with Gabe yesterday after I went to the motel. I didn't want to be around him. There isn't anyone here who understands but you. *Aerosol.* Remember?"

She started crying again, and a voice came into the background, soft and gentle, and then the phone rustled and Cindy's mom came on.

"Gertie," she said quietly. "Cindy's really hurting. If I book you a plane ticket for the weekend, do you think your dad would let you visit?"

"Yes," I said. "Of course, I mean, I want to be there. But I'll pay you back. I get paid tomorrow."

"I'll send you the ticket when it's booked. It would mean a lot to Cindy."

"Can you put her back on?" I asked. "I want to tell her . . ."

But my voice trailed off.

I just wanted to tell her I loved her.

July

"YOU DON'T HAVE TO STAND UP, MOM."

My bag is packed, and Ciarán stands by the door spinning the car keys around his finger.

"I can lean my legs against the couch," she says.

She rises slowly, held up by muscles she can't feel. She trembles at the work of staying upright, palms pressing down on the air around her for balance.

It's been easy to forget how tall she is, five eleven at least, even as fragile bones make her shrink. As she rises to her full height I see the person she used to be, and the strength it had taken to rebuild her life after she left my dad. I hug her tightly, gripping her shoulders when we part, and then her knees buckle from something neither of us can feel and she collapses back down on the couch.

"Please consider taking your shot," I say.

"Okay."

"The doctor said you can start again anytime."

Her eyes squint with a scowl and a sigh forces its way through her nose. "Don't babysit me, Gertie."

"*Fine,* fine," I say, knowing she won't take the drug, knowing I'll have to start over on convincing her when I come home. "Sorry. I'll be back soon. Don't let Ciarán give you a hard time."

"All right, now," Ciarán says, "time to get going, Gertie."

I grasp Mom's hand once more. I get her to smile.

I've never felt like a real New Yorker. Once, after years living there, I was walking east down Delancey and thought I was looking at the Manhattan Bridge. That's on Canal. But you can't be accused of being a fraud if you never claimed to be the real thing.

After landing at JFK I get the feeling, as I always do, that New York recognizes me. I balk at how easily I fit right back in, remembering Mom's prophecy that soon she'll let us go and we can move back. As I ride to Cindy's house on the train I strike a manner of detached sternness I always associate with real New Yorkers, the look that says you know your next five moves. By the time I'm climbing up Cindy's stoop, I drop the act and, almost giddy, allow her four-story house to swallow me whole.

"Gertie!" Cindy answers the door wearing jeans that look expensive and a tailored white oxford, fully grown now into the casual elegance she's always possessed.

"You're four years late," she'd said to me and Ciarán when we moved to New York, one hand cocked on her hip as she stalked through our new apartment. She's light-years ahead of me, this girl who moved to the city at eighteen and never looked back. I step inside the house that's completely theirs, no buzzers to different apartments mounted on the brick exterior, just one dead bolt on the front door.

I sink into her hug, squeezing her tightly. A noise from above catches my attention, and I look over Cindy's shoulder.

"Dr. Bryan!" I exclaim as she comes down the stairs, still wearing her scrubs.

"I hate that you and Ciarán call me that," Willa says.

"I know, I'm sorry." I open up one arm and pull her into our hug. "We're just so proud of you for saving so many lives."

I hold the two of them, breathe them in. It wasn't my soulmate I met in Sioux Falls. It was Cindy's.

From the living room comes the sound of squawking. Frankie, their green-cheeked conure, bobs up and down on her perch. Cindy detaches from us, coos as she lifts the bird out of the cage.

"I forgot how loud Frankie is," I say.

Willa sighs, but smiles, too, as she watches Cindy transfer Frankie to her shoulder. "She's insufferable. But she makes Cindy so happy."

Louisa, their au pair, slinks gracefully down the stairs, holding Eleanor, who's wearing the pink dress and bow I sent her for Christmas, sizing way ahead of her age with the hope I could see her wear it. She's ten months now, and the outfit is still too big.

I reach for the baby, folding her in my arms. My face fills up Eleanor's dark eyes. I'm new to her all over again, and she takes me in, and I take her in. She has skin and hair the color of almonds. Willa carried her but the donor they found must've looked like Cindy—there's a hint of that same tough beauty in her.

"Are you leaving this little nugget with me, too?"

Willa snorts. "No."

"Louisa is coming with us," Cindy calls over her shoulder, beckoning for me to follow her into the kitchen, where glasses are waiting for wine and a pot of Bolognese bubbles on the stove. "We redid the guest room, Gertie, it's sumptuous. I can't wait for you to see it."

Willa catches my eyes and rolls her own. "Oh, Willa," I laugh, putting my hand on her arm as we follow Cindy.

In college, Cindy inherited a fortune from her dad's father. Since the age of twenty-one, she's had a man in her employ whose job is to turn her money into more money.

"Where's Charles Wallace?" I look around for the feathery, long-snouted dog that usually charges to the door barking whenever anyone arrives.

"Upstairs, hiding," Willa says. "He's seen the suitcases."

"Poor thing. Oh!"

Louisa swoops by, scooping Eleanor from my arms and wiggling her down into a high chair at the kitchen table. "It's time for your dinner," she says to the baby.

"Louisa and Cindy have Eleanor on a very tight schedule," Willa explains. "Very unlike my free-for-all childhood."

"Mine, too," I say.

We clink the glasses Cindy hands us. I look between the two of them and think it's a miracle we're all here together, that our friendships not only survived but became something more. That one good thing came out of that trenchantly terrible summer, a neat stitch in its heart.

"You're good with her," Cindy says later, though all I'm doing is handing Eleanor things she wants but can't reach herself.

"I can't believe Willa had a baby during her residency."

"It was really important to her," Cindy says. "We've talked about me carrying next. Have you and Ciarán thought more about having kids?"

Dinner's been eaten, the dishes done, and Willa is upstairs packing. Charles Wallace, the borzoi, sulks into the living room and sighs as he jumps on the couch. I sit on the floor, the dog rests his head on my shoulder, and I hold Eleanor in my lap, my arm around her belly. I take a sip of wine from Cindy's irreplaceably fragile glasses. There are words I could say, but I only half understand how I feel about them.

"Ciarán would be such a good dad," I finally get out, "but it's been about a year since we talked seriously about it."

"So he wants them."

"Ciarán and I are always going to choose each other over everything else," I say. "Is that a bad trait in parents? He *would* have them, but he's accepted we might not."

"You *don't* want them?"

"How could I have a kid? Eleanor's the only baby I could ever love." I plant kisses on her fat cheeks; she giggles and flails. "Can we film her eating ice cream for the first time?"

"She can't have ice cream," Cindy replies. "You're deflecting."

Outside, the moon climbs its scaffolding of light. It's a chilly night for July, and a fire crackles in the hearth. I sink my toes into the plush rug. Eleanor begins to fuss, and Cindy takes her from me, and without the baby's warmth my skin turns to gooseflesh.

"I don't know if I'd be a good mother," I say. "And since my mom moved in, I feel like we have to choose. Take care of the generation before us or the one after. I don't think we could do both."

"You could do both," she says. "You and Ciarán can do anything."

"I feel so old already." I rub my forehead. "But I know in ten or twenty years I'll be mad at myself for thinking thirty-one is old."

"Typical Gertie," Cindy says. "Living in any time other than the present."

I stretch my legs out beneath the coffee table and arch my back against the couch. "Don't worry. I'm here."

Eleanor's head falls back against Cindy's pale pink shoulder. The curtains are open and through the glass I catch the shadowy faces of people walking by, looking in, and I bristle from the exposure, but Cindy hates a curtained room, the heat of its containment.

In a different world I would want children. It's not just me as a parent that I doubt, but the world at large, our chances for survival, and how our children will be required one day to shape their pains into a story they can live with.

"I found something I wanted to show you," I say, stretching to reach my purse without getting up. "My mom had it in her things when she moved in."

I pull out a Polaroid. Framed in the square are our dads, with Ansel in the middle, an arm around each of them.

"This might've been the last photo of the three of them together before Ansel got sick."

Cindy smiles weakly. "That's your grandpa," she says, turning the photograph toward Eleanor, who looks at it, unfocused. Cindy nudges the photo onto the coffee table with the tips of her fingers.

"These parallel lives." She sighs. "I think about Ansel sometimes, more than seems rational for someone who never met him. What would've happened if he'd lived?"

"It's a lot of responsibility to put on a dead man, but everything would be different," I say. "I mean everything."

August

THE PAST

MRS. FELLOWS SENT AN EMAIL WITH THE CONFIRMATION NUMBER FOR A one-way plane ticket to Detroit, leaving the next day. We could figure out the return date when I got there, she wrote. *Or maybe you could just stay since school starts soon?*

The memorial was Sunday, four days away. Annemarie told me to give my dad the details, in case he could join, but I'd put it off, surprised that I had to be the one to tell my dad his best friend had died.

I told Anthony I needed to miss some shifts for a funeral, but I didn't tell him I might not be coming back. Though Adam and I hadn't spoken since the night we went to Vermillion, he was the only person I planned to tell—breaking our silence to let him know I'd be gone forever. Eventually the news would get around to everyone, and at least Lucas wouldn't think he had the power to drive me out of town. I was leaving because I had people other places.

I rode my bike to the high school where Adam had been working, a brown brick building with a looping drive and an empty parking lot. The day was humid, half sun and half thunder, and I slipped into the deserted school where everything was partially shut down: The lights had been dimmed, the cafeteria was closed off by wire gates, and fans stationed throughout the halls blew warm air around. My footsteps echoed as I searched for the library; if Adam was installing computers, I figured he might be there.

I found it, and the smell of books wafted out into the hall. Light streamed through a curved wall of windows, and there Adam was, arms stretched around a computer as he untangled cords and fit a plug into the back of a monitor. He looked up.

"How'd you get in here?"

I shrugged. "No one at the front office."

Dust floated around his head like a busted halo. He smiled. I tried to smile back but seeing him reminded me of what Lucas had said about me, that I was a slut. I hadn't expected to think of that, looking at Adam, and I wanted to hear him refute it. But that would mean saying it out loud.

"Sorry to just show up, but I have something to tell you." I sat in a rolling chair on the opposite side of the table where he was working. I spun in a slow circle. "I wanted you to know, at least."

"What is it?" He wound a cord slowly around his fist, looking like he hoped whatever I was about to say had nothing to do with him.

"I'm leaving tomorrow. I don't think I'm coming back."

The sun made Adam squint and he shaded his eyes against the glare as he typed something into the computer he'd just booted up. "Is it your dad?" He sounded frustrated—angry, even.

"No. Cindy's dad died."

Adam straightened; the clipped edge in his voice softened with sympathy—and maybe relief. "I'm sorry."

I wanted to break his gaze, so I flipped open a dictionary on the table and pinched the Bible-thin paper between my fingers.

"I know that Lucas found out about us," Adam said. "I hope he didn't give you a hard time."

Us. I squeezed my eyes shut until they hurt.

"I don't want to talk about Lucas," I said.

"I know. But I never would have told him, you know that, right? I was ready, you know, to let it all just go away."

I faltered, and then I recovered.

"Don't feel bad," I said. "No use regretting something you didn't have the chance not to do."

Adam laughed and the laugh echoed in the big, empty space. He hoisted himself up onto the table next to my chair and looked down at me. "Everything is always so intense with you."

There was blame in what he said to me. I shrank, ran my thumb along the edge of the dictionary, planting it in the space carved out for each letter.

"Will your dad be okay without you?"

"I hope so," I managed to say.

Adam cracked his knuckles. In response to the silence, he pulled the dictionary from underneath my hand and opened it to a random page, spinning his finger in the air until it landed on a word. With closed eyes, he said, "This word describes your future."

"I don't think I like this game," I said. "Let me guess. It looks like you're in the *d*'s. Your finger landed on *doomed,* didn't it?"

"No," he said. *"Dorky."*

"It did *not.*"

"It *did,*" Adam said, snapping the dictionary shut.

"You're lying! My turn, give it to me."

We were slipping into our easy way of being together. I planted my finger on a page.

"Mariner," I said. "And *I'm* not lying. Ever thought about joining the navy?"

"And a thousand thousand slimy things lived on; and so did I."

"I didn't know you were a Coleridge stan," I said.

"See? You got the reference. You *are* a dork."

Adam looked at me, but I hadn't come here so we could look at each other like that—I'd had enough, done enough, I was leaving. But kindness, when you were aching for it, could shape-shift into all kinds of feelings—and most especially into ones you'd already banished. He stood up and opened his arms for a hug, and I stepped into them. He put his hand on the back of my head, and for a moment I thought he might kiss me, but a cart rolled down the hall outside, startling us apart. Adam coughed, I studied the big clock on the wall. Adam smiled, but I knew, and he knew, that the moment had passed, and I was going to leave in a minute, and I might never come back.

"It's probably better this way," he said.

I stood up and lifted my hand in a half-hearted wave, and on its way down he caught it, squeezed it, and let it go.

That evening, I folded my clothes into the suitcases that had spent the summer pressed into the corner of the apartment. If my dad came home, I would tell him I was leaving and give him the Narcan. I'd let him know about Mike's memorial; maybe he'd get a plane ticket and come with me. I'd imagined all of his reactions, but most of all I wanted him to ask when I'd be back.

I retrieved all the things I'd left lying around the house. I lingered outside on the balcony, where I'd passed so much of my time looking out at the endless horizon and for a short time thinking I might be able to find a place in it.

My phone's ringing waterfalled off the balcony. It was Cindy.

"I'm so happy you called. I'm packing now."

The line crackled, the reception fuzzing in and out.

"Can you hear me?"

Her voice sounded like a sigh. "How are you?"

"Fine. I said I was packing."

"Right," she said. "Look, is everything okay?"

"What do you mean?" I asked. "I—"

Another sigh from her cut me off. "You know, I called you just now hoping you'd deny it. I would've believed you. I'm so stupid."

"Cindy."

"The worst part might be how much you claim to care about me. And it was all just utter bullshit."

Fear took the shape of two hands around my neck, twisting tighter and tighter. I was afraid if I spoke, I'd throw up.

"Gabe told me everything." There were tears crowding Cindy's voice. "But it's not just that. Now that fucking photo of you is going around and *everyone* knows. The whole school. As if it wasn't already hard enough for us there, Gertie."

"*Cindy.*"

I could barely get her name out. I was as frozen as I'd been sitting outside Alice's house that night with Gabe. The dead branches scratching the sky, cold seeping into my bones from the ice-hardened steps. Hell wasn't hot. It was absolutely freezing.

Cindy breathed hard on the other end of the line. "Don't you have anything to say?"

"I'm so, so sorry," I said desperately. "I made a terrible mistake. My dad was leaving. I was really lost. I wanted to tell you, I swear."

"You know what, I don't want to hear any more from you. I just wanted to tell you not to get on the plane tomorrow."

"*Please* let me explain. I'll come home and tell you everything. It was a mistake, Cindy. I fucked up."

"Don't bother. I'm just happy we didn't spend the summer under the same roof."

"I never wanted to hurt you."

"But you did, Gertie. I'm hanging up. Don't call me back."

And then she was gone. Her words echoed in my ears, and my heart plunged when I thought of what her face might have looked like when she saw the photo Gabe had taken of me. He'd told me he'd deleted it. I'd believed him.

Why? I texted him. *Why did you tell her now?*

Gabe replied with a simple message: *Check ur messenger.*

I skipped between apps. A little red *1* icon was anchored to the screen. When I clicked on it, my own face stared back at me—the face from that night in December, smiling, undressed, making the biggest mistake of my life.

But Gabe and I weren't alone in the message. Gabe, who'd looked up photos from the lake party that I'd been tagged in, who had found me even in my new life, had included Lucas, Austin, Adam, Willa, and Jill.

I was dating her best friend when I took this, Gabe wrote, followed by a shrug emoji.

There it was, his threat made real, like blood on a No Trespassing sign. Lucas replied almost immediately: *That tracks she's a slut.*

One by one, tiny faces appeared beneath the message, telling me they'd all seen the photo. The last face to pop up was Adam's. Five faces, five daggers stabbing me.

Who the fuck does this girl think she is? added Austin. *She's not even that hot.*

Jill and Willa removed themselves from the thread. I removed myself, too. There was nothing I could say that they'd believe. I'd never even had a real boyfriend, I just didn't know how to say no to people. These boys, their minds were made up about me, but did I really deserve *this*?

The screen went dark and I rubbed a smudge off my reflection. I heard noise from within and turned around to see my dad inside. He was looking down at my suitcases.

"Are you going somewhere?" he asked.

"No," I said. I turned back around to watch the sky as it coated itself in bronzer. "Don't worry about it."

August

THE PAST

I WOKE UP IN THE MIDDLE OF THE NIGHT TO A CROWD OF TEXTS PILED ON my lock screen.

Cindy told me you're not coming—is everything OK?

I was surprised Cindy hadn't told her mom the truth. Annemarie's love for me was so precarious that she would never in a million years defend me if she knew I'd hurt her daughter.

And then there was a long text from Gabe.

U stopped talking to me and then Cindy dumps me because she says I don't get it but I was there for both her and u and it fucking sucked that u both just ghosted and how did I end up the bad guy. Fuck u Gertie.

I wondered if Lucas and the others were sharing the photo, if it was popping up in other threads, small ghosts born in different parts of the city that would grow up to stalk me. They'd never leave me alone. I'd never be able to make myself unrecognizable to them.

The pool was closed, but I went down to it anyway, climbed over the low padlocked gate, and dangled my feet in the water. When

Cindy and I were younger we'd go to the city pool during the summer and float in the deep end with our arms limp, pretending to be the dead girl from one of the sinking scenes in *Titanic.* She drifted through a flooded, icy room in her white nightgown as though she'd slept through it all, dead before she even woke up.

The hot concrete. Ice cream from the snack bar. Cindy's dad alive, idling in the parking lot as we dragged ourselves through cold pool showers and back into our clothes. The window down and Mike's arm hanging out, hand slapping the car door to the beat of whatever he was listening to, whatever he'd be forced to turn off in favor of Rihanna. Our nail polish coming off in sheets from the chlorine, littering the back seat. Leave-in conditioner spritzed into our stringy wet hair. Having no idea at the time that it was a day that would become a memory.

I wanted to be anywhere else—with Jamie, who is sitting in the dark, too, shivering alone in a cell in a city by the sea.

A man comes to see her, predictably villainous with his calm demeanor, resting his elbow on an arrow slit in the fortress where they're keeping her, looking not at her but at a churning sea beneath them.

"I'm told," he says, "that you've become close with my son."

Jamie grows pale. "Your son?"

So there are secrets Hayden kept as well.

"Is he alive?" she asks.

With little pause the man replies: "Hayden made his choice. Now it's time you make yours. I can send you home—but I need you to tell me everything you know."

He looks at her.

"I won't open the corridor for you," she says. "Even if I could, I wouldn't."

He sucks his lips inside his mouth as though tasting her words.

Her trial lasts one day. Hayden's father sits in the gallery, silently watching as she's sentenced to burn at the stake. They don't tell her when. She read somewhere that Joan of Arc's heart didn't burn along with the rest of her body. The executioner found the whole muscle nestled in the ashes, so intact it was practically beating. But Jamie's not Joan of Arc, and her heart will burn with the rest of her.

How did this happen? she thinks.

But there's someone on her side, even if all they can offer is a quicker death. They come to her cell one night, wearing a dark hood that falls low over their face. A vial appears, extended through the bars. "It's from Hayden," a low voice whispers.

She drinks it. It's bitter.

July

THE FUTURE

CHARLES WALLACE SITS WITH ME ON THE STOOP, AND WE WATCH THE FOUR of them—Willa, Cindy, Eleanor, Louisa—pile into a cab. Cindy runs back once more to kiss my cheek and scrunch Charles Wallace's face between her hands, and then they're gone.

"You ready to have a fun time with your auntie?" I say to the dog, scratching his ears. He looks at me sideways, his long anteater snout pinched in a grimace, but he follows me up to the top floor, where branches sway against the window and a long wooden desk is built into the wall. I open my computer, but Frankie starts to scream at having been left alone downstairs, so I go and get her. Back in the office, I try to concentrate while Frankie marches over the desk. I'm very aware of Charles Wallace eyeing her. "He won't try to eat her, as long as you don't leave them alone together," Cindy said, but in my mind I can see the snack-size bird's sun-shot head disappear into Charles Wallace's open maw.

It's easy to get distracted by thoughts like this, especially since the past keeps a tight grip on my story; I pry its fingers loose one by one. The problem, though, is that hell is you *and* other people, and even from the vantage point of my forgiving memory, I don't always like myself in the story I'm telling, and the guilt-bound part of me would have me show all the bad parts. I can't handle much of that today, so I put Frankie away and take Charles Wallace for a walk, first snapping on little bootees that make him prance miserably.

"Your moms say your feet are sensitive, sweetie," I say.

We pass a middle school as it lets out. On the corner, waiting for the light, I listen to a boy as he gossips with his friends and eats a Cup Noodles he microwaved at the bodega.

They're talking about someone from school. "She's so hot," he says, just as a girl his age rounds the corner. She catches his eye.

"Not you," he says to her. Then, under his breath, but audible, I'm certain, because I hear and so she must, too, he adds: "*Definitely* not you."

So kids can still be mean, if you're wondering. Not always the woken-up pumpkins their parents would have you believe. Would he care if he knew she might remember this forever? When you're young you hold on to everything, every wound. Being old means you get over it on the train home.

I hope this is the worst of it for her. For a while, anyway.

August

THE PAST

ADAM DIDN'T TEXT ME. NO ONE TEXTED ME EXCEPT FOR WILLA. AND GABE, who wrote: *Gertie, I'm sorry, that was fucked what I did, I lost my mind.*

I deleted the text and blocked his number. I should've quit Hy-Vee, too, and spent the rest of the month in the dark of my dad's apartment, but I'd paid August's rent already and was completely broke. I also needed proof that what was happening to me was really happening, so I went for my usual shift, and my manager was relieved to hear I didn't go out of town, because he hadn't been able to find a replacement for me. With stiff fingers I scanned all the things people were buying while, a few feet away, Austin and Lucas leaned against Jill's lane. Lucas fixed me with a dark stare and stalked off toward the back of the store.

At home, my stuff was once again spilling out of my suitcases, the Narcan back in its hiding spot in a zippered pocket. I called my mom, but she didn't answer. It was the middle of the night in Europe, but I still imagined her phone ringing, unheard, resting on the deck with the open sea moving water busily from place to place. Sea spray leaving droplets on the screen. Or else the phone was dead or without reception. An artifact from her old life.

I went out to the balcony at the time my plane was supposed to be taking off. Above, there was nothing but dried-up contrails from takeoffs against a thin-looking sky, like someone had watered the blue down to make it last longer. I shouldn't have stayed out there, but I kept looking for my flight. I opened a text from Cindy's mom.

Cindy won't tell me what happened. Are you getting on the plane? Should I come get you?

I replied to save her a trip to the airport for a girl who wasn't showing up.

I'm sorry, Mrs. Fellows. I couldn't come.

A plane arced overhead, and my heart tore apart. It probably wasn't even my plane, but I could feel the chill of the air-conditioning and the smooth vinyl seat that would've been mine.

Everyone was calling me a slut, and the word took up sullen residence inside me. Just something about me others believed to be true.

The plane disappeared from sight. That secret, aborted maneuver I'd never told my dad about. I sat there with my phone and gave social media a wide berth.

Cindy's mom called. I let her leave a voicemail. She said she was worried, she'd called my mom because she felt something wasn't right about all this, but she hadn't been able to get through. Wasn't there a satellite phone for emergencies? she wanted to know. Would I send the number? And she wanted to talk to my dad—what was his new cell? *Call me,* she emphasized.

I wished Cindy would tell her the truth so she could go back to hating me.

Sorry I missed you, Mrs. Fellows. I really wanted to come. Please don't worry about me. I'm so sorry for everything. I love you and Cindy. I'll pay you back for the ticket.

I sat alone for a long time until my dad came home and joined me on the balcony. I still hadn't told him about Mike. Mike, who had been one of Uncle Ansel's best friends, too, the only person left in my dad's life who had known him. Someone owed him the truth, and I was the only one here to tell it.

"Dad?"

He looked up from his book and waited for the rest of my thought.

I bit my lip until I tasted blood. "Mike died," I said.

He looked right at me and blinked. "What?"

"Mike died. A couple days ago."

"You just found out?"

"Yes. No. I wasn't sure how to tell you."

He took his glasses off and tapped them on the cover of the book in his lap. *Life and Fate,* it was called, and a barcode from Siouxland Libraries was stuck to its cover.

"I didn't know how to tell you," I said again. "And Cindy's mad at me for something I did. I miss Mike. I know how much you loved him."

I could see sadness sinking into my father's face—deeper than his face, into his heart. "Mike Fellows was a good guy," he said. "One of the most important people in my life."

My dad was a somber person, but I'd never heard him sound like this, so funereal. I started crying—for my dad, for Mike, for Ansel, for Cindy, for everything. I felt my dad's arms around me. "It's okay," he said soothingly. Then, more to himself: "It's okay. He's with Ansel now."

That only made me cry harder.

"We can't lose you, too," I sobbed. "That night in Vermillion, Dad, I was worried you were going to be dead when I got there."

"Don't worry, Gertie."

I shrugged out of his arms.

"Dad, we need to get you help."

"Please," he said softly. "Just let me grieve my friend."

Fury spun inside me, miasmic. My dad sat beside me looking devastated, but I couldn't let him be. There wasn't time to let him be.

"I didn't know what to do," I said. "Tell me what I should've done, what I should do next time."

"There won't be a next time."

"Who was that woman?"

"It doesn't matter."

"It *does* matter. She was the only one there to make sure you didn't die."

"I'm sorry you had to get involved in all that, Gertrude, but I'm telling you everything is fine. Please drop it."

Gertrude, the name reserved for when I was in the deepest trouble. I didn't heed the warning. I couldn't.

"Things are getting to a point I can't handle anymore," I said.

"I'll be more careful."

"Are you using more because I'm here?"

"Don't be ridiculous."

I moved my chair nearer, but the closer I got, the further within himself he retreated.

"I think we should call Mom," I said.

He'd been drifting away but he raced suddenly back to me, a slingshot released. His anger trembled just above the surface of his skin, stormy and dark. I recoiled, shrinking from the malicious energy that buzzed around him.

"Go ahead," he said sharply. "I'm not her problem anymore. She'll just bring you home."

"Come *on,* Dad. Is there a place I can take you, that could help?" I tried to reach for his hand, but he moved it away.

"Please, Daddy," I said through tears. *"Please."*

"I'm not going to tell you again," he said, shoving his chair back as he stood. "Drop it. You can't stay here if you don't."

His movement washed over me as he opened the door and closed it behind him. I froze for a moment; in the aftermath of his anger, mine was burning, smoking out grief over Mike and putting pressure on all the things that for so long I'd kept myself from saying, all the words that formed a hot diamond of cruelty in my heart. I wrenched the door open, thundered after him. He was in his room, putting his wallet in his pocket.

"You're so pathetic," I screamed, the pain of it nearly doubling me over. "So fucking weak."

My dad looked at me with sad calm.

"I'm *done,*" I cried. "Go ahead and kick me out. You'll never fucking see me again."

He sighed deeply, blinking quickly. Then he smiled, almost mocking, like he knew something I didn't, and moved past me toward the door.

July

THE FUTURE

I TAKE CHARLES WALLACE EVERY PLACE HE'S ALLOWED; UNFORTUNATELY, my doctor's office in FiDi, where I've made an appointment for my annual exam, isn't one of them.

"You really need to find one in Michigan," Ciarán said when I told him I was going to see my doctor.

The waiting room is mostly empty at eight A.M., and I sit by the window that looks out over Trinity Church's graveyard. I would find the proximity unsettling if not for the fact that this cemetery is very old. Death looks better with age. Nothing creeps me out more than a brand-new headstone, a pristine mausoleum. A knot of people stand over Hamilton's grave. I'm not judging. It's something Dad would like, seeing where Hamilton is buried, something I would like as long as I could see it with him.

After my appointment, I retrieve Charles Wallace and take a long walk to meet my friend Naomi in Red Hook. Naomi shows me the cover for her new book, which suits it perfectly. "It's going to be huge," I say, touching her arm.

She asks what I'm working on.

"Oh, you know," I reply, "it's sort of YA, sort of a fantasy."

"Wait, you write YA fantasy now?"

"More or less."

"What a pivot."

I appreciate that she at least tries not to look startled. I suspect she believes I don't have the chops for genre. I don't offer any other details—there will be time for that.

"I can't believe you're gone," she says over coffee. "It's weird not to have you in New York."

"There's nothing easier to believe in than someone's absence." I smile as I say it because I know it will annoy her.

The art studios by the harbor are open today. Charles Wallace is forbidden to enter some of the rooms—the ones with delicate pottery and lacy glass baubles—while others welcome him warmly, though perhaps bringing him was a mistake, since I have to buy a hand-stuffed velvet deer, which he lunges for and beheads in seconds.

After we leave the studios we stand by the water and watch high tide come in.

"Lately, I've been keeping a candle lit while I write," Naomi says, "even in the daytime. There's something primordial about it. I feel less lonely."

"That's so dramatic. I approve."

I don't feel lonely when I write, though I could stand to. In fact, my brain usually feels like Grand Central at rush hour. Chaos, and people sweeping in and out, and if I'm lucky, at the end of the day I've transcribed one legible feeling.

Going north on Van Brunt, we pass the funky jeweler's where Naomi's husband bought her engagement ring. "Let's look at diamonds," she says.

They let Charles Wallace come in. He's still carrying his new headless toy, no longer art, but he sits by a glass case and stares at the glinting stones. I kneel and take a photo with him; the camera catches a burst of light glancing off the jewels. *With Aunt Gertie he gets whatever he wants,* I caption the picture, and then post it to Instagram. Living in New York isn't all about whims, but opportunities for pretending do present themselves. You turn your back on the graveyard and the sea and go into the jewelry shop and life is all summer days, dogs, diamonds.

August

THE PAST

HY-VEE AGAIN. BUT I WAS SO NUMB. HOURS FELL AWAY IN CLUMPS, AND I didn't really remember the details once they were gone. School would start in a few weeks, an eternity at the end of which I had to go home and see Gabe again, and face what I'd done to Cindy.

A guy came to my register carrying a six-pack of beer. He looked way too young to buy it.

"Really?" I said. "ID, please."

I almost didn't ask, because I didn't actually care. Instead of pulling out his wallet, the boy pulled out his phone.

"No, I need, like, photo ID from the government."

He looped his index finger into the neck of my shirt and pulled it forward, shoving his phone into the gap he'd made. I heard the snap of his camera.

"Stop it, stop it!" I pushed his hands away, my voice a panicked whisper. He stepped back, his face sleazy and serene, and he looked at the photo he'd taken. I brought my hand to my chest. My heartbeats tripped over one another as they escaped up my throat. A ringing in my ears rose and faded. His laughter echoed, far away at first, and then loud and real. His laughter wasn't echoing—it was multiplied by other voices.

Lucas and Austin. They were the ones laughing, the echoes I thought I'd heard. They stood by the doors and looked at their friend, who held up his phone, and his voice boomed: "One more for the collection."

I tried to shape my rage into words. But none came. The boys were gone before I could form a syllable, giddy with pride over what they'd done.

A man flipping through a magazine nearby averted his eyes.

I picked up the receiver of the phone near my register without bringing it to my ear. I could call the police. The boy's beer still sat on my conveyor belt, getting warm. I could smash the bottles on the tile floor. I could run outside and smash one against his skull. I wanted to. I really wanted to.

I put the receiver down. I turned off my light and went to Anthony's office. In a quiet, shaky voice, I told him what happened.

He was only there because the night manager had called in sick. He slapped his pen down and briefly I thought he was angry on my behalf, but then he said, "So it's your friends playing around? Look, Gertie, don't encourage them, and don't make a mess."

"It wasn't playful. I didn't want him to do it."

"I can't do anything about someone who doesn't work here."

"But it happened in the store. And Austin and Lucas were there."

Anthony asked if the boy touched my chest or just my shirt. I faded away from him after that. Floated to my locker. Floated from the store. I sat at one of the picnic tables outside, afraid to leave, afraid I'd run into Lucas, just afraid.

For the first time, the idea of moving to Florida with Vaughn didn't strike me as terrible. The teeth had been taken out of my hatred of him.

My expectation that Adam would have texted me by now was humiliating. He had to know how I was reeling from the photo. He'd probably guessed Cindy had seen it, too. When I told him about Gabe on the balcony that night, he'd said, *You don't have to tell me more.* I thought he was being nice, that he didn't want me to have to talk about something painful, but maybe he really *didn't* want to know. Maybe he was tired of knowing.

Without writing or calling, my mom emailed me a ticket home for Labor Day. Two weeks away—it wouldn't be hard to ride the rest out alone. I lay on the floor of my dad's apartment in front of the vent that purred with lukewarm air-conditioning and looked at the ticket on my phone. Adam and I had been friends, sometimes more than. I still thought about him. I still wanted some kind of closure, still wanted to know why he'd left me alone.

An alert from my night sky app told me the space station would be visible over Sioux Falls that night. I took it as a sign and texted Adam, asking if he wanted to find a place outside the city to watch it.

I'm sorry you got caught up in this, like, interstate drama, I added, *but I thought we could talk. It's been really hard.*

It took hours without a reply for me to realize I wasn't going to get one. I heard, finally, what he really meant when he'd said, in the library, *Everything is so intense with you.* It was too messed up. My dad was too messed up. I was too messed up. And I'd opened him up to ridicule from the people he had to live with. He was done risking anything for me.

I felt brittle, like old lace. I began imagining worse than he could ever say. In my mind he tore me to pieces. He must have known what I'd do with his silence, but he wasn't going to text me to put an end to it.

There was love on the surface of what we'd had, but beneath, all its bones were broken.

July

THE FUTURE

A TEXT ARRIVES FROM ADAM. HE MUST HAVE SEEN MY POST ABOUT CHARLES Wallace and diamonds in Red Hook. He asks if I want to get a drink.

In college, Adam changed majors from economics to finance. He got his MBA, moved to New York, became an investment banker, fulfilling the vision of himself that had consumed him throughout our years together: He would one day become the man who would take care of me. He was always telling me I wouldn't have to worry about anything, that he would support me and my poor career choice, but with time his support began to feel like a threat, this promise of money that lay somewhere in the future and that I'd be a fool not to want.

By the time Adam arrived in New York, Ciarán and I had been in Brooklyn for a year. I thought the city was big enough that I'd never see him. But Adam is the type of person who will stay in your life forever, if you let him—and, often, people let him, because he finds ways to be blameless. Who knows? Maybe he is, or is sometimes.

He wrote to Willa not long after he arrived, and soon he was around again, all of us at a bar in FiDi full of finance bros.

"Your one is lovely," Ciarán said quietly as he shook Adam's hand, nodding toward the girl he'd brought. Cindy's head nearly fell off her shoulders, her disdain was so vibrant.

"She's so young that when I asked her how old she is, she said, 'I'm a sophomore,'" Cindy said viciously under her breath. We laughed, and I felt bad for laughing because Ciarán wasn't wrong, she *was* lovely, and in fact I felt worried for her from the moment she opened her arms to hug me. She knew about me, she wanted me to like her, or needed me to believe my presence in Adam's life didn't faze her.

"What?" Ciarán whispered as we slid into the booth. "You look freaked."

That Ciarán and Adam were getting along so well, becoming *friends,* crackled before me like a live wire on the ground. I wanted to stomp on it and die in the process.

"You don't need to go out of your way to be nice to him," I said. "She's *so* young."

"Someone has to make sure he doesn't commit white-collar crimes." Ciarán laughed, watching Adam as he got up to buy the first round, leaving his new girlfriend talking with Willa. I slumped in the back of the booth, shoulders rounded, and Cindy leaned over and asked if I was okay.

"We're going to have to limit this sort of thing," I whispered back, and as I spoke Adam returned with four beers clenched in the spaces between his fingers, and there was something about him that wanted so desperately to be liked that I softened.

"I got you a vodka soda, Gertie," he said, gesturing to where it waited to be collected at the bar, alongside a cosmo that was for his girlfriend. She looked at the drinks, panicked, then at me, and when she saw I was watching she looked at the table with shame.

You—or someone—could argue I had treated Adam badly in the

end, but that part of our life was over. I did my best to keep him at a distance. Our meetings were as infrequent as holidays and only in groups, at parties or dinners, and once, in New York's only betrayal of me, by chance on the subway.

He more or less stopped trying, so I'm surprised to hear from him now. I didn't tell him that Ciarán and I left New York, though he's guessed somehow, or Willa told him.

Can we get a drink while you're here?

"What do you think?" I ask Ciarán later. "And don't accuse me of not making a decision. I really want to know what you think. You like Adam better than I do, after all."

"That poor man," Ciarán says.

"You always say that."

"Maybe." I can hear Ciarán walking somewhere, the noise of traffic accompanying his voice. "If I'm being honest, I think he never moved on."

"And you're okay with me getting a drink with him?"

"I don't mean to say I think he's in love with you still," Ciarán said. "But I don't think he ever found ways to get over what happened. It was a big thing, you know, the trauma you both went through that summer, and so young."

"It's been a long time," I say. "And he hardly went through anything."

Ciarán stays quiet, leaving me to guess what he's thinking. Maybe he wishes I could muster more empathy. Maybe he's thinking about the things I haven't gotten over either.

I decide not to reply to Adam. My time here is short, my writing going well, and I'm starting to understand things about the story that I didn't before.

Adam texts again, and as I read what he's written, I realize with a sinking heart I will have to see him.

Sorry to text again. I know you're probably busy. I was going to tell you in person, but I wanted you to know that Austin died.

Hearing Austin is gone stabs a hole in my memory of that summer, scratching him out, another disappearance. I shouldn't be so affected, but I've never been able to make death come naturally to me. It opens a chasm of *no longer* and *never again* and *never got the chance*. Tears fill my eyes, almost against my will because I never liked Austin. I write to Adam to suggest a place.

August

THE PAST

THE SPACE STATION WOULD LOOK LIKE A PLANE BUT MOVE MUCH FASTER.

Alone, I biked outside of Sioux Falls to where the city's modest lights wouldn't reach. I dropped my bike by the side of the road and lay down in the grass on the other side of the ditch. The sun was still fading, the moon was a shadow, and the stars waited backstage. Tired of feeling sorry for myself, I decided to feel grateful that at least Adam, through his silence, had told me the truth, and I could seal off the door of the room where we'd lived.

I held my phone above my nose and rotated it. The night sky app found the space station beneath me, through the earth, and then it burst over the horizon. I dropped my phone. A bright blinking light, traveling faster than I'd been prepared for. It took my breath away, that object up there, filled with people who were going about what was for them just a normal day at work.

Then it disappeared, lost to more northerly skies, but I watched for a long time after it had passed, startled only by my phone vibrat-

ing against my chest, and I saw the last thing I expected: a call from
my mom.

"Hello?"

"Hi, honey." Her voice sounded far away.

"Is everything okay? It's late there. Or early?"

"I know. I couldn't sleep. I'm on deck, beneath the most beautiful
night sky, getting toward morning, and I thought of you, and then I
saw that I had service."

My own night sky shone. A swarm of midges looked like mist.
Her sea breeze, my prairie breeze—I closed my eyes and felt both at
once, together in the same place. Then her faraway voice came back,
and I felt the distance again.

"Are you there, Gertie?"

"I'm here. It's funny, Mom. The space station just passed overhead, and for like a second I was closer to it than I am to you."

Vaughn was sleeping below deck. My dad was somewhere. It was
just the two of us, me and Mom, again.

"France was divine," she told me. "I wish you'd seen it."

"It sounds beautiful."

"I haven't even told you anything about it!"

"I got your postcards. And just the names. Saint-Tropez. Like it's
made of topaz and diamonds."

"You don't pronounce the *z*."

"You're so worldly," I said. "Knowing when not to pronounce *z*'s."

My mom laughed. "Yes, I speak fluent French and Italian now."

She told me about the seafood, the oysters, the champagne she
didn't drink but that she admired on other tables, bubbling over the
gold-plated rims of the flutes.

"There's nothing as beautiful as first light on the sea," she said.

I imagined her glittering world. And then I remembered that
Annemarie had called her. "Did you get a message from Mrs. Fellows, by the way?"

"No, I didn't. Voicemail has been wonky. Should I have? Is everything okay?"

"Mr. Fellows died. He overdosed."

My mom fell silent. For a moment I thought I'd lost her.

"Oh, honey. I'm so sorry. Are you and Dad going back to Michigan?"

"They already had the memorial."

"Your dad didn't want to go? You should've called the satellite phone, we would've gotten you there."

A tear pushed through my closed eyelids. "You said no satellite phone unless it's an emergency."

"Well, Gertie, that would've counted."

"It's hard to tell," I said. "I don't know what will make you mad."

"I didn't mean for you to feel that way. You can always call."

She said she'd call Mrs. Fellows when she next made landfall. As her sky got lighter, mine got darker, and I was about to apologize to her, just for everything, when the call dropped. She'd call Mrs. Fellows, and who knew what would be said. I'd lowered that drawbridge, come what may.

I wondered which star was mine and Cindy's, the one she'd bought for us. I couldn't remember which season it was visible in. I bet Cindy wanted to scorch it off the map. Knowing she hated me, knowing I'd hurt her, gave me this feeling like I'd never be able to go home again.

The closest thing I had to going home would be to send Jamie to hers. She felt very real to me, as soon as I thought of her back there, waking up on the banks of the pond near her house, a made-up place that I knew as well as my own home.

She immediately throws up. An iron hand squeezes her stomach. She shivers and burns. The poison she took had killed her in the Underworld, but here it was just enough to make her sick. There, in the distance, will be her house, and on her body is her old yellow dress, and on her feet her pair of Converse. Her bracelet is back on her wrist, its links catching the sun.

Her phone comes back to life, too. Months have passed but no one noticed she was gone or knew that she'd had to kill and maim and fight to survive. To everyone else, she'd lived a normal version of herself that summer, but that girl was a stranger to her. On her nightstand, she finds a thin, sparkly gold chain with a circular pendant dotted with tiny chips of crystal that form the Gemini constellation, her zodiac sign. It's a gift from a boy she is apparently in love with. She's never heard his name before. Only hours ago she'd known more clearly than she'd ever known anything that she was dying. It hadn't been mysterious, there hadn't been a bright light. She was simply leaving.

All her memories are of Hayden and the Underworld—not Brandon, this boy she's dating, not the parties she sees in her own Instagram photos. She can't remember her life here because to her it doesn't exist.

The boy comes to see her. He pushes a strand of her hair behind her ear and kisses her. Jamie's surprised, she almost recoils, but she doesn't. This is her first kiss with him, but not his first kiss with her, and that feels wrong in a way she doesn't know how to react to. She's living two months behind him, and in that time she fell in love with someone else.

Would any world feel real to Jamie, ever again?

Would any world feel real to me, ever again?

July

THE FUTURE

I WAS THINKING ABOUT YOUR ANTIQUE SHOP EARLIER TODAY, I WRITE TO Mom. *I remember running around in it when I was little. That was probably annoying.*

You were very good.

She's blurring the edges of the past, smudging out the cracks, like the bad stuff came and made her who she was, and now she's unmaking herself and all of us.

What was your favorite piece you ever bought?

An 18th-century tea caddy.

That's older than God.

It still smelled like tea!

I remember talking to her that night, lying in the grass as the space station sped overhead. After the call dropped, after I thought about Jamie going home, I found the resolve in myself to get up, get my bike, and pedal back to my dad's. He wasn't home, but I knew soon I would finally find the right thing to say. I remember his face when

I next saw him. (But I also remember music, bodies.) I went home right after work. (Spilled beer, fruity acid surrounding my tongue, a sweet drink placed in front of me.) I stayed up late, writing on the balcony. (Someone's room, not my own.)

I remember going home.

August

THE PAST

I HADN'T SEEN MY DAD SINCE OUR FIGHT. HE TEXTED ME TO SAY HE WAS with his friend in Vermillion. I didn't answer.

I went to work because it was the one thing I could count on, and at the end of my shift I was planning to give my notice—summer was over, I was going home—but Anthony stuck his head out of his office and asked me to step inside. His face was set in a grimace.

"What do you need?" I asked, sitting down across from him.

Anthony put both his hands on his desk and spread his fingers. His mouth twitched, pushing his frown into a deeper one.

"I reviewed security footage from the *incident*." Anthony looked at the corner of the ceiling as he spoke. "And I talked to some of the other associates on the floor that day."

"Okay," I said.

"I'm not saying that kid shoulda did what he did, Gertie, but from what others have said, you're the common denominator in a lot of drama going on this summer, drama that's causing rifts between staff members."

Anthony's eyes, like two flies, landed on me.

"I didn't start any of it, though," I said.

"I appreciate that. But, Gertie, there's something to be said for a general level of comportment in this job. This is *customer service*. This is where people shop for food for their families."

Anthony's face morphed, like he wasn't looking at me but at some image of me he'd seen somewhere.

"Are you still talking about what happened in the store? Or the other photo?"

"Wait a minute, now. I didn't see it and I'm not gonna see it, but unfortunately that's a fireable offense, Gertie, to share that on store property. I'm sorry, but you can't continue working here. And as a word of advice, you need to be smarter about the situations you put yourself in."

"I didn't share it. I didn't take it. It wasn't me."

"It was *of* you. That's the whole point."

I dissolved into smoke. I twisted my fingers to try to stay solid, but I wished I weren't alone with Anthony. I wished my dad were there, or my mom. Or even Mrs. Fellows. Someone who would step between us and say this wasn't my fault.

"Okay," I said. "I'll take my last paycheck now before I go, then."

"You'll have to come back and pick it up on payday, since you didn't sign up for direct deposit."

I was about to stand up and leave, obey, but I knew that I was never going back there. Not if it was the only store in the world that had any food left would I ever go back there.

I pointed to his binder of checks.

"I need the check now, or I'll ask the police to follow up about the sexual harassment of a minor in your store."

It was a moment in which I was changed. In which I demanded something that was mine.

Anthony muttered something under his breath, so low that I

couldn't quite hear it, but I got the idea. He pulled my time sheets up on the computer, ran them through the payroll system, and cut me a check. As soon as it was in my hands I swept out of his office, let the door slam behind me.

I grabbed my bag from my locker and burst through the swinging plastic doors with their foggy porthole windows and went up to the row of registers where my old friends were stationed. Austin had his phone in his hands, scrolling. Jill leaned on her conveyor belt, and Lucas scowled when he saw me coming. Willa wasn't there; she'd been distancing herself from them ever since Gabe sent the photo.

The photo. I knew Austin had it on his phone.

"Hey, Austin," I said. "Can I borrow your phone?"

He was surprised enough that he loosened his grip. I reached out and slapped his phone from his hand. It landed on the floor with a clatter, and I stomped on it until a spiderweb of cracks spread across the screen. His background photo hiccuped and disappeared. The photo of me wasn't gone, but seeing his dark, cracked screen still felt like a victory.

July

THE FUTURE

I TELL ADAM TO MEET ME AT A BAR IN CROWN HEIGHTS, NEAR THE APART-
ment where Ciarán and I had lived for eight years. I go early with
Charles Wallace so I can walk around our old neighborhood, hoping
to see some of the stray cats I used to feed. They don't come out,
maybe because of Charles Wallace, but I stand outside the brownstone where we had the garden level. I remember the day we moved
in. It had been snowing, and while everything was a mystery it also
felt like ahead of us there was nothing but runway.

"Gertie."

Adam sees me first from a table on the terrace of the trendy spot
on Prospect Place with a cocktail list that includes glasses smudged
with rosemary. He stands up, and when he hugs me he puts his hand
on the back of my head like he used to. My face comes up to his chest
like it always has.

Charles Wallace presents himself to Adam for affection. Adam ruf-
fles his fur, and I sit down across from them.

"What happened?" I ask. "To Austin."

"You warned me," he says. "Years ago. When Austin started using."

"When did he die?"

"Three months ago."

"He was clean last time we talked," I say, but I know: That no longer matters.

"That was forever ago," Adam says.

He raises his eyes to me. They lie still on my face.

"I can't believe Willa didn't tell me," I say nervously, pulling away from his gaze.

"I didn't tell Willa."

The silence extends until it's broken by our server. I order a martini, and Adam says he'll have the same. The initial shock of discomfort from being near him leaves me scattered, and I take him in as I try to put the pieces of myself back together. He looks the same as he always has. It's hard to find the age in him, except for the furrow in his brow and the creases that come with it, although he's always had that, even when we were kids, his expression of stern composure. Today, though, he looks disheveled, far from the suave banker look he'd perfected upon arrival in New York—brown oxfords, hair slicked back, button-downs and zippered vests. Now his shirt is wrinkled. His glasses, missing a nose pad, sit slightly lopsided on his face. The loss of Austin is written on him. They'd tried so hard to be different that sometimes I hadn't seen one in the other at all. Now I can. The person Adam had come into this world with had left him here alone. Despite knowing better, I want to remove some of his pain.

"I'm sorry," he says. "We don't have to talk about Austin. I know you didn't like him."

Does he think so little of me?

"He was your brother, Adam. It doesn't matter if I liked him."

"Well, I would like to talk about something else." Adam sighs. "I'm too angry still."

"Okay. We can talk about something else." But we sit there with Austin's death hanging over us. It's been years since we were this alone together. Years since we had anything to say to each other that hadn't grown out of failure or pain or our basic incompatibility.

"I don't understand why you had to leave New York." Without much else to say, Adam retreats to the familiar space of the ways I'm wrong. "Why your mom moved in with you."

"We didn't have much of a choice. She's sick."

"Did your parents have a choice, when they basically had you fending for yourself at sixteen?"

His anger, whomever it's for—me, Austin, my parents—surges as he speaks. There are people passing by, so close they brush against the low metal fence at the edge of the terrace, and I look into their passing faces to forestall what's coming next: defeat, accusations, a pointless afternoon, the same old drama.

"It's not really that simple," I say quietly into my lap.

"It kills me that you're doing this to yourself again, Gertie. Giving everything to someone who's never given anything to you."

"That's not true."

"Isn't it?" he asks, with a little meanness in his voice. "I know you never believed it was hard for me, too, being your friend, witnessing that stuff, but it was. All those times I tried to give you a way out—" He cuts off, pinches his eyes shut, and shakes himself free from his thought.

"How do you even have time to take care of her?" he asks. "Don't you have to work?"

He says it as if it's a crime that I have to work. I think about lying, or just getting up and leaving, because we're lost somewhere between *the past can't be changed* and *the past can always be repeated.*

"I got let go." I tell him the truth, giving him the chance to pounce on it. I want to know if he's the same as he was.

"Jesus, you guys must really be struggling," Adam says. "This is what I mean—you have enough on your plate. I can't believe Ciarán isn't putting a stop to this."

"We agreed together that we would do this. It's what family does—our family, anyway."

"He should be protecting you."

"Adam. Look at me. It's not your problem."

Whatever Adam was about to say next falls soundlessly between us. He clears his throat and starts over.

"It makes me sad, that I couldn't tell you about Austin right away." I hear it: that deep hurt he reserves only for me. "We were so close, once. Remember how easy it was to talk to each other? In my memory, it's like we were one person."

"We suffered for it."

"Don't you ever think of us still?" The misery deepens in his face.

"I think of those years all the time," I say. "But not in the way you mean."

"We were friends, too." His voice is quieter now, as though it doesn't matter if I hear. "I miss that."

"What happened was really hard. I'm not saying it wasn't. But it's better this way—you met Helen."

Adam waves my words away. "We broke up after Austin died."

"I'm sorry to hear it."

"I never had time for her. I know you thought she was too young for me."

"A little." I smile. Adam returns it, small and thin.

"I wonder what would've happened if you hadn't had to go meet a guy who can charm a brick off a fucking wall." He slaps the table, and the dull thud rouses Charles Wallace, who looks up at him with startled eyes. "In fucking Spain."

I can't help the sigh that rushes out of me. Adam has always seen what I did as a betrayal. I hoped by now he would have recognized it more for what it was: growing up.

"I didn't come here to rehash all of this," I say. "I came here because your brother died, and I'm very sorry about it, and I know this sort of thing can be hard to talk about with people who don't know—"

"Is it terrible?" Adam laughs through his nose and brings his eyes up to look at me. "That I used Austin's death to get you to see me?"

We've barely touched our martinis, brine from the olives glistens on their surface, and looking at them, looking at us, disgusts me. We're playacting the past and doing a bad job. But we're different now, or I am, and I know enough to know this agony is no longer inevitable.

"What would you have me do?" I ask. "Leave Ciarán?"

Ciarán's name in my mouth silences him, as it always has. Adam looks like he's having a hard time keeping himself together, made mad by all he wants to say.

"Do you remember," I ask, "what happened the first time you told me you loved me? What a disaster it was?"

He looks down into his drink. "My recollection must be different from yours."

"Must be," I say, and then, because I want him to have to sit with the memory, whatever his version of it is, I excuse myself to go to the bathroom, away from this torrent of guilt and rotten love.

I can stay hidden only so long; already someone is testing the handle. He'd told me he loved me my first year at Michigan, and somehow saying it made our passion desperate, rough. Hungry and eager. Fast. He held my hair tightly at my neck, leaving my throat exposed. My fingers left marks on his skin. I wanted him to tell me he loved me again, to feel the rush in my abdomen and the little bit of anger beneath it.

"Tell me more," I'd said.

"I hated it." He'd been breathless. "In Sioux Falls that summer. I hated that everyone could have you except me. You were such a little slut."

I'd frozen beneath him, stunned and silent, pulled through the cold tunnel of time. I'd looked at Adam but didn't recognize him. I'd been trapped. I'd begun to struggle, desperate to shed him from me, and he, startled, didn't move right away.

"Why would you say that?" I'd cried, inhaling hot tears. "Why did you have to say that?"

It was dirty talk, tossed out stupidly, meant harmlessly, but I'd almost started to feel I was more than who had claimed to possess me.

Adam, who'd been there for Lucas and the photo and the slut-shaming, who loved me, saw me the same way as everyone else. I left his apartment and for months after that we didn't talk, but I returned to him, because with those words he'd sent me back into the skin of the girl I'd been. And I stayed and stayed until finally I freed myself.

I never forgave him. Maybe I still haven't.

I leave the bathroom, brushing by the person who's been waiting. Once outside, I'll tell Adam again that I'm sorry for his loss, and I'll gather my things, untangle Charles Wallace from underneath the table, and I'll leave.

But our table is empty when I get back, except for the dog and a stack of bills, far more than needed, a *fuck you, you poor bitch*–sized stack of twenties. Charles Wallace whines, the whine turns into a yawn, and he presses his nose into my legs.

"You poor baby, left here all alone by that mean boy." I kiss his snout. "I bet it was very scary."

I stand for a moment and stare at the money, his cold leverage, at the end of the day all he could really ever offer, and suddenly, despite the anger heating up inside me, I feel very sorry for him. I also feel that finally, at long last, he's becoming someone I'll never speak to again.

I arrange the bills into a neat stack. When the check comes, I pay with my card and leave the cash as a tip.

August

THE PAST

I WAS ON THE BALCONY. I REMEMBER I WAS ON THE BALCONY, SLEEPLESS, looking through the deep night as though I could see through it to September, when I'd be back home. I was thinking about my book. I think I came up with the ending that night at Rolling Prairie.

Maybe Jamie has sex with Brandon, her alleged boyfriend. She's not even sure if it's their first time. She'll try anything to feel like this world, this life, is real. She tells her boyfriend she loves him, but she sees Hayden's face as she does.

I'd always imagined that Jamie would rescue Hayden from the Underworld. Alone one night, she'll see the corridor glowing, and she'll go get him, and bring him back. I'd also always known that if this did happen, if they found themselves together in Jamie's world, they wouldn't last long.

Her boyfriend finds her with Hayden, calls her a slut. She and Hayden start to argue about everything—the war and the secret Jamie kept; Hayden's father, who'd delivered her to a death sentence; whether they ever loved each other. And then Hayden tells Jamie she should've left him to die in the Underworld. That had been his plan all along, to die for his hopeless cause, and she robbed him of his chance at that bankrupt valor.

These problems were so big, so deep and loud and tumultuous, I could drown in them.

In her dreams she's the sniper and the target. In her dreams she can't save Hayden, or herself. The shock and confusion and adrenaline that flooded her when she first came home have worn off. It had kept her from thinking about the war. Now she can't stop smelling death. The darkness around her grows and steals her sleep. It steals her breath. It steals her belief that she's tried her best to do the right thing.

She and Hayden have only one choice—to leave, head for California, like I'd planned from the start. They get on a bus and disappear west, gazing out the window at a vast desert and the straight posture of the sky. Jamie wonders what their lives will look like in three months, or three weeks. If they'll survive. If they'll still be in love. Anything was possible. She'd died, after all, and here she still was.

The sun rose over Rolling Prairie, making me squint fresh-squeezed light out of my eyes. My memory blurs here. I saw my dad's car pull slowly around the building, toward the parking lot. I waited to hear him come inside, prepared to chastise him about his absence, but playfully, so we could move past our fight and find the things that needed to be said.

He didn't come inside. Twenty minutes passed. Childish, I thought, that he was avoiding me. I was numb from a long, sleepless night—but after a half hour a small tangle of fear drew me up and led me downstairs.

My dad's car gleamed in its spot by the mailboxes. Burning fuel from the tailpipe rippled in the air. He was sitting in the driver's seat, sleeping.

I tapped on the window. "It looks like you and I had the same sort of night."

I tapped again.

"Dad?"

His eyes didn't open. I knocked hard on the window, but he still didn't wake up.

"Dad!" I pounded the glass with flat palms. The door was locked, the parking lot empty.

I flew inside and upstairs, I could barely breathe as I tore open my suitcase and the sealed sprays of Narcan poured into my lap. There was a hammer in one of the kitchen drawers. Back downstairs, I smashed the car's back window, slicing my palm open on a shard of glass as I reached through to unlock the driver's-side door. The car alarm screamed; trapped heat rushed over me, a sudden force of energy released. My dad's fingers were limp in his lap, tinged blue beneath their nicotine stains. I took his face in my hands, his breath barely grazed my palm. My fingers shook, and at first I missed his nose, and I thought my heart might explode, and he would die because I didn't know how to use the one thing that could save him, and then I pushed the tip deep into his nostril and hit the plunger.

I took his wrist and waited. I stared at Lincoln's face on a penny that had fallen between the seat and the door, looking as stern as rigor mortis. A car rolled by, but its driver didn't notice me. Two minutes passed, then three.

A stronger beat hit my fingers, and I sank to my knees, my face in my hands, my whole body racked with sobs. I found my phone and dialed 911, and I told the voice that answered where I was. When they arrived, I was sitting on the pavement in a pile of glass.

The biggest risk factor for dying of an overdose, I learn later, is having survived one.

In the ambulance a paramedic bandaged my hand, and when we got to the hospital, they whisked my dad into the ER. I sat on a bench outside and held my arms against a chill I was only imagining. Blood soaked through the bandage; the cut was deep. The sun was as cold as ice, a jagged hole in the blue parachute of the sky. A pair of pink ballet flats appeared beside my feet. They belonged to a woman with a hospital badge on her hip, brown hair swept up in a bun, bright pink blush on pale cheeks.

"It's nice to meet you," she said. "I'm Sarah. You can come with me."

The voices of the paramedics swam back to my ears. One of them had asked me questions during the ride, and part of me received them, answered them, but all I remembered was tracing the patterns of blue in my dad's face as I spoke.

Sarah took my arm and led me into the hospital. We passed through the emergency room. A curtain swished, and a pair of feet caught my eye, and I thought they might belong to my dad, but a doctor glided into the cubicle and flicked the curtain shut behind him.

"This way," she said, not releasing my elbow.

"Wait," I said. "Can I see him?"

"Soon," she said. "What happened to your hand?"

"I had to break the car window."

With a rush of turns and the groan of an elevator, we ended up in a small office with a stiff maroon couch. A coffeepot sat on a bookshelf, its cord grew toward the floor, and the room was full of the smell of burned coffee and hot printer toner. Loose papers crept onto Sarah's computer keyboard. One window looked over the parking lot, its blinds pulled halfway up.

"Okay," she said, dropping into the chair behind her desk. "Who can we call? Is your mom home?"

My sinuses burned. I swallowed over and over until I found the voice to say, "She's traveling in Europe."

Sarah frowned. "Okay. Other family?"

"None," I said. Saying so made me feel ashamed, though I didn't know why.

"Close friends?"

"My dad just moved here. We lived in Michigan—well, I still live there, technically, with my mom." I dug my fingernails into my palm. "Can I see him?"

"So your parents share custody?" Sarah asked, scribbling on a form she'd pulled from her desk drawer.

"My mom has sole custody."

Sarah slapped her pen on the desk. "We need to get your mom on the phone."

"She's sailing. I mean, she has a satellite phone, but she's some-where on the Mediterranean. I don't remember where exactly she is right now."

"What's the number?"

I pulled my phone from my pocket. "I can stay by myself," I said, "until my mom can get here."

It was like I didn't say anything at all, the way Sarah ignored me. She scribbled down the number, licked her finger, and leafed through a pile of papers on her desk. As she rose, she clicked her pen and said she'd be back after she made the call.

"Why can't you make the call in here?"

"It's better to have a minute alone with your mom. To explain things. It might be difficult for her to hear."

"That's an understatement," I muttered. What would my mom say, really? And what did I want her to say? I couldn't go back to my dad's. Or Willa's or Lucas's or Adam's. No place felt safe, except maybe one. Cindy's.

Even though she hated me, the thought of her, her house, her dog and cat and even Annemarie—it all felt so safe. And I wondered how much longer we could go before it would be too late to talk to each other again. Soon we'd get used to being apart, the way you could get used to anything with enough time.

"Wait," I said to Sarah. I opened my silent text thread with Cindy. *Aerosol.*

August

THE PAST

I COULD ONLY WAIT SO LONG. SARAH WOULD ONLY WAIT SO LONG.

My heart skipped. Cindy was typing.

What? she wrote.

It was all I needed. I turned around quickly. "When you call, will you ask my mom if Mrs. Fellows—if my friend's mom—can take me? Back in Michigan. Just until my mom gets back."

Sarah raised her eyebrows, but she nodded. I turned back around. A withered succulent sat in a clay pot on the windowsill. Bubbles clung to the side of an old water glass on her desk. I trickled a few drops over the plant. I wondered if Cindy had told her mom about Gabe yet. The thought of it made me want to walk out, leave the hospital, before Cindy and her mom closed the door on me forever. Cindy hadn't agreed, after all, she'd just responded to a text, maybe more curious than worried, like, *What the fuck did Gertie do now?* And it would be so easy to slip away. I was halfway to the West Coast. I could just keep going. As long as I didn't run into Sarah, I could be on a bus before anyone realized I was missing.

The line between reality and fantasy blurred. What threshold did you have to reach before you left your life—just abandoned it? What pushed you to that point, and was there a wire for each of us, somewhere down the road, waiting to be tripped? Some moment when you realized there was nothing left to do but run?

There in Sarah's office, I finally felt like I couldn't run anymore—even if I wanted to. That was the difference between me and Jamie. All I could do was turn around, go home, but for Jamie there was only forward. Maybe meeting Hayden had been a glitch the universe never should have allowed—but it had happened, and there was no going back.

The idea of the two of them running away made my own life seem calmer. I was different from them, and it hit me as though I were realizing it for the first time. I'd put myself in them, but I wasn't them. They'd taken on lives of their own, and all the feelings I'd projected, magnified, twisted, belonged to them now. And they could change. They didn't need me anymore. Their renaissance would have to happen someplace they'd—I'd—never been. Renaissance, or else their dark age—after all, they are runaways with no jobs and only a little cash, and they'd have to deal with the things they'd done.

When Sarah walked back in, she nodded.

"If we can get Mrs. Fellows on the phone, we might be in business."

"Okay," I say, "but, like, I'm not leaving today, though, am I?"

Sarah wedged her way through the tight spaces of her office, back to her computer, where she started typing as soon as she sat down.

"We'll see what she says. Your mom doesn't want you to go back to your father's." She typed something into the computer.

"My dad can't be alone," I said. "I mean, if I hadn't found him today . . . I *almost* wasn't in time . . ."

Sarah looked surprised that I was surprised. She lifted her hands from the keyboard and clasped them over the center of her desk.

"He's not alone. We're getting your dad the help he needs. You're not responsible for anything. Does that make sense?"

No, I wanted to say. Nothing made sense. But Sarah's fingers had returned to the keyboard. She asked for Annemarie's number, and with the phone between her ear and her shoulder she started out by saying, "Hello, I'm calling from Sanford Hospital in Sioux Falls . . ."

Her voice faded away as a buzzing rose in my ears. My vision blurred. It was like my life here was a clerical error, and now it was getting whited out. The sky reeled in its constellations; blue days and hot nights and rainy afternoons spun backward, starting the summer over. The prairie packed up shop and drove away, a touring carnival that was moving on.

"That's good news," Sarah said.

I looked up at her.

"Okay." She'd said *okay* a hundred times, and so crisply. She dropped the phone in its cradle.

"You can stay with your friend."

"What about my dad? Can I see him?"

"The doctors need space to monitor him. Narcan wears off. They just need to do their thing."

"But can't I just look in on him?"

She didn't reply, but a doctor stopped us on our way out of the hospital and said he'd been looking for me. He asked me if I knew what my dad had taken and how much. He asked me if we could sit down for a few minutes. Sarah sighed but let him talk.

I didn't know for sure, but in my mind I counted the pill bottles and needles and little glassine bags. I described what I'd seen, what I'd guessed. I told him about the night in Vermillion, and how he'd come back to life on his own then.

Sarah interrupted. "We can't expect her to answer all these questions."

"I'm just trying to paint a picture," the doctor said. "She's our only source of information. And she did tremendously today." He looked straight at me. "You saved his life, you know that, right?"

"Please, can I just see him?"

The doctor looked at Sarah, and Sarah sighed.

"Let me make a call." She stepped away. When she returned, she said, "*Briefly*. Your mom doesn't want you hanging around here."

"Your dad'll be okay," the doctor said, leading me to the elevator. "We just gave him another dose of Narcan. He's stabilizing, things are looking very good. You did wonderful, young lady."

"Thank you," I said. "Thank you for telling me."

As we rode the elevator, I saw the name tag on the doctor's white coat. Dr. Bryan.

"Is there any chance you're Willa's dad?" I asked.

He made a surprised sound as he nodded. "I am."

"She told me you worked here. Tell her thank you. She's been really nice to me."

His face changed. I left him by the door to my dad's room and stepped inside. A hospital gown stretched across his chest, an oxygen mask covered his face. He wasn't awake. His eyes were shut but in the expression of a nightmare. If not for the mole on his forehead, I might not have recognized him. My hand hovered above his arm. I touched one finger to his shoulder.

"I'm so sorry, Dad," I whispered. "I didn't mean it, what I said. You'll see me again really soon."

I gathered my things in my dad's apartment. Our two chairs on the balcony were angled toward each other, like always. Sarah was waiting in her car to take me to the airport. Strips of light fell in through the windows, and the clock on the stove glowed. There were things in my purse that I took out and placed on my dad's desk: my Hy-Vee badge and the last paycheck from Anthony. I signed it over to my dad—something my mom had taught me how to do—and placed it neatly next to the keyboard. *For rent*, I wrote on a Post-it that I stuck over Anthony's signature.

The printer spat out my boarding pass. I put my Hy-Vee shirt in the trash. I deflated the air mattress, tried to fit it back in its box but couldn't.

The day had turned into a quiet afternoon. I saw different versions of myself all over the city as Sarah drove me to the airport. I extinguished them one by one, pinching them out like little candles.

"Bye, Sarah," I said outside the gate. She'd insisted she see me get on the plane, and because I was a minor, she was allowed to. The plane lifted me up and away.

I left for the last time.

July

THE FUTURE

THE BIG SQUARE FOOTAGE OF WILLA AND CINDY'S HOUSE IS THE CLOSEST I've felt to the aloneness of Sioux Falls, the long hours on the balcony, where I imagined what I looked like to someone on the ground as I imagine now what I might look like if someone cross-sectioned the brownstone like a dollhouse. I'm on the top floor, the smallest part of the house, because I prefer close spaces when I write, trapping thoughts before they can escape, and from here I can see down to the street and over to the French café on the corner, glasses of wine just visible on the tables like teardrops of garnet. Above, the sky is a woman who lives alone.

A candle is lit on the desk, Naomi's tactic for rejecting loneliness. In Sioux Falls it was me and the prairie, the clothes I wore over and over when I couldn't find quarters for the machine, and ashes, ashes, ashes blowing from Dad's tray in gusts of wind. And a mired feeling, believing this part of the story would play on loop, never becoming anything else, until gunpowder and a spark came together to destroy it.

When I first started writing this book, I resisted looking its people up online. I worried that seeing how they'd changed would disrupt the work of my imagination, and I wanted all changes to be my own, our futures a mystery the reader could never know. I would be the one to offer redemption, or not.

But I caved to the temptation to see them in their lives.

Lucas was invisible on the internet; I never found him. Jill had settled serenely in Oregon, her photos glossy and perfect with no identifiable shadow of real life. Gabe was living in Arizona. He had a wife and a baby. There were old photos of him at a Black Lives Matter protest. So perhaps he'd become a better person. I wondered if he saw how serious what he'd done was, how much trouble he'd be in today for sharing a photo like that. Or maybe he saw his past only as a contradiction, and he'd wiped his slate clean.

We all had a different summer from the one I remember, the one I'm writing about; after all, everyone is the main character in their own life, just as I am in mine—all of us, maybe, trying to strike that sweet spot of being humble and also a hero in this sad and deadly world.

I did the best I could. And now, after years of fighting who I was then, who they were, who my dad was, I'm ready to make something beautiful.

part
three

August

THE PAST

WHEN I LANDED IN DETROIT, I DIDN'T FEEL LIKE I'D ARRIVED HOME. I FELT LIKE everything had changed, and I had nowhere to go, even though Annemarie was flagging me down at baggage claim.

In the car, I told her about my dad. And about Gabe—though I left out the photo, which I wanted to forget more than anything.

"I feel like I tricked you," I said. "I should've told you the truth before I came. Do you hate me now, too?"

"I hate that fucking Gabe kid is who I hate," Annemarie said, clutching the wheel, thrusting her eyes over her shoulder as she changed lanes. "Excuse my French."

"But Cindy hates me for it. She doesn't want to see me. And I get it, really. If you think it's better, I can stay at my house. You can take me there."

"Nice try," she said. "We're going home, and you and Cindy are going to talk this through."

"But that's not fair to Cindy."

"You are kids and you'll do what I say. You don't get to decide whether or not you cut someone out of your life." She laughed a little to herself. "That's my decision."

"I really don't think she wants to talk to me yet," I pleaded.

"I'm going to make her."

I wanted to tell her: *Please don't. Please don't make it worse.* But then I saw the future unspool, me and Cindy never talking, never apologizing or forgiving, going our separate ways and then, all of a sudden, we wouldn't remember things about each other anymore. We'd have forgotten on purpose.

Mrs. Fellows parked her SUV on the curb outside their house, turned off the engine, and looked at me. "We'll get your bags later," she said, and I started to ask why, but then I saw Cindy standing on the lawn, Ralph the dog bounding in circles around her, his rope toy strangled in his mouth, looking at me eagerly because Cindy was ignoring him. Steve the cat was stationed sphinxlike on the porch railing behind her, yawning in the dusk. The last of the summer's fireflies short-circuited above the grass. I dropped my backpack and walked toward her.

"You answered my text," I said. "You saved me."

I stopped in the middle of the yard, waiting to see if she'd meet me halfway.

"I'm so sorry," I said.

"You said that already."

"I don't expect you to forgive me yet."

"Good. Because I don't."

"It wasn't right, what I did."

"It wasn't right what both you and Gabe did."

"Exactly—I know it was my fault, but it was Gabe's fault, too."

"Don't bring him up."

"You brought him up."

"Whatever. I'm going inside."

"No, wait."

"What?"

"Don't go in yet. Please."

"I'm getting mosquito bites."

"I have bug spray in my bag." I gestured to my backpack. "Do you want some?"

"You brought your own bug spray to South Dakota?"

"I mean, I didn't know if he'd have any."

He. We fell silent.

"It was awful, Cindy. Being there. I couldn't help him. He didn't want my help."

Cindy's face fell. "I couldn't help mine either."

"I should've been here. I think about what I could've done differently this summer, this year, and your dad would still be here and—"

Cindy knocked a tear away from her cheek. "Don't do that. It's not fair to me. I know you think you're trying to help, but it ends up making things all about you. You *saved* your dad, and, like, I know this sounds fucked up, but it makes me feel even worse about being too late to help mine."

Cindy's eyes flitted to her driveway, where her dad's car was parked. Just sitting there, back at their house, where he wasn't. She was right, for the first time I glimpsed how she was right. All this time. Blaming myself had made things about me that weren't about me.

"I'm sorry I wasn't there for the funeral," I said.

"I told you not to come."

"I shouldn't have listened."

"Maybe that's true," she said.

Her face slipped into a small smile, a loss of footing she corrected quickly.

"The photo," Cindy said. "That sucked, Gabe sharing it with your friends there."

"You know about that?"

"He showed me the messages. Thought it would make me forgive him or something, like I'd be happy he made you suffer."

That part hurt. "I didn't know that."

"But, like, your friends defended you, right? Or Adam at least?"

"Willa did." I shook my head slowly. "But no one else. Not even Adam. There were things that happened, Cindy—"

My voice choked on tears. When I started to tell her Cindy closed the distance between us and put her arms around me. I held her like I was about to lose her. Like I could stop her from becoming a stranger one day.

"Do you remember your trampoline?" I asked quietly.

Something had made me think of it; maybe it was the dusk, turning into the dark of its vinyl. The trampoline had been in Cindy's backyard; when one of its legs cracked, Mike had sawed it apart and dragged its pieces to the curb.

Cindy pulled away, the start of a smile on her face. "The one that came unwelded?" she asked.

"Nuclear winter," I reminded her.

Years ago, a night one summer. The temperature had dropped into the forties and we put on winter coats and lay on the trampoline for hours, taking selfies and drinking hot chocolate.

"Look at this one," Cindy had said, tilting her phone toward me. I was wearing sunglasses and a puffy coat. "You look ready for nuclear winter."

"A dry nuclear winter indicates a wet nuclear spring," I said. "Plan accordingly, farmers."

We'd laughed at everything back then.

"It feels like forever ago," Cindy said now. She put her arm through my elbow.

"Are we going to be okay?" I asked.

She laughed at me. "Obviously. We already lived through nuclear winter together. Remember?"

"You can never *really* touch anything, not in the way you think," a former science teacher had said, his description of how electrons repel each other. "You'll only ever hover near."

Cindy and I came close, though, the soft boundaries of our atoms overlapping. We walked toward her house with our arms linked, the dog and cat brushing past us to reach the door first, mosquitoes landing on our faces, our feet crushing the grass. We closed the door against the night.

July

CIARÁN CALLS AS I'M MAKING DINNER IN CINDY'S KITCHEN. A BUTTER SAUCE simmers indulgently on the stove; a rich spoonful coats my mouth elegantly. Frankie watches from a playstand set up for her outside the kitchen, while Charles Wallace splays diagonally between the cabinet and the island, staring at me with a look that says if he's stuck with me he might as well love me.

Jostling wet hands in a dish towel, I answer the phone and put Ciarán on speaker with the knuckle of my pinkie.

"I'm making our favorite chicken," I say. "I wish you were here."

Ciarán's warm voice fills the kitchen. The chicken breast sizzles as I lay it flat in a burning hot cast iron. I keep one eye on it and listen as Ciarán tells me about his day. I hear him shuffling through the house. I hear the closing of a door.

"Listen," he says after a short silence. "I need to tell you something. It's about Carla."

"What happened?" A dose of panic pulls me up straighter.

"Nothing, she's fine," he says. "I debated not telling you until you're back next week, but I thought it'd be better to give you a heads-up."

"Ciarán, what's going on?"

"I found this stash of pills. Xanax, but, like, a lot of them. Her doctor in Florida prescribed them—just a one-pill-a-day prescription, you know, but it looks like she wasn't taking them, just putting them away."

A tendril of smoke rises from the pan, winding itself around me. The fuel shimmering in the hot sun comes back. The broken glass in the parking lot comes back. The blood from my sliced palm comes back. I can feel it trickle down and hit the delicate skin of my inner wrist just as it had then.

"Do you want me to toss them?" Ciarán's voice nudges me.

"Would you put Mom on, please?"

"I knew I should've waited to tell you," Ciarán says. "Let's just think what to do a bit. I'll throw them away right now if you want and we can talk to Carla together when you're back."

"I need to talk to her."

"Maybe it's not what you think. You know she's always been in an insecure place when it comes to healthcare. She didn't have it all those years."

He's trying to see the better possibility, as he always does.

"You keep telling me she's not serious about ending her life. I'm telling you she is. I need to talk to my mother, please, Ciarán."

He's fighting to ignore me. I can hear it in the sigh that fills the line.

My mom's voice comes on against the bright clean marble and steel of Cindy's kitchen. "Hi, sweetie."

My phone still rests on the countertop. I plant one elbow on either side of it, my head in my hands.

"Mom," I say. "What's going on?"

"Ciarán's cooking dinner."

"The pills, Mom." My voice grows louder. "Your stash of pills."

Charles Wallace scrambles to his feet, looking for the danger. Mom says nothing.

The siren approaching Dad's apartment. The hammer on the ground next to me in the parking lot. There'd been a penny on the floorboard of the car, Abraham Lincoln looking on.

"What are you doing with all those pills?"

"You gotta have a stash," she says, her voice playful.

The first tear falls on my phone's screen. "After *everything*? How could you, after—and Ciarán had to stumble on them like that? He changed his whole life for me, for us, and you're just going to let us *find* you?"

"It's okay, sweetie," she says.

"Don't *fucking* call me sweetie. What do you mean, it's *okay*?"

"It's not for right now," she says. "If at all possible, I'll go the medically sanctioned route. These are just in case things get bad. I won't be that burden on you."

"You've got to be joking. Ciarán and I could go to jail if we let you do that, Mom."

"Don't be ridiculous. As far as anyone else is concerned, you know *nothing*."

"I want you to throw them away."

After everything that happened. The loop, endless. An alarm shrills and I register vaguely that the kitchen has turned dusty gray with smoke. Out of the corner of my eye I see Frankie take flight. Charles Wallace scrambles from the kitchen, looking for quiet. I stand frozen over the phone, watching the chicken blacken, waiting for the flames to burst open and burn us all down.

I grab the pan, cursing the hot handle, and throw it in the sink. Steam hisses as I blast it with cold water. Beneath the blare of the alarm, I hear my mom say, "Gertie? Can you hear me? Are you okay?"

That night I hold my burned hand above me in the dark, turning it over in shadow. After coaxing Frankie down from the top of an armoire, I rode the train one stop to the urgent care, where they covered my palm in antibiotic cream and wrapped it in a bandage. My pulse throbs in the burn's hot center, and my phone is on the pillow next to me, Ciarán's voice coming through it.

"Is Mom okay?" I ask.

"She's glad you're okay, and that you didn't burn Willa and Cindy's house down. I am, too, for that matter."

"I'm so mad at her. She's being so practical about it, like it's nothing."

"She's really scared of what's going to happen."

"Aren't we all?" My hand falls into Charles Wallace's feathery coat. I've been letting him into the bed even though Cindy told me not to. He lifts himself halfway and flops back over on my chest. "Isn't that life?"

"I know it must be hard for you to hear her say stuff like that," Ciarán says. "Believe me, I don't much want her to off herself in our house either. I don't know what to say other than I hope she doesn't get worse."

"She's always done this. Prepare for the worst and barrel toward it with this absolutely insane drive."

"I hate to tell you, my love, but you're quite similar."

"Maybe," I admit. "Not as much, though, the longer I'm with you."

It's almost harder to hear his voice than not. Aloneness I've always been able to do, but phone calls with Ciarán these past two weeks have made me remember how I felt when I was unsure he'd ever be mine. Unsure that together we'd take our lives and make them livable.

August

THE PAST

ANNEMARIE DROVE ME TO MY HOUSE THE NEXT DAY AND WAITED WITH ME
for my mom to get home from the airport. We sat on the front porch.
The For Sale sign swung in the wind, looking weatherworn after its
many months stationed in our yard.

When my mom turned in to the driveway, she was blurred behind
tinted glass, but I saw her wave. Mrs. Fellows and I stood up to meet
her. She looked at me, held up her hands, and, almost with a smile,
she said, "I don't want to know." Then she came toward me with
open arms and hugged me.

She asked if she could talk with Cindy's mom for a minute, so I
went inside and watched them through the window. Their mouths
moved. My mom reached out to touch Annemarie's shoulder as she
wiped tears from her eyes. And then Annemarie left, and my mom
came inside.

She looked past anger. She looked at me softly.

"It's a nice night to sit in the backyard," she said.

We pulled the two white plastic chairs on the patio side by side. They were chairs just like the ones in the garage and on my dad's balcony in Sioux Falls.

"Did I ever tell you the story about the first time you slept through the night?" my mom asked.

I shook my head. "I know I was a terrible sleeper. I put you through hell then, too."

"You had just turned one. For a whole year, I didn't get to sleep through the night."

"I'm sorry," I said, and I really did feel bad.

She picked at a scarred bit of plastic on her armrest. Her long, thin face was without a smile.

"One evening, when your dad was out of town, I stopped at the liquor store, because I'd reached a point where I thought I could have just one glass. I bought champagne, and I thought, 'Who would want to drink a whole bottle of champagne alone?' It'd be easy to do it moderately." She paused, remembering. "I put you to bed, and I asked God to take care of my baby."

The wind picked up pieces of her hair and made them dance above her head.

"You slept," she said. "I couldn't believe you slept."

I'd never heard this story before. I could see my mom with her legs crossed on our couch, and the champagne, extraordinary and effervescent, boasting the patient rise of its bubbles: a perfect thing. I could feel the cool fizz on my tongue, the small needly feeling as it passed down my throat.

"You didn't need me that night," my mom said, "not too different from how you don't need me now."

"I need you, Mom," I said. "Obviously I need you."

"I just mean you've always been independent. You could always sense when your parents were going off the rails. Your dad was sober then, but I was afraid to call him. I didn't want to go to sleep, because what if you got hurt and I didn't wake up? I didn't know who to call. I was so ashamed, so I called a suicide hotline."

"Suicide hotline?"

"I didn't want to hurt myself. But I was afraid if I called anyone else, they'd take you away from me. So I called a place where I wouldn't have to give my name, but maybe they would help me anyway."

Her voice trailed off. She was far away in a memory, her chin tucked into her chest. A bat swooped across the sky, a bulb of darkness on a string. I tried to think of something to say that would remind her she was here, alive.

"They convinced me to call your dad," my mom finally said, "and he called my sponsor, who stayed with me until morning and then took me to rehab."

"I didn't know," I said, unable to find any other words.

She shook her head slowly. "I wish I could say it was the last drink I had, but there were a few more for a few more years."

"For how much longer after that was Dad sober? Before relapsing for the first time."

She brushed a mosquito off her knee. "I don't really remember. Maybe a couple years. You were still young." She paused. "I love your dad. I know it doesn't seem like it. I don't know how to say it, but we needed each other at one time, and it worked then, but then it stopped working for me. I wish it had worked. I'm sorry it didn't."

"He doesn't know how to take care of himself," I said.

"It's true. He never learned. First he had his parents, and in New York there was Ansel. Then me. And then you this summer."

"It's just hard," I said. "Because he's going to use if he's not happy, but there's no way for him to be happy when he's alone."

"I know," my mom said. "It doesn't make sense. But it's something we all go through."

I looked at the tops of the trees, the way they brushed against the sky, almost touching but not touching.

"Do you think he meant to?"

"Meant to what?"

"Overdose."

"I don't know. Your father has always been depressed. I can only imagine the loss of Mike hit him hard."

"He's never found anything that's worked for his depression?" I asked.

"No. Lithium did at first. You probably remember those days. But he'd go on and off it because it gave him tremors. Was he taking anything for it while you were there?"

"I don't think so."

"He's getting help now," she said firmly, as though forcing herself to believe it. "I'll stay in touch, help him set up his rehab."

"That's nice of you," I said.

"It's what he would do for me if the situation were reversed. It's what we always do—switch places. Who helps, who needs help."

She looked lonely sitting next to me. I hated that I was only now realizing how much empathy she had.

It seemed useless to fight anymore. In two years, I'd leave home, probably, to go to college. Could I really ask her to give up on a new life when I was on the brink of starting one, too?

"I don't want you to be sad, Mom," I said. "I want you to be happy. If that means marrying Vaughn, you should."

"I don't know what happy looks like anymore," she said. "One day, though. One day, I'll be back to my old jovial self."

"Me, too," I said. "Maybe one day I'll be jovial again."

She laughed. I reached my hand between our chairs, and she took it.

"Don't worry," she said. "It's the bad stuff that makes you who you are."

I leaned my head back and opened my face to the sky.

"Cindy's mom mentioned something about drama with Gabe and some of the kids out in Sioux Falls. What happened?"

I closed my eyes. "Everything's okay, Mom."

"Is it really, sweetie?"

One day, I promised her, I would tell the whole story.

July

I TEND TOWARD LISTLESSNESS IN CINDY'S HOUSE FOR THE NEXT TWO DAYS, thinking about my parents and the lives that didn't turn out as they thought they would. *It's just in case,* Mom said, *it's not for now,* in the same way it had seemed Dad was always going to get clean down the road, and I lived every day on edge because of it. They were like rioting birds, trapped in my gloved hands. Both of them trying to take flight. She didn't want to kill herself, she'd told me fifteen years earlier, in the garden of our old house, but if you call the suicide hotline maybe a part of you does. It's a choice we all make every day, staying alive—some of us realize it, and some of us don't.

The day before I leave New York, I leash up Charles Wallace and we ride together in a cab to Seventy-second and Fifth and head into Central Park, winding our way inward so we can sit on the slabs of schist, worn into waves by glaciers, that overlook the Lake and the Central Park Boathouse, though Charles Wallace would rather be off-leash and zooming. I'll walk around with him until nine P.M.

when the leash hours end, slip his glow collar around his neck, and let him run on the Great Lawn, but for now we sit in the thin, even sunshine and watch turtles slip murkily beneath the surface of the water.

I know so little of my mother's life before she met my dad, who by trouble or charm had always sucked all the air out of the room. All that talking with him was what made me feel I knew Ansel so well, even though we'd never met, even though more than the whole of Ansel's lifetime has gone by since he died. I often feel Ansel's presence in the city he never saw change.

I didn't look for Ansel's novel until my mom's house had sold and the rooms were being emptied. It was the summer after my sophomore year; a few months later, I would comment on Ciarán's Instagram and we'd start talking again, but at that time I still believed Adam and I would always be together. I'd borrowed his car and driven home to help with packing. Any things I still had left there, which weren't many, would have to go. I had nowhere to put them, and Vaughn didn't want them in Florida.

I escaped to the basement as Vaughn and Mom began to argue. Tucked away in a damp corner were a few boxes labeled *Ansel* in handwriting I recognized as Mike's. The pages of the manuscript had gone brittle with age; the strikes from the typewriter faded, blurry. The title, stern and all caps across the top of the page, was *People Other Places*.

In the center of the basement was a steel support pipe that Cindy and I used to swing around, pretending we were pole dancers, and I settled against it with Ansel's book in my lap.

It was hours before Vaughn found me and asked why I hadn't finished cleaning out my room. I didn't care. Ansel had written a love story, one I hadn't been able to put down. The protagonist was a man named Richard, and the story began in his youth as an only child growing up in Detroit. His mother was a poet, aloof and lost in her own words. The nuns who led his classes slapped his knuckles with rulers for much less than what he'd get for the secret in his heart. He studied journalism at U of D Mercy and afterward left for New York. At *Time* he fell in love with a man, but, soon after, that man was killed in Chợ Lớn while covering the war. New York City was Richard's refuge, and he found hope in knowing the people he met there, who were an eclectic mix, like any good friend group in literature.

The book soared in a turmoil of loss and love and renewed hope when, after years of being alone, he met someone new.

And then he got sick.

The story grew darker, and as I read I was sure it would end tragically. I felt tears in my eyes, anticipating it, Richard's death waiting like an orderly at the end of a hospital hallway. And then Ansel flashed forward, no justification offered, to a future far off. A future of old age and calm. A future where two bodies that have moved through decades are still moving. Their pills for blood pressure and arthritis are small tokens of achievement on porcelain plates next to steaming cups of coffee in a sun-drenched kitchen. Ansel had veered away from what I thought was inevitable, giving no explanation because none was needed. I would've felt scolded for believing in the end I'd projected, except Ansel's writing was so gentle with me. His book answered a question I'd felt but never known how to ask: What do you do when oblivion is chasing you?

The answer: You write what couldn't be. Ansel might have been dying, but in his last months he wrote something that would outlive him. His book might be my biggest influence, though I know of no one else who has read it.

Ansel and my dad, their past in New York, were so mythic, and Ansel's book only heightened the fame he possessed in my mind, the connection I'd felt as a writer who'd come after him. Because of this, Mom had faded into the background. I'd let her fade. Now her easy acceptance that her life is over makes me feel like I know less about her than ever. In real life, as in books, people can be thin, poorly written, and it's not always their fault if they are.

I take out my phone and text her.

You were living in Ann Arbor when you met Dad, right? I haven't asked you what it's like to be back.

I've always liked Ann Arbor.

Did you live in an apartment? A house?

I lived in that white turn-of-the-century Foursquare down Plymouth Road, between the old schoolhouse and the cemetery. It's really in Dixboro not A2. The one with the picket fence and hydrangea bush in the front.

You lived there? I know that house.

I'm sure I said something.

I don't remember it.

Maybe I said it to myself. I liked it there. It had a dirt cellar. We lit off fireworks in the backyard during the summer.

Sounds nice.

Once I was driving home from a party and I got pulled over by a cop. I was drunk, but it was a different time back then. He let me keep driving and followed me home to make sure I got there. As soon as I turned in to the driveway he just drove off. Didn't even tell me not to do it again.

I'm glad you were okay. I pause, debating whether or not I should bring up Dad. *Dad would drive drunk and high, and it wasn't even that long ago. I worried so much that summer.*

I worried, too, she writes.

Do you think there's a chance Mike was using before the car accident? Or was it really all Dad's fault?

I don't know, Gertie, Mom writes. *Maybe it's better not to think about it.*

It's something Dad would say, too. And that's one of the fundamental differences between me and my parents. I'm always thinking about it, whatever *it* might be. Endless turning over of what happened and how it could have happened differently—that's what has made me who I am.

I dial her number and listen to the ringing in my ear. She answers.

"I'm going to write about your stash of Xanax," I say. "So everyone will know I'm complicit and I will get in trouble if you do it."

"Well don't do *that,*" she says.

"Will you throw the pills away for me?" I ask. "You could live another twenty years. Or more. That's a long time."

"I hate that you're still worrying about this," she says. "How is your hand?"

"My hand is fine. My hand is nothing. Tell me what we can do, Mom."

"You're too funny," she says. "Ciarán asked me a version of that question last night. You're both very kind. You've been saving people your whole life, Gertie. You don't have to worry about me. I'm not your father."

There's a wedding at the boathouse; party guests spill out onto the patio, flutes of champagne glittering in their hands. One drops and breaks, and I remember the sound of Dad's car window breaking. The slab of stone beneath my thighs as hot as the asphalt parking lot in Sioux Falls. My hand bandaged now; my palm bleeding then.

Mom's voice breaks through the memory. "I've lived a wonderful life," she says. "I had some great experiences."

"Please," I say. "I need to be able to save you."

December (Again)

THE PAST

RIGHT BEFORE THE HOLIDAYS, A LETTER FROM MY DAD ARRIVED FOR ME. MY mom brought it in from the mailbox and handed it to me without saying anything. She blew a kiss and left me in the garage.

Alice's annual party was that night. I wouldn't be caught dead there. The cold reminded me of last year's; being outside was like kissing someone who'd just been pulled from a frozen lake.

Cindy was on vacation, her annual ski trip, except this year she was actually looking forward to being with her mom. My dad's chair was still in the same place in the garage. I sat in it and watched a snowfall as it made its way to earth.

This letter was the first from him, a months-late reply to one I'd sent him right before school started, when he was still in rehab. I wrote him because Cindy said, offhandedly, but in a way that pierced me, "I would write if I were in your position. But that's me."

And it somehow felt like hurting her not to do it.

I didn't know what to say or how to be angry with him. It was like everything I felt about the summer was trapped in an elevator, and the intercom wasn't working, so instead of finding an argument, or telling him I forgave him, or asking for forgiveness, I just wrote as though we were having a conversation on the balcony. I told him about how Cindy and I tried to read *War and Peace* at the end of the summer, so we could brag about it, but we gave up after twenty pages. The book made us wonder if we weren't literary enough to move to New York City—*since you're a former New Yorker,* I wrote, *I need your opinion on that.*

When weeks passed with no letter in reply, and then months, I began to think he was angry. Angry because I'd come to Sioux Falls, angry because I didn't let him die, angry he was on the long, slow march of recovery that would consume him every day, and I'd put him on that path. For the first month after his overdose, my mom called him once a week to check in, but he never asked to talk to me, and I never asked to talk to him.

"He needs to figure out how to make his amends to you before you start speaking," my mom said to me. "If you talk to someone without making amends, you'll keep talking to them without making amends."

I didn't agree with her, I would've rather he called me, even if he wasn't ready to make amends.

I turned the letter over and looked at the flap without opening it.

Snow collected on the shoulders of the For Sale sign, which was turning geriatric in the front yard. Vaughn had gone to spend the winter in Florida, and my mom said she would decide at the end of the school year if we were going to join him or stay in Michigan. If we did move, it meant I'd leave for my senior year. It was almost too strange to think about the future when I was still living the last summer over in my head. When I hadn't been able to leave it behind. Even though I was *this close* to leaving it behind.

And then, in October, Adam texted me.

I'm sorry about everything that happened between us.

When the text landed in my phone, Cindy and I were sitting in the cafeteria, alone at the end of a long table. There was still buzz about Gabe and the photo, though not as much by then. Mostly, people had moved on, especially when they realized Cindy and I were staying friends. We loved shocking them in that way; we felt like good feminists because of it.

I turned my phone toward Cindy and whispered to her, "What do I say?"

Cindy had one of her knees pulled up to her chest, her arm wrapped around it, and her eyes swooped from her math homework to my phone.

She studied the text, her mouth slightly open. She looked up at me and laughed a little.

"What are you laughing at?"

"You," she said.

I looked at her blankly.

"*Nothing,*" she said. "Obviously, you say nothing."

I put my phone facedown on the table so I couldn't see the screen.

"Look," Cindy went on. "I get that Adam was nice, or sort of, but he could be pretty dismissive of you, and he wasn't there when you needed him the most. Everything was just so toxic. You shouldn't get mixed up with those people again."

"You're right," I said, moving my phone into my bag. And I knew she was. Still, the text was like a magnet. My brain kept getting pulled back to it.

Looking at my dad's letter, I wondered how the post office had read his sloppy handwriting. It was a miracle this got to me. My thumb slid beneath the envelope flap.

Hi, Hon,

Thank you for such a nice, long letter. I guzzled it all down in one long swig. Then I went back to it and read it in sips. It took me some time to write you back because I'm sure you know I feel bad about this summer, and it doesn't feel good to feel bad, and I knew writing you would make me deal with those bad feelings, so I put it off. Here we are.

I was in a halfway house through October, but now I'm back at the ranch, much to Sabrina's dismay, but the lease isn't up until February, and I made the payments while I was gone, so she can't do anything about it. It's surprising how much money you save when you're not paying fifteen bucks a pop for oxy. I'm just kidding. I'm not surprised.

We never really talked about Mike. It's difficult for me, so I won't spend much time on that, but know that I am going through the steps of grief. I'm trying to work out how I fit into a world that contains neither him nor Ansel.

Are you going to apply to college next year? You mentioned New York last summer—is that still the plan? I'm dreaming smaller. I'm contemplating a move back to Michigan, pending my job search here. There's not much to report, except that I had a star-cross'd interview at an ad agency in Oklahoma two weeks ago, in-person after three phone interviews. It was my first time on a plane since before I moved to Sioux Falls, and the flight was turbulent, scary, and packed with sweaty, suffering travelers jammed into a regional jet, the CRJ-200, an aircraft favored by airlines for its range, low operating costs, short takeoff and landing capabilities, and, most especially, the number of cramped, miserable passengers it will hold. I asked the flight attendant if we were experiencing extreme turbulence. He replied, reassuringly, that no one had ever survived extreme turbulence. Then, on the way from the airport to the office, I got lost. I asked three people which way was north. No one knew. All that to spend three hours being asked in nineteen different ways what my greatest strengths were. Finally, frustrated, I replied my greatest strength was that I wasn't an asshole. Needless to say, I haven't gotten a call.

The flight back was the same as the one there.

I did make a new friend at a meeting last month, and she helped me pick out a pair of new glasses, which I wore to a bar for open mic (I had a Diet Coke), during which I received blank stares from a crowd of people I suspect are not Gordon Lightfoot fans, nor interested in the Edmund Fitzgerald or any Great Lakes shipwrecks for that matter. But I'm glad I went, and I'll go again. And thank you, to you and your mom, for shipping my guitar so carefully—you didn't have to do that.

Your mom told me she thinks you're keeping secrets. What's up with that? She asked what I'd thought of how you were acting over the summer. I of course have little knowledge of what you got up to in Sioux Falls, for all I know you ran for mayor, so I told her I thought you were just being a teenager, plus we'd put you through hell, but not to worry because your writing will be the better for it. She hung up on me.

I should've gotten to know your friends. Bike-boy and the others. I saw you with them sometimes—once I went to Hy-Vee and you were outside with them on your lunch. I don't think you saw me, or maybe you pretended not to see me. They looked like cool kids, and I thought you were too cool for cool kids.

All this to say, if you're OK, I'm OK, but are you OK? It might make you feel better to tell me—no judgment here, as you know. And your mom's anxiety can be formidable. I'm here—really, this time.

Love,
Dad

P.S. I was looking at files on the computer and came across some of your novel pages. I hope you finish it. I want to find out what happens to those time travelers. Hayden is not as cool as he thinks he is. Jamie is very cool.

. . .

As I turned the letter over to check the back of the page, which was blank, I thought of what my mom said about talking before making amends, and I wondered, *What does making amends even mean for us?* Conversation—that was how my dad and I had always connected, always loved each other.

I read his letter a few more times—in small sips, like he said. The first person I thought of telling about the letter was Cindy. The next was Adam.

I didn't listen to Cindy in October. For the whole day after Adam texted, my phone gave off a heat I could feel even when it wasn't in my hand, and in my mind grew the slow acceptance of the fact that I was going to respond to him. I sat on my bed that night with my thumbs on the keypad.

I didn't realize how much I needed to hear that until you said it. You really hurt me.

After I pressed send, I threw my phone on my pillow and plunged forward onto the bed, buried myself in the sheets, my heart pounding, regretting I'd written, wanting him to write back, hoping he wouldn't.

Then my phone rang.

"Adam?"

"Wow," he said. "It's good to hear your voice."

"Really?"

"I didn't think you were going to reply. I would've understood if you hadn't."

"I didn't think I was going to either."

It took a long time for me to fade from conversation after I'd left, he said. Lucas mentioned the glass in the parking lot, my dad's car sitting there with no window, and after that Adam went to the apartment and knocked on my dad's door. But I'd already left.

"Why didn't you text me?" I asked.

"I don't know," he said. "I was embarrassed. I didn't know what to say. Awful, I know."

We talked late into the night. I stayed on the call because to end it would risk putting out a fire that was keeping me warm. After that, his texts kept coming and I kept replying to them. We never brought up the summer. But stalking these new conversations were all the rest of them. I couldn't block them out, but I couldn't stop talking to Adam either, and I didn't know why I was making myself relive the worst summer of my life. My dad's apartment, Hy-Vee, the lake, Lucas's apartment—these places popped up in my dreams, the types of dreams where I tried to move but couldn't, and I woke up kicking with leaden legs, and I wondered if I was my own stalker for putting myself through that again.

Still holding my dad's letter, I opened a text from Adam that he'd sent yesterday. A photo of a big maize-and-blue envelope from the University of Michigan. *Welcome* emblazoned on the front. The packet was addressed to Adam.

You didn't tell me you applied! I'd written back almost immediately.

His next text was still sitting in my phone, and I still hadn't replied.

Start over with me?

He was waiting for me to say something, but I didn't know what to say. If I said yes, he'd make his decision because of me, and I didn't want that. Or, I wanted it, but knew I shouldn't want it.

And if I said no? Or, some version of no; some version of anything except yes. Maybe he'd stop texting me. Maybe that was a good thing. Because already I was imagining the drama, and how delicious it would be, and bad, what people would say if they heard we were together—but it wouldn't matter because we would be different people with different lives. It made me a little dizzy, thinking about it. The good and bad of it. The silliness of it. The secrecy of it. Was it possible to start over with someone if that person was part of the reason you needed to start over in the first place?

Some version of me stood at the edge of the cliff, arms windmilling, and I walked up behind her. Did I push her over, or pull her back?

epilogue

July

THE FUTURE

A FANTASY WRITTEN DOWN CAN NEVER CHANGE THE FUTURE, BUT IT WILL change the past, that place where forgiveness really lives.

I could have written a book of callous distance, everything shaved away but me and my father. That might fit better with what's considered dignified—a woman relaying trauma in a way that's palatable to others because they need to understand it only in principle. I've been to that place in my mind, it's a desert, safe to walk through only at dawn. So I allow that summer to be everything that happened and more—fantasy, boys, bars, parties, betrayal, death—because to remove one piece would be to diminish the rest. Regarding sentimentality, I'm guilty as charged. I want lushness and mess, lava at the core, and sweat.

My dad cared about me and my mother, but honesty required a down payment he couldn't afford. He wanted to live but he didn't, so now I give him what he couldn't have: the dignity of surviving to see a world that had grown more likely to forgive him.

Because in truth I didn't arrive in time that morning in Sioux

Falls. I didn't go home after Anthony fired me. I went to a bar by myself, knowing, as I had before, that I would find a way for them to serve me. When I told an older man my real age, it took the space of two drinks for him to convince himself it was okay.

I found my father covered in light, the sun like a bucket of water thrown over his face to wake him. I broke the window, as I did in the story. I fumbled the nasal spray and held his face in my hands, as the fictional version of myself had done, but the first dose of Narcan bloomed through a dead man, and so did the second. His breath never grazed my skin, his pulse never restarted in my hands. I sat with his body while I waited for the ambulance to come. The paramedics pronounced him dead in the ambulance. I rode with him to the hospital. When I apologized for the last thing I'd said to him—*You'll never fucking see me again*—it was to his body; he wasn't alive inside, he didn't hear me. With Sarah, the social worker, I texted Cindy *Aerosol* as a different kind of shrapnel tore through me.

Everything would've been different if Cindy hadn't told me about the Narcan, and what I mean is: I wouldn't have been too late to save him because I never would have been able to save him at all.

I said early on I'd be truthful when I wanted and not when I didn't. If I hadn't been coming home from a stranger's apartment at dawn, I would have been asleep inside. In no real story would I have been in time. No real story, but quietly, in the upstairs of the Brooklyn brownstone, I wrote him alive again, felt the pulse come back, both his and my own.

There was no letter from him to read on that cold December evening. No conversation, no amends. That fall I mailed him the pages of the novel I wrote on his balcony, with no return address so they wouldn't bounce back. I wanted him to see what I'd done, even if he wasn't there to see it. I wanted him to know there was imagination in me, even if he wasn't there to know it. Jamie and Hayden had lost the war and run away, but they had each other. They would figure out a way to live in the same world. And, in a way, isn't that true of all people in love?

Imagination, then, is the torch in the tunnel—not the light at the end of it, but something in your hand that you've lit yourself.

On my last morning in New York, I take Charles Wallace for a walk to pick up a draft of the new book, which I've had printed at FedEx. CW grabs a smooshy stress ball from a basket near the floor, slobbers all over it, and I have to buy it. But I don't mind.

You were there, the stack of pages seems to say. *You saved him.*

But there are sacrifices to be made. I had to take from my mom to keep my dad alive. Her story fell to the side, overlooked as mothers' are, and I didn't write about the part where instead of setting up his rehab, she settled his affairs.

Mom feels fulfilled, she told me when I called her from Central Park. It's a hard fact to accept when there's so little bright, visible joy—but more likely I haven't looked closely enough. A drop of happiness sterilizes a lot of pain, iodine blooming in water. Her resilience is stunning; I'm not sure I have half as much, which is why I'm having such a hard time understanding her right to die with dignity, why I'm placing another unfair burden on her: I'm forcing her to live because he didn't. There's a difference, she's trying to tell me, between suicide and being ready to go. But I'm going to be stubborn about it. Practically, we don't have a choice—*Unfair as it is,* I want to tell her, *you have to live.* I also want to tell her: *There are years of joy left. A family to live with.* "We were apart for fifteen years," I told her, watching an argument break out between wedding guests at the boathouse, "so I need at least fifteen more from you."

This time, I don't want a story. I just want real life. Because I can only do this once, raising someone from the dead. It's taken everything. There won't be another book like this.

Cindy and Willa return from the Bahamas, a flurry of bags and laughter and exclamations over Charles Wallace and Frankie, who abandon me immediately for their moms, but I'm just as happy to trade them in for a few moments with Eleanor in my arms.

"What did you do?" Cindy exclaims, pointing to the bandaged hand that holds Eleanor to my chest.

"I burned it."

"You need to be more careful," Cindy says, shoving her suitcase toward the stairs with her knee.

"Please," I say, half laughing, "don't say that to me."

The pages of my manuscript stick out of my bag, packed and ready for the airport. I'll have to change names, of course, and other details. The grocery store will become something else. A movie theater, or a TJ Maxx. No one will be fooled. Cindy will be miffed I brought my dad back to life but not hers. Willa will smirk at her father in the hospital telling me I'd done so well. The others, if they read it—well, I don't plan to ask them what they think.

Willa closes the front door, shutting out the noise of the street. Through a hug, she asks me, "Did you do any writing?"

"A little," I say.

acknowledgments

ENDLESS THANKS TO MY AGENT, DANIELLE BUKOWSKI, FOR HER DEDICA-
tion and advocacy.

To Jesse Shuman, my brilliant editor at Ballantine, who was a true
partner in this project and whose vision for the book inspired, en-
couraged, and sustained me. I'm so grateful.

To the whole team at Ballantine, including Kara Cesare, Kim Hovey,
Jennifer Hershey, Kara Welsh, Elena Giavaldi, Emma Thomasch,
Abdi Omer, Debbie Glasserman, Sam Wetzler, Pam Alders, and Cara
DuBois; as well as Hasan Altaf for the excellent copyediting.

To the Hawthornden Literary Retreat, where I finished this book,
for the gift of time and a space to write. And to Johanna Lane,
Meghan Dowling, Maddy Routon, and Kij Johnson for the dinner
conversations; as well as to my colleagues at *Public Books* who covered
for me while I was away.

Atomic Hearts grew from a short story, "Aerosol," that was pub-
lished in *One Teen Story*. Special thanks to Patrick Ryan and Lena

Valencia for being interested, way back when, in a story about a teenage girl who wants to write a fantasy novel. Thanks also to Michelle Hart, who read a first draft.

To generous first readers, Sarah Blakley-Cartwright, Elizabeth Gaffney and her novel workshop at A Public Space, David Busis, Aaron Fai, Kiik Araki-Kawaguchi, Kyle Francis Williams, and Rachel Dugan. To Laura Kasischke for the epigraph and the friendship across decades. And to Sidik Fofana, Nick Fuller Googins, Maria Kuznetsova, Allison Larkin, Rachel Lyon, Kristen Radtke, Asako Serizawa, and LaToya Watkins for the early support.

There are a few moments in this book adapted from a blog called *Storytime* that my father kept during the last five months of his life. I'm glad he wrote these stories down:

- The Woodstock story on page 104
- The dad joke on page 164
- The letter on pages 323–25

Overall, *Atomic Hearts* is a work of fiction. I've changed names, characters, places, dialogue, and incidents—all of which are the products of my imagination and are used fictitiously.

And, finally, thanks to Frank Cosgriff for the years of love and laughter.

about the author

MEGAN CUMMINS is the author of *If the Body Allows It*, awarded the 2019 Prairie Schooner Book Prize in Fiction and longlisted for the Story Prize and the PEN/Robert W. Bingham Prize for Debut Short Story Collection. Her stories and essays have appeared in *A Public Space*, *Guernica*, *One Teen Story*, *Ninth Letter*, *Electric Literature*, and elsewhere. She is the managing editor of *Public Books* and an editor-at-large at *A Public Space*. *Atomic Hearts* is her debut novel.

megancummins.com
Instagram: @meganmcummins
Bluesky: @megancummins

about the type

This book was set in Bembo, a typeface based on an old-style Roman face that was used for Cardinal Pietro Bembo's tract *De Aetna* in 1495. Bembo was cut by Francesco Griffo (1450–1518) in the early sixteenth century for Italian Renaissance printer and publisher Aldus Manutius (1449–1515). The Lanston Monotype Company of Philadelphia brought the well-proportioned letterforms of Bembo to the United States in the 1930s.